THE WARP CLOCK

A TIME TRAVEL ADVENTURE

NATHAN VAN COOPS

For my parents, Marilyn, Kevin, and Peter, because you don't truly comprehend the love a parent has for a child until you become a parent yourself. Now I get it.

Want to be the first to learn about new books by Nathan Van Coops? Join the subscriber team at www.nathanvancoops.com and receive a complimentary chronothon short story. You'll also get access to the monthly newsletter, Facebook groups, and exclusive member content. Join your fellow time travelers today, because yesterday may be too late!

1

"It's a pity that with all of time and space to be explored, we have such a brief opportunity to enjoy it. But I'd rather have a fleeting life filled with wonder than an unremarkable eternity." -Journal of Dr. Harold Quickly, 2018

They say time travelers never die.

They're wrong.

I suppose there's an argument to be made that as long as one time traveler still exists in the universe, none of us are ever really gone. From that traveler's perspective, our lives are immortal strands in the fabric of history, waiting to be revisited.

Or maybe that's just what I think about during funerals to make myself feel better.

At least I'm not the one in the casket today.

Around the room people are wiping away tears and speaking in hushed tones, but I don't recognize most of them. If they were really so close to him, would they be acting this sad? They have to know there are other versions of the man still out there in the multiverse, alive and smiling.

Maybe he just won't return their calls. It's hard to mourn for a guy when I have plans to meet him for dinner.

Tall windows stream sunlight from overhead. This venue is very him, not just architecturally, but quite literally, since they've named the building after him.

The Dr. Harold Quickly Center for Temporal Sciences.

The gathering hall is crowded. If you're going to have a funeral service for a time travel scientist, I suppose it's only right to invite his friends and family, but it must be hard to plan a guest list when they are showing up from a dozen different timestreams. The servers at the hors d'oeuvres table in the back look overwhelmed.

Mym is somewhere around here. Several of her, actually. As I scan the room I spot multiple versions of her curled blonde hair and smiling eyes. Each one of her is chatting with different attendees that have come to pay their respects.

Must keep track of which one is my wife . . .

I fidget with the ring on my finger. Still feels a bit new thinking of her that way, even though it's been a while now. Mym has an app running on her phone that knows the real time we've been married, otherwise I'd never be able to keep track. With all the jumps we've made since that day I couldn't even guess. But I remember our wedding ceremony like it was yesterday. I've been back twice to visit. I could recite our vows by heart if I needed to. Maybe that will buy me some forgiveness if I lose track of an anniversary.

The line at the front of the hall has finally diminished to fewer than a dozen people so I move toward the casket and wait my turn.

They've done a nice job with the holo-projections. The image of Dr. Quickly smiling serenely near the front of the room looks nearly lifelike. I suspect ASCOTT put a lot of money into the presentation. The Allied Scientific Coalition of Time Travelers donated the building and made a big fuss about hosting the official funeral. After the service, the casket is getting buried in the Dr. Quickly Memorial Rose Garden. I catch sight of the new director of ASCOTT, Jermaine Clevis, looking smug as he greets guests. He must feel that hosting the funeral of the most accomplished scientist in the history of time travel will be good for his reputation. He might feel less inclined to believe that if he knew we stuffed the casket full of sandbags.

When it's finally my turn to pay my respects, I run my hand over the casket. The glossy mahogany has some sort of smudge-repelling varnish. I absentmindedly trace the words "Hi Doc" on the finish. Moments after I pull my hand away, my fingerprints disappear. It's a cool feature but it's overkill. Not like he'll see them anyway.

I slip my hands back into my pockets and check out the simple photograph perched on a stand next to the casket. Mym brought it along to contribute. The man who has taught me everything I know about time is smiling back at me in black and white. The 8x10 photo shows Harry just a bit older than when I first met him, a gray-haired senior citizen with cheerful eyes and a Florida suntan. Despite the building bearing his name, I know all this formality was never his style. The man in the photo wouldn't be caught dead in this place.

"He's not in there, is he?"

The voice comes from beside me and I look down to find a little girl standing next to me. She's perhaps nine or ten. Her light brown hair is tied back in a ponytail and she's wearing red Converse All-Stars. She has a dress on, but also leggings. I glimpse the edge of a T-shirt under her collar as well. I get the impression she just pulled the dress over her regular clothes to fit in at the event.

"You know Harry?" I ask.

She nods. "He told me he wants to be buried under a big open sky in Montana. Not in a lab."

I observe the little girl with curiosity. She's wearing a tiny canvas backpack with colorful patches on it.

"I like your shoes," I say.

"I know." The little girl glances around the room and then grabs my hand. "Come on. I've got to tell you something, but not here." She pulls me toward the side exit. I catch Mym's attention from afar and she has a puzzled look on her face. I shrug and let the little girl pull me outside. She stops just beyond the second set of glass doors and looks around. The building is surrounded by a concrete walking path and a lush garden. Other than a few squirrels chattering in the tree branches, we seem to have the area to ourselves.

"I think this is okay, but we have to be fast." She swings the backpack off her shoulder and reaches inside. After a few moments of searching, she extracts half of a door handle. Next, she reaches into her pocket and removes a watch.

No. Not a watch. A chronometer.

The device looks a lot like a wristwatch but this one is too big for a child. The fobs and dials on the side can move the bezel and a series of concentric rings. It definitely does a lot more than tell time. I know an Abraham Manembo chronometer when I see one, and this has to be some of his finest work.

"What's your name?" I ask, studying the girl with new curiosity.

"You don't know me yet," the girl replies. She dials the settings on the chronometer, then adjusts the height of the door handle in her hand. "You need to grab my shoulder."

"I appreciate the invitation, but I can't go anywhere right now," I reply. "I've got my wife inside and we're in the middle of this event."

The little girl looks up at me with an exasperated expression. "You can trust me. We're on the same side."

"Same side of what?"

The girl frowns. "I knew you were going to be difficult."

I cross my arms. "Look, as much as I enjoy making new friends, you can't just go zipping off through time with strangers at a moment's notice. I try not to anyway. Hasn't worked out well for me in the past." I consider her chronometer again. "Who are you here with?"

The girl gives me a look that is suspiciously close to an eye roll. She sighs and offers me the door handle. "Here. You take it then. This side up."

Confused, I extend a hand and accept it. It's copper-plated and looks old. "What do you want me to do with it?"

The girl grabs me by the wrist and pulls it lower. She reaches for the chronometer pin. "I'm Piper Travers. You're my dad, and I'm here to save you."

2

"As a time traveler, your native timestream is like your address. It's your way home. And also information that it is best not everyone knows." -Journal of Dr. Harold Quickly, 1996

"Uh-uh. Not falling for that," I say, snatching the little girl's hand away from the chronometer just before she presses the pin. "Especially after that comment."

The girl squirms in my grasp and I pocket the door handle.

"Don't! I need that!" she exclaims.

"Just hold up a second, okay?" I release my grip on her wrist and she backs up a step. "Piper *Travers*, you said? You've got some explaining to do."

"There's no time!" she says. "You have to come with me now!"

"Not without you telling me what's going on." Looking at her, I can't help but recall what she said. *I'm her dad?* She certainly fits the part. She's got my darker complexion but there are definite hints of blonde in her hair amid the brown. The shape of her eyes as well. They aren't the exact color of Mym's, but they are familiar just the same.

But I don't have a daughter.

"Look, I know it can be confusing with so many of us running around, but I think you might have the wrong version of me. There are a couple other Myms inside. Maybe one of them is your mom?"

"You said you'd always help me. Whenever I needed you. You said always!"

"And I will help you," I reply. "Just tell me what's going on."

She stands on her tiptoes and cranes her neck to see through the glass doors and into the crowded hall. "They'll be here soon. I don't want them to see me."

"Who?"

"The bad men," she says. "They're coming. That's why you've got to help me fix things, before it's too late."

"Fix what? Look, why don't you come back inside with me real quick, we'll grab Mym, and we can all figure this out together."

Piper looks skeptical and consults a watch on her wrist. "I can't go back in there. He's going to find me."

"Who is?"

"The Gladiator."

"Gladiator?"

Her eyes widen as she looks through the doors. "Oh no! They're already here."

I look inside but don't see what she's talking about. Scanning the crowd, it looks like a normal collection of dark suits and dresses. A couple of synthetic people have shown up, but no one who looks like a gladiator.

"Which ones are . . ." I turn to Piper again but she's gone. She's running across the lawn, headed for a line of shrubbery at the edge of the commons. "Hey! Wait!" I take one last glance inside, trying to locate Mym, but I don't see her. I sprint after the little girl and race across the lawn to catch her. She gets down on all fours and scrambles through a gap in the hedge. By the time I reach it, she's back on her feet and running through a playground on the other side.

"Hey! Where are you going? You need to tell me where to . . ." I push myself through the shrubbery and run after her, but she crawls into the bottom of a twisting tubular slide. The squeaking of her sneakers resonates out of the tube. I finally enter the playground and wait for her to emerge from the top of the slide, but the sounds inside the tube cease.

I stick my head inside the bottom of the slide and try to see up the curve. "Piper? Come back out. You didn't tell me who is after you. Who's this gladiator person?"

The tube is silent. I climb the ladder for the platform at the far side and peer down the interior of the slide. Nothing.

I scan the playground. Jungle gym. Monkey bars. Good stationary objects. I check the metal bar at the entrance to the slide. Sure enough, there is a small, slightly damp handprint. Good anchor, especially if you aim for nighttime when it's likely to be unused. Someone taught this kid the basics and it seems awfully familiar.

"Piper?" I call her name one last time, then slide down the tube just to be sure. When I emerge from the bottom of the slide—my clothes crackling with static electricity—I stand up and look back toward the gathering hall. The Gladiator?

I find the gate to the playground and break into a run along the walking path back to the building. A sense of foreboding is rising in my stomach. I yank open the door and scan the hall for Mym. I spot Abraham near the casket paying his respects. The old watchmaker and long-time friend of Harry is standing quietly at the side of the casket, perhaps praying. But as I watch, a bald man walks up behind him and grabs him by the back of the neck. The next moment both of them vanish into thin air.

Holy shit.

I search the room for the right version of my wife. This is bad. There are more people here than when I left, but no one seems alarmed yet, despite the sudden disappearance of the man and Abraham.

Where are you, Mym? I push my way through the crowd, knocking plates of hors d'oeuvres out of people's hands in my haste to find her. A tall man on the far side of the room has his eyes on me and is headed my way. There's a woman with a tight black Afro talking into a device on her wrist and moving in from my left. I spin around and check every side of the room. There. Chatting with Jermaine Clevis near the far exit. Thank God. I move that way but I'm not alone. Someone else has seen her too. A muscled man whose suit coat seems a size too small is pushing his way through the crowd ahead of me. He's almost to her. Luckily, he's cleared a path behind him. I rush forward and reach his back just as he's walking up behind Mym. Jermaine has his eyes locked on my wife and doesn't seem to notice the approaching threat. The big man has one hand behind his back clutching some kind of remote. His other hand stretches for Mym's neck.

I kick the back of his knee. Hard.

The man loses his balance and crashes to the floor. I leap over him and wrap my arms around Mym. "Hey, babe, I think it's time we go, don't you?" I pull her toward the exit before she's had time to object. "Good to see you, director!" Jermaine's mouth is hanging open. I nod to him as I back through the exit door. It swings open for me automatically.

"What are you doing?" Mym exclaims.

"We gotta go," I say. "Right now."

The big man I toppled is on his feet again and in pursuit. The room is in turmoil. A few people are rushing for the exits. Mym takes one look at the scene and doesn't argue. We sprint down the outside walkway past more ASCOTT offices, headed toward an open parking lot on the far end of the sidewalk.

"You have any anchors on you?" I ask.

"We just left my bag in there," Mym replies.

"That's not good." I fumble in my jacket pockets but only find the copper-colored door handle I took from Piper and my portable degravitizer.

"Where did you get that?" Mym asks, indicating the door handle.

"Long story." I slip it back into my pocket.

"We're not using it?"

"I don't know where it goes."

Mym glances back the way we came. The man in the suit is still after us. Two more people have exited the hall after him and are pointing our way. The woman with the Afro is still talking to someone via a wrist communicator.

"We'll have to get out of here the linear way," I say, pulling my MFD from my pants pocket. The multi-function device resembles a phone from the early twenty-first century but with a lot more capabilities. I quickly summon a vehicle. It starts blinking its way toward us on the map screen.

"Who are these guys?" Mym asks. "Can't we just confront them?" I can tell she's sizing up the man running toward us. Mym might be petite but she knows how to handle herself, and I don't doubt she could give our pursuer a few surprises.

"Can't let them grab us," I say. "Saw them blinking people out of the building. They grabbed Abraham. Stay on guard for pop-ups."

As if on cue, the bald guy I previously saw inside appears directly in front of us on the sidewalk and immediately reaches for me. My fist connects with his nose and sends him stumbling back. The woman with the Afro appears on the sidewalk behind Mym, but she's ready too. Mym delivers a kick to the woman's abdomen and sends her tumbling into the grass. The big man in the suit is barreling toward us in a more straightforward assault. He lunges for Mym, but I step in front of him and jab the degravitizer at him. I jam it against his forehead, then press the button.

He screams and reels away.

That'll give him something to think about. Let him try jumping us out now and see which parts of his face don't make the trip.

The woman gets up from the grass and I aim the degravitizer at her. She keeps her distance. The device is only effective at a range of a couple inches but our remaining attackers stay clear. Neither is eager to have any gravitites yanked from their bodies. Besides being painful, it will negate their ability to jump us away.

My phone beeps to alert me that our car has arrived. The bald man I punched has recovered and is blocking the walkway toward the parking lot. I move toward him, still brandishing the degravitizer and keeping Mym close. He backs away slowly.

"You know we'll find you again," the man says. "You won't be able to run forever."

"Just keep away from us," I reply, "or you'll regret it."

The man smirks and moves aside. I maneuver to the auto-driving car that pulls up to the curb. Mym scrambles inside and I follow her, sliding onto the seat next to her. I slam the door.

"Lock doors," I command. The car complies.

"Who are these people?" Mym asks, watching them cautiously through the window.

"Drive. Nearest expressway," I tell the car. It begins rolling and we leave the trio of our attackers on the sidewalk discussing our departure. The big man is rubbing his forehead and scowling at me. "I don't know." I finally respond to Mym's question. "But we need to get lost before they find a way to track us."

A contingent of ASCOTT security guards is racing across the grass aboard a golf cart. Our attackers spot them and quickly disperse in different directions. We pull away before I can see anything else.

Our car moves into the vehicle lanes headed east toward the expressways. I take a moment to orient myself. We're in Los Angeles in 2165. Thousands of miles and a century and a half from home. Not my first choice in places to be attacked. The car picks up speed as it pulls onto the expressway, and we join the flow of other automated traffic headed north.

Mym watches the cars behind us, but it doesn't appear that anyone is following us. She enables the car's anti-tracking setting anyway, just to be sure.

"What on earth was that about?" she asks.

"No idea. But whoever they are, they're bad news." I reach into my pocket and pull out the door handle I got from Piper. "One more thing." I look Mym in the eyes. "I met our daughter. She's in trouble."

3

"The #1 reason I love time travel? Easy. Sleeping in. Go ahead and schedule that meeting for 6am. I'll be there well-rested, sometime after I've finished lunch." -Journal of Dr. Harold Quickly, 1998

"You lost her?" Mym says. "You met her for five minutes and you already lost her?"

The conversation isn't going very well. I'm wishing the auto-driving car had a little more room for me to escape Mym's intense questioning.

"She's quick on her feet. You would have had a hard time catching her too," I say, recalling my pursuit of Piper through the playground.

"Why did she only talk to you?" Mym asks. "I would've helped her too." Her expression is questioning, maybe even a little hurt.

"Look, I'm pretty sure she was just confused. There were at least three other versions of you at that funeral. She was probably trying to talk to one of them. We aren't having kids for a while yet, so she's definitely not our daughter."

"If someone wasn't always dragging his feet, she could be," Mym mutters.

"I'm not dragging my feet," I say. "We haven't been married that long. We have the entire universe and all of time at our disposal. I'm not even totally sure I want kids. Excuse me for not wanting to get tied down just yet."

"Time travelers can have kids, Ben. It's not that hard."

"I get that. And I'm with you. Eventually. But not yet. This girl must belong to some future version of us, or else coming back in time would change things. The odds that we'd have that exact kid in a few years are like an infinity to one."

Mym frowns. "Then why did she come back to talk to you? I assume she'd know that."

"Like I said, she was probably confused. She was scared of those guys showing up to grab her. Maybe some other version of us got nabbed at the funeral and they were her parents."

"Why show up there then?"

"I don't know. Maybe she's following instructions? Did you have a contingency plan with your dad when you were a kid, in case something ever happened to him?"

"We had hundreds of contingency plans. It was a whole playbook."

"Any of them say to go find an earlier version of your dad and ask for help?"

Mym furrows her brow. "Yeah. We should go talk to my dad and ask for help."

I smile.

Mym consults the car's navigation menu. "Where are you taking us?"

"I was thinking we'd try your safe house in Santa Barbara. There's a Tachyon pulse transmitter there. We can make some calls and get some answers. Whatever is going on with this girl's parents, maybe we can figure it out and get their kid back to them."

Mym peers out the windshield. "So we're doing the whole drive? Not skipping it?"

She and I usually skip long car and train rides by simply jumping to the point when the vehicle is about to arrive. Auto-driving cars have made planning arrival times much easier. Usually I'd be happy to skip, but with an unknown quantity of bad guys after us, the idea seems more dangerous than usual.

"I'd like to keep my eyes open for surprises," I say.

"What's the plan after the safe house?" Mym asks.

"We'll have to find Piper again and see if we can figure out what she knows, but I'm guessing she'll be looking for us too. If she's smart, she'll try to contact us again. Let's hope our alternate selves didn't raise a quitter."

"We don't know our own future in very much detail," Mym says. "Especially now that she might have changed it. Hard to say when she might be able to locate us again."

"And we have to assume the thugs at the funeral probably nabbed your bag while they were there," I add. "They'll have your MFD and a lot of your personal info." Mym's multi-function device has a variety of time travel apps and information about our travels. I'm not excited about it being in other hands.

"It's locked," Mym says. "They won't be able to use it without me."

"That's the problem. They might already have you." I tell her about the bald guy making Abraham vanish. "We have to assume they could have versions of me too."

"You think anyone they grabbed will give up our locations?"

"Depends on how bad these people really are, and what they're willing to do to get what they want."

"And we have no idea what that is."

"Not yet," I reply. "But we're going to figure it out in a hurry."

"That little girl is facing these guys all alone?"

I take her hand and give it a gentle squeeze. "Not for long. We'll find her."

The bustling city of Santa Barbara has grown a lot since my century, but it still has a lot of its original charm. Mission-style archways and beach culture have remained. Despite the addition of the metaspace and its myriad scenic diversions, the sunny coastal weather and the allure of the Pacific Ocean have kept people's attention.

California is also a leader in "Natural Beauty Zones" where meta enhancements have been unplugged to remind people to stay invested in "authentic nature." People who have grown tired of the digital universe can go retro and just sit around enjoying the scenery. It's good to know an old-school time traveler like me can still find a few places to fit in.

The safe house is an unassuming apartment off State Street that sits above a surf shop. I've been to it a few times throughout the century, but it hasn't changed much. Viewed through my meta-sunglasses, the digital façade has new beaches featured and the surfers in the recordings are performing tricks that would have been unheard of in my time. But when we enter the store, the long-haired bro behind the counter seems like he would fit into any number of *Point Break* movies they've remade in the last hundred years. He's shirtless and sandy and lights up at the sight of Mym.

"Yo, Miss Quickly! Good to see you. We've been keeping the place tight and right, yeah?" He scoots around the counter and spreads his arms. "Business is up as you can see." He points to the nearly empty surfboard racks. "The tour tots been bangin' up the rentals a bit, but I keep 'em going on. You been getting our rent okay?"

"I'm not checking up on the store today, Chex. Just headed upstairs to get some work done."

"Right, right," Chex replies. "Gots to keep those digits in the plus column and all that." He looks at me and tosses his hair out of his eyes. "Sup, mango."

"Ben," I reply, extending a hand.

Mym makes straight for the door at the back of the room and unlocks it with her fingerprint. Chex's eyes trail her a little longer than I appreciate before finally coming back to me. He shakes my hand.

"And she's *Mrs. Travers* these days," I add.

Chex stares at me blankly for a moment, then finally nods. "Oh, freaky. You're the mister to her S? Right and tight, mo. Right and tight." He holds a couple fingers up in what might presumably be the latest version of a hang ten symbol. That or it's something rude I've failed to research about this decade. Either way, I just smile.

"Catch you later... mango," I say.

"See my man go!" Chex shouts and hops back across the counter. "Tight and right." He goes back to minding the front door.

I find Mym upstairs running through recent activity logs for the safe house. The converted apartment is one of our less-frequent hideouts, but that doesn't mean it hasn't had traffic. With any number of past and future selves roaming the fractal universe, even the out-of-the-way locations can be hotspots depending on the decade. It pays to stay alert. I walk up behind Mym where she's viewing a display projected on the wall. "Any sign of company?"

"I'm checking now. Running a scan of authorized access codes."

I glance around the apartment. Unlike Dr. Quickly's safe houses, which tend to resemble libraries full of knickknacks, Mym's personal spots are tidy and modern. Dr. Quickly has stuck to analog time travel methods—photos and carefully catalogued anchors—but Mym has embraced the digital age, combining her father's methods with modern tech whenever possible to streamline the process. We've begun creating new spaces for the two of us, but this one was set up well before she met me.

I locate the temporal spectrometer and start running a test on the copper door handle. If I'm lucky, it will be from a timestream we can track.

"How old do we think our daughter needs to be before we let her time travel alone? Would we have given her a personal access code or do you think she uses one of ours?" I ask.

"If she's using our accounts for everything, she'll be harder to track," Mym says. "She should still have a user access file somewhere though, at least for fingerprint and retinal scan locks. I'm not finding anything in the records here. No reference to a Piper Travers accessing this space."

The temporal spectrometer results from the door handle don't match any known timestreams either. Another dead end. I frown. "What about call logs? Any evidence that we've used the tachyon pulse transmitter to call anyone named Piper?"

"Good idea," Mym says, running the search of our call logs. The program pings back a result right away. "Oh wow. We do have a record of making a call to a Piper Travers number."

"When?"

Mym blinks at the call line. "Um. Right now? This is like ten . . . eight seconds from now."

She looks at me and I shrug. "Okay. Let's do that."

She hesitates for just a second, then addresses the call management system. "CMS, call Piper Travers."

The tachyon pulse transmitter in the corner fires up and starts clicking through its transmission warm-up. We get a ringing and then a bit of static.

"Hello?" Mym says.

There is a faint murmur that sounds like someone muttering to themselves, then the TPT clicks and the line goes dead.

I look to Mym. "You think the transmission failed?"

"I don't know. It sounded like someone might have picked up for a second."

She is about to try again when we get an incoming call. The COM screen lights up with the ASCOTT logo, a variety of scientific instruments on a shield over a field of green.

Mym makes sure our location settings are off, then picks up the call.

The reddened face of Jermaine Clevis appears on screen. I'm not sure if he's angry, concerned, or simply out of breath. "I'm so glad I reached you. Terrible, terrible day. Are you safe?"

"We're safe enough for now," Mym replies.

"Good. Very good," Jermaine says, wringing his hands. He appears to be in his office. He glances up to someone out of frame. "Yes. Of course I have to show them. It's . . . well, if there's any way to avoid it . . ."

"What's happened?" Mym asks. "More abductions?"

Jermaine nods vigorously, then shakes his head. "No. Not more than we know of, but there have been developments. We caught one of the perpetrators, mind you. Found him still on the grounds. He hadn't jumped away."

"Getting degravitized in the face will do that to you," I comment.

Jermaine apparently doesn't hear me. He keeps glancing at

something on his desk. "Miss Quickly. Or rather, Mrs. Travers as I should say." He gives an apologetic sort of grimace. "It seems the abductors left a message for you."

"For me?" Mym asks. "Why me?"

Jermaine runs a hand through his feathery hair. It sticks out in odd tufts afterward, perhaps the result of some dislodged hair product. "I don't know where to begin exactly, but it seems we had a serious security breach."

"I'd say so," I mutter.

Mym swats at me. "Shh. Let him speak."

"It's rather grim news, I'm afraid." Jermaine straightens up and tries to compose himself. "These ruffians gained access to some sensitive electronic documents. Documents regarding you."

"What sort of documents?" Mym asks.

"They have to do with your father," Jermaine says. "They pertain to a certain device that was in your father's keeping that ASCOTT had a vested interest in. A device intended to safeguard the manner in which Dr. Quickly and other analog travelers conducted themselves in time. I suspect you know to which device I'm referring."

Mym's eyes narrow. "I do, but what has that got to do with ASCOTT? Or with me?"

Jermaine swallows hard and winces. "Well, it was really more a matter of record keeping on our end. Updating the files regarding your father's legal date of death. A technicality really. We just wanted to be accurate about the ownership of the device in this timestream."

"My father's will clearly states that his possessions remain the property of his other selves, or if none are able to claim them, then they pass to me."

"Of course. And that's what we have in our files, but during the update of our records, some information was compromised. Information that should have been confidential was exposed to third parties. Information about your father's device. I'm afraid its existence is no longer a secret."

"What device?" I ask. "What are you guys talking about?"

Mym turns to me. "A long time ago, Dad designed a tool. A

safeguard against the improper use of his chronometers. It's a sort of temporal tuner. All the chronometers we use are tuned from frequencies determined by this one device. Dad named it the warp clock."

"Aren't all time travel devices tuned to specific temporal frequencies?" I ask. "Why is this device such a big secret?"

Mym turns to Jermaine. "I need to pause your transmission for just a second, director. Hold tight."

Jermaine puts up a hand to object. "I have more—" but the rest of his words stay frozen in his mouth as the transmission freezes.

"The warp clock is how our chronometers get made in the first place," Mym says. "There was no one we could trust with that."

"Well, Jermaine obviously knew," I say. "Who else knew about it?"

"Just Abe that I know of. He's the one who actually built it. He needed it to fix the chronometers and create more. Other than that, I can't think of anyone who would know about it."

"Why all the secrecy?" I ask. "Just to keep other people from making chronometers? Was that ever a major threat? Seems like they are pretty complicated for anyone else to fabricate anyway."

"Tuning new chronometers is not all that the warp clock is good for," Mym replies. "It also turns them off."

"Off?"

"They wanted a failsafe. Just in case chronometers fall into the wrong hands or someone needs to shut a time traveler down. If you have the warp clock, you control all of the chronometers that were tuned from it."

"Why would Abe build something so dangerous?" I ask. "Isn't that a bad idea?"

"It was actually ASCOTT that wanted it created," Mym says. "And Dad agreed to it. He thought it was the best solution to the problem. A compromise we all could agree on."

"What problem?" I ask.

"The problem of us," Mym says, her gesture encompassing both of us. "The problem of unregulated time travelers. When ASCOTT formed, they wanted to keep anyone from operating outside the jurisdiction of the central streams. Outside of ASCOTT's control. Even us."

"I thought that ASCOTT always left Harry alone on account of him being the father of time travel. It would be like the Federal Aviation Administration trying to fine the Wright Brothers or something."

"But that's exactly what they wanted to do," Mym explains. "They did want to regulate us. Make sure we followed the rules and didn't create a bunch of paradoxes and new timestreams. They were convinced no one could be trusted to regulate themselves. Even Dad. That's why Abraham's warp clock was the compromise."

"How so?" I ask.

"Dad agreed to the compromise because he thought it wasn't a bad idea to have someone he trusted to keep him in check. He knew his limitations, but he saw the potential for danger and didn't want ASCOTT to be the ones with their fingers on the button. He felt better about it being Abe."

"Like Superman and Batman," I reply.

Mym just looks at me, confused.

"Superman gave Batman some kryptonite to use on him if he ever went crazy and needed to be stopped. Abe's like Quickly's Batman."

"Sure. If that's how you want to see it," Mym says. "But now the word is out that it exists. I wouldn't be surprised if every criminal in the time travel universe wants to get their hands on it."

"What do they plan to do with it?" I ask.

"Not sure I want to find out." She turns to the screen and unfreezes Jermaine again.

"—information to give you," Jermaine continues, seemingly unaware we've been gone. "Let me finish what I meant to tell you before you go."

"We're listening," Mym says.

"They've sent their demands. These attackers from the funeral. They want you to turn over the device to them, or they'll hurt more of the hostages."

"More?" Mym says. She moves closer to the screen. "They've hurt someone already before we even got their demands?"

"They sent a video," Jermaine says. "I'm afraid it's rather shocking and graphic. I have to warn you."

"Just tell us who they've hurt," I say, my stomach in knots recalling the men making people vanish from the funeral. "Was it Abraham? One of our other friends? Who else do they have?"

Jermaine looks even more uncomfortable. He clears his throat and finally responds. "It's you, Mr. Travers. They've killed you. And if you don't cooperate, they mean to do it again."

4

"Don't forget that when you are skipping around in time, you miss people. And you may also be missing out." -Journal of Dr. Harold Quickly, 2272

"What do you mean, they killed me?"

Jermaine still looks uncomfortable. "I'm going to transmit the video file to you now. Watch it when you decide. Like I said, it's quite disturbing." He looks down at his desk. "Okay. Transmission sent. You have our deepest sympathies."

Did he just try to console me about my own death?

"Let me see this video," I say.

Mym hesitates, then activates the play button on the virtual view screen. A scene replaces Director Clevis's office. The video is jumbled and poorly focused. A handheld camera is bouncing around the scene at a nauseating speed but finally settles on several figures in the center of a room with stone walls. It may be some sort of basement. The men in the frame are masked, some with ski masks, others with more elaborate methods. Oddly, one is dressed in a Hawaiian shirt. The man in the center of the frame is wearing a heavy metal helmet that is dome-shaped with circular eyeholes. The helmet flares at the neck but successfully covers all but the glassy eyes peering out. He is the first to speak. His voice has a vaguely echoing quality inside the helmet.

"Mym Travers. This message is for you alone. You will hand over the warp clock at the location we tell you, at the time we tell you, or people you love will die." He gestures to the man with the camera. "Feed in the video. Show her the price she'll pay if she refuses."

The man with the camera fumbles with something, causing the view to dip. We spend several seconds looking at the floor while he attempts to play the video. The man in the helmet grumbles something, then the man with the camera straightens it again. "There were two files with the same name for some reason. Not sure why they sent it twice. Okay, here we go."

The video jumps to a different scene. A dim room, the walls are wood. Could be a cabin. Two men are tied to chairs. As the camera zooms in on the face of one man, I recognize myself. Only it isn't my face—not exactly. This man is older than me, perhaps a decade or more. A sprinkling of gray hair has made an appearance on his stubbled chin and his hairline has receded somewhat. The lines around his eyes are more pronounced as well. But there's no denying it's me. The camera pivots and focuses on the second chair. This man has his head down, but someone grabs his hair and pulls his head up to look at the camera.

Mym gasps.

This one is me too. I can't be sure if it's my current timeline. There could be any number of versions of myself roaming the fractal universe, but this version can't be far off. If we differ in age, it doesn't look to be by much. My other self glares at his captors and begins to say something, but the video cuts to a different scene.

Two men are now standing near a wall, hands bound with canvas bags over their heads. The men have been secured to posts in the ground. Someone near the camera speaks.

"They didn't say which one. I guess we get to pick."

A rifle barrel pivots into view, though it's not a modern gun. It appears to be a musket of some kind, the type you'd find at a Revolutionary War reenactment. The cameraman backs up a step and more of the man with the gun comes into view. He's wearing old-fashioned attire as well—a collared coat with epaulettes and shiny buttons. The coat has long tails. He has a modern mask, however, a rubberized face like you'd see in a Halloween costume store. This one might be George Washington or some other colonial figure. The man lifts the musket to his shoulder, aims at the man on the right, and squeezes the trigger.

The blast from the gun sends a cloud of smoke billowing from the barrel.

The shot hits the man on the right squarely in the chest, and he collapses immediately to the ground. His hands are still linked to the post. His body hits the ground with a meaty thump.

"Oh my God!" Mym puts a hand to her mouth.

The other captive has flinched and ducked involuntarily and now shifts from side to side trying to ascertain what has happened.

"Okay, you got that recorded, right?" The man in the rubber mask turns to the cameraman. "Send that back."

The camera pans to the ground and the figure of the man lying there. A stain of blood has already begun to wick through the fibers of his shirt. I can't tell which version of me it was. The only distinguishing feature that can be discerned is that the me on the ground has a tear in the knee of his pants—otherwise, they are dressed nearly identically. The second me is cut loose from the post and yanked forward by the rope. His bagged head pivots as the man in the mask nudges him with the barrel of the rifle.

"You bunch of bastards!" the me in the hood exclaims.

The video goes black.

A second later, the scene of the men in the stone-walled room reappears. The man in the metal helmet steps closer to the camera. "We are capable of getting to anyone you love, Mrs. Travers. The choice is yours. Hand over the device, or watch them die. Don't waste our time."

A set of temporal coordinates appears on screen for several seconds, then the video ends.

Jermaine Clevis's office comes back up on the view screen. He's watching us intently. Evidently he's still been able to see us even while he was off screen.

Mym is standing shell-shocked, her hands covering her mouth.

"I'm sorry to be the bearer of such evil news," Jermaine says. "But I knew you would want to be informed right away."

"You have any idea where they transmitted this from?" I ask. I key the download feature on my lenses to save the file.

Jermaine frowns and shakes his head. "It came through a variety of channels that we've been unable to track. I can have our historians take a look. We may be able to narrow down the timestream and time period a bit if we study the imagery, but I didn't know whether you'd be willing to share these images with anyone. I thought it best to get it to you directly first."

"We can't have this out," Mym replies. "Not without knowing who's involved and how they got their hands on Ben." She turns to me. "Are you okay?"

I realize I've barely moved since the video ended. "Yeah. I'm okay. It's just . . . that was really surreal."

"It's possible that those versions of you may be from different timestreams," Jermaine comments. "They may have nothing to do with your present trajectory in time."

Mym reaches for the transmitter controls. "Thank you for contacting us, director. We could use some time to weigh our options and discuss this."

"Of course, of course," Jermaine says, putting up his hands. "Please rest assured that the resources of ASCOTT are at your disposal. Please let us know how you would like to proceed."

"We'll be in touch," Mym says and signs us off from the transmission.

She turns to me and just stares at my face. The mask of courage she was wearing with the director is already slipping.

I step forward and wrap my arms around her. "I don't know what that was, but we'll figure it out."

Mym encircles me with her arms and hangs on. "That was one of the worst things I've ever seen."

My eyes drift to the empty wall where the screen was projected. "I know what you mean."

After the better part of a minute, Mym finally relaxes her grip on me.

"These guys clearly mean business," I say. My mind is reeling from what we've witnessed. "We're going to need help with this one. We need to warn as many people as we can. Prevent them from taking any more hostages."

"And we need to find our daughter," Mym says.

I think about the little girl who disappeared into the slide at the playground. Alternate future or not, she's still family. "Yeah. We can't let them get their hands on her."

"They already have all they need for leverage, but she's just a kid," Mym says. "If they had her too . . ."

"Don't worry," I say. "These aren't the first loco time travelers we've been up against. They're going to find out they're messing with the wrong people. We're going to find her first."

Mym exhales audibly and turns back to the controls of the tachyon pulse transmitter. "Okay. I'll start making some calls."

"I'm going to make us something to drink." I walk around the corner to the kitchen where I am out of sight and rest my hand on the refrigerator door handle. The image of the gunshot flashes through my mind again. It's almost as if I can feel the impact in my chest. Some version of me is going to die that way. It could be me. Is it me?

I open the refrigerator and find nothing helpful. There's a bottle of vodka in the freezer but nothing to mix it with.

I'm not that desperate.

I fill the teakettle instead and set it atop the electric stove burner. I pull up the downloaded video on my meta lenses and watch it again. Colonial musket. Torn jeans. Gun smoke. The blood seeps through his shirt. I watch it over and over again, seeing the body of my other self hitting the ground.

The kettle starts to scream.

I make two mugs of tea and affix a positive expression on my face before walking back around the corner. I hand Mym her tea. "So who do we call first?"

Then the incoming call chime starts to ring.

5

"Appreciate each year and decade you live through. Relish its quirks and eccentricities. Many time travelers would cross centuries and expend fortunes to experience what you take for granted." -Journal of Dr. Harold Quickly, 1972

"They're prison escapees," Carson says. Mym has pinged him with the tachyon pulse transmitter looking for advice, and his response was immediate. Of the time traveling friends we have, Carson is the most tuned-in to the criminal underworld, ever since he got a job in the future hunting down rogue time travelers.

"Time travel prison?" I ask.

"It's called Rookwood Penitentiary," he replies.

We're talking to him remotely via the TPT, but he's enabled metaspace calling, meaning it looks like we're occupying the same space. My meta lenses have transposed his setting over ours. I'm still not entirely comfortable using the metaspace, but Carson has adapted to it lately and likes using it for all of his calls. He commandeers the image matrix and transports us virtually to Rookwood Penitentiary.

"It's mostly used for cons running afoul of ASCOTT," he explains.

"Everything from gambling infractions to illegal organ harvesting. It can't hold inmates forever, unfortunately, but it keeps the worst of the time travel criminals off the streets and flagged on the Grid. The inmates have nicknamed the prison 'Time Out.'"

"Cute," I mutter. I study the virtual view of the prison's exterior. It looks like a fortress, but obviously not impenetrable. "Too bad it couldn't hold these guys."

"Yeah. The breakout happened fast. They had help, obviously. It's a network of criminals." Carson pivots us to a top-down view of the prison, making it seem like we're floating hundreds of feet overhead. I grab Mym's shoulder involuntarily. Carson doesn't seem to notice my discomfort. "Seven escapees that we know of, plus whoever was helping them on the outside. The press is calling them 'The Tempus Fugitives.' Good news is, the guy you zapped at the funeral was a big clue. He was a legal parolee, so he didn't trip the flagging system, but his affiliations helped clue us in to what he's been involved with."

Carson flashes us back to his current location and starts rummaging around in some cabinets. I release Mym's shoulder and she pats me gently on the back. We appear to be in a warehouse of some kind. There are a number of vehicles parked behind him and a wall of tools. My virtual self is partially embedded in a truck so I take a step sideways, not liking the idea of being fused with something, even in the metaspace.

The cabinet Carson is looking through has a lot of electronics and some power packs. "It's around here somewhere," he mutters as he sifts through items. "Ah, here we go." He holds up a data key with a logo on top in the shape of an eye. The eye has some familiar-looking rays coming out of it. "Confiscated this a few months back. Took it from a parole violator we caught scalping used concert tickets before rock shows. Seems he's involved with the same underground group that sprung these guys. The parolee you zapped was a member of this church—The Way of the All Seeing Eye. Sometimes it's called the Church of Providence. They adopted the 'Eye of Providence' as a symbol, but it's not really a church in the traditional sense. These guys are involved with a group worshipping A.I. and the eventual technological singularity."

"They want to worship an artificial intelligence?" I ask.

"Idea's been around a long time," Carson says. "Since the early twenty-first century, actually. But this is a more evolved version. They assume that when the singularity happens, the A.I. will essentially be a god. They want to get on its good side now. A lot of the time that means sucking up to whatever A.I. they think might have a chance to evolve.

"Hard to say if these cons were actually devout members or not, but they were using a church-run communications network to talk to each other. There must have been some code involved that the guards missed. In any case, the guys using the network figured out a way to connect with the outside and plan their escape. Now they are on the loose."

"And murdering people we love," Mym says. "Why are they coming after the warp clock?"

"From what you tell me, a device used to control chronometers would be highly valuable to escaped convicts. If they got their hands on some chronometers, they could stay off the ASCOTT radar permanently. ASCOTT only tracks Grid users and people using Temprovibe time traveling devices. That makes chronometers prized possessions for criminals. They could use them to get out of the central streams, hide out, and ASCOTT would never find them."

"They have to know we could use the warp clock to shut those chronometers down," Mym says. "So it makes sense that they want it. Once they have control of the warp clock, they won't have to worry about being stranded somewhere."

"Exactly," Carson replies. "They're staying off-Grid and out of sight for now. Not sure how they're getting around, but from the video you showed me, we can assume they have at least two chronometers now. If you were to shut them down remotely, I'd say goodbye to our chances of getting the other versions of you back."

"They grabbed Abe from the funeral too," I say. "If they force him to give them more chronometers, that might be as many as they could want."

"More reason they want control of the warp clock," Carson says. "If they get that, they're free and clear. Nothing to stop them from disappearing into the multiverse and causing whatever mayhem they desire. If they get the ability to retune chronometers and operate off-Grid, there's no telling how many new timestreams they create," Carson says. "The potential is unlimited."

I consider what he's saying. As much as I've disliked ASCOTT's methods over the years, the de facto governing agency for time travelers has done a reasonable job of avoiding paradoxes. The Grid tracking system they invented keeps travelers from jumping into one another, and the Temprovibe time traveling devices themselves are rigged to only function in certain timestreams. Thanks to ASCOTT's interference, most of the fractal universe is still unexplored by time travelers, and therefore largely untampered with. A breach in that dam could unleash a flood of time travelers into other streams, creating untold numbers of paradoxes. It wouldn't necessarily be catastrophic for the universe, but there would be no putting the lid back on it once it happened.

"I'd say good riddance if they weren't taking our people with them," Mym says.

"So what's the plan?" I ask. "I feel like we have to warn the others. Anyone wearing a chronometer seems a likely target for these guys, and I hate to say it, but the closer they are to Mym and me, the more likely they are to get hurt."

Mym frowns. "I'm putting people in danger again. Just by knowing them."

I put a hand on her shoulder. "Hey, this isn't on you. Not one bit."

"Why now?" Mym asks Carson. "Why come after us at this period of our lives? They don't seem to have gone after my dad. Why go after us?"

Carson rubs his hands over his head, failing to straighten his unruly, red hair. "I've run into it before. It's sort of a moral code. A certain segment of the underworld seems to follow it. Nobody goes after Quickly. It's like they consider him to be, I don't know . . . Grandfather Time. I think they respect that he's the one who opened this world to them and they don't want to mess with that. Harry Quickly is a hero."

"So the criminal underworld has more respect for Harry than ASCOTT does?" I ask. "They apparently never trusted him. That's why we're in this warp clock business to begin with."

"What can I say? He's a man of the people," Carson replies. "I've been to the houses of cons who have his picture on the wall, like he's the pope or something."

"But that respect apparently doesn't fall on his family," Mym says.

"Well, not the in-laws anyway," Carson says, looking at me.

"How about his granddaughter?" I ask. "Any hope they'll leave her alone on principle?"

Carson frowns. "I wouldn't count on it."

Mym unfolds her arms and seems to have made a decision. "Okay, let's get everyone we know into the Central Streams. That way if they do manage to get their hands on the warp clock we won't be completely stranded. We could use Temprovibes if we had to. We wouldn't be able to get everywhere we want to go, but we won't be completely trapped in one timestream. Everybody stays close to home and hides out till we figure out how to get these other Bens and Abe back."

"That could work," Carson says. "I can get on the horn and spread the word. What about your missing future daughter? I looked around a little but couldn't find any information on her."

"I think we should handle that," I say. "She found us once, there's a good chance she'll keep trying. Once we have her, we can get to a central stream and keep her safe."

"And I still need to locate the warp clock," Mym says.

"You know where it is?" I ask.

Mym gathers a few items off the table to stuff into her bag. "I've only seen it once before, but it doesn't matter. It won't be there now. Dad never kept it with us. He and Abe kept it in a solitaire somewhere. I'll have to ask him to get me there."

It's been a while since I've heard the term, but I'm familiar with solitaires. They are timestreams deliberately cut off from others. No organic ways in or out without already having an anchor from there.

"You plan to give it to them?" Carson asks.

"Do I have a choice?" Mym asks. "They're killing people. Killing *Ben*. I can't just let that happen."

Carson doesn't argue. He closes up the cabinets he's been rummaging through and adjusts the video feed to show us back in the apartment. "Okay, I'll do what I can on my end. I'll see what else I can dig up on these guys and call you when I have something new."

"Be safe, man," I say.

"You too." Carson gives me a long look, seems like he's going to say something else, but then just nods and signs off.

Mym turns to me. "You good with this plan?"

"Except for the part where I have no idea where to start," I say. "That kid could be anywhere right now."

Mym fidgets with the straps on her bag. "I don't know how to find Piper, but I know someone who might be able to help us learn more about where your alternate selves are being held. That's something I'd like to sort out. If they took Abe, then he might be there too."

"Any plan is better than no plan," I say. "Yours wins."

"I have a place to start, but it will involve a bit of a trip. Your chronometer charged up?"

"Ready when you are."

Mym sets to work degravitizing an anchor from her collection and moves it to a table. I rest my hand atop hers and give it a squeeze.

Mym double-checks her chronometer settings, and I do my best to not think about the musket and the gunshot and the way the man in the hood thudded to the dirt. The bloodstain seeping slowly through his shirt . . .

"Ready?" Mym is watching me.

"Yeah. Let's do it."

Mym presses the pin and we blink.

6

"Sometimes I'm asked which year has the best food. Many argue the merits of cuisines from specific decades or timestreams. I'm personally still trying to recreate a lasagna I tasted in 1825." –Journal of Dr. Harold Quickly, 1980

A red light is flashing in the corner of my right sunglasses lens. Disconnected. Wherever we've jumped to, there are no metaspace features. I pull the sunglasses off my face and look around.

We're in another safe house. Europe somewhere, if I had to guess based on the living room decor. Ambient noise from the street is coming in through the open window, but the curtains are covering the view. "Quiet," Mym whispers, holding a finger to her lips. "Follow me." She pulls me through a doorway into a small bedroom and closes the door till only a crack of light remains. She peers through it.

Being roughly a head taller than Mym, I'm able to stand behind her to see what she's looking at. A few moments pass, then a door somewhere else in the house opens and footsteps sound along the floorboards. They grow muffled when they reach the living room rug. Two people step into view. One is Mym, but she's a teenager, fourteen or fifteen at most. The other person is Dr. Quickly.

"You think that was enough time?" the young Mym asks.

"It would seem so," Dr. Quickly replies. "Assuming you get a chance to use it one day."

The young Mym is making notes in a journal. "You really think we'll need anchors in this decade? We hardly ever come up this far."

"More reason to have safe places to jump to," her father replies. "The most dangerous times require the most preparation." He looks our way and notes the door we're hiding behind. His eyes narrow slightly as he studies the crack we're peering through. Mym eases the door shut. The scientist's voice still carries from the other room. "Now come on, let's get out of here. Plenty more stations to set up. Let's see if we can get a few more in before lunch."

We wait till the sound of their voices stops, then a few minutes later, emerge back into the living room.

"You guys had quite the system," I say.

"Dad had me setting up anchors for most of my adolescence," Mym replies. "I was so sick of taking anchor photos by the time I was sixteen, I never wanted to make another jump."

"I guess you grew out of it."

"I realized the perks outweigh the hassles."

"Where are we?" I move to the window and open the curtains. I'm looking down from the third floor onto a narrow street lined with shops. The stonework around the windows of the long building across from ours is weatherworn and old, a relic from a prior century.

"We're in Florence," Mym replies. "We need to visit a friend and get some advice. I've been thinking about that video."

"Pretty hard not to," I mutter.

"While you were making us tea, I ran a basic net search on images in the video, trying to get clues on where they were keeping you, er, them. I didn't get any hits on the video itself, but something came back on the gun. It looked old. Authentically old. It's possible it was a replica, but I'd like to find out. It's a strange choice of weapon in any case."

"This helmet guy and the one in the costume obviously have a flair for the theatrical," I say. "Do you think the gun looked American Colonial? Or maybe French?"

The Warp Clock

"I want to find out," Mym says. "I have a friend who works at the Uffizi, and she might be able to give us some answers."

"Linear friend or time traveler?"

"Sophia is linear, but when it comes to the past, she's as good a historian as I've ever known—time travelers included."

I pull the curtains back across the windows to leave them the way I found them. "And she lives here in Florence?"

"She used to," Mym says. She checks her chronometer. "She's dead right now, but we won't let that stop us."

It takes a series of jumps using anchors from the Quicklys' collection to get us farther back in time. Even with our chronometers plugged into power sources, they are heavily drained by the time we arrive in 2075. We've dialed back the clock on the city of Florence, but the effect is less evident here than in other cities. Florence seems to age at its own rate, and it has never been fast. After a quick change of clothes using the wardrobe options at the safe house, we head into the streets and make our way toward the Uffizi Gallery.

The Ponte Vecchio is crowded with tourists shopping for jewelry. The historic bridge still features wooden shop fronts with elaborate iron hardware on the doors and windows. Mym pauses briefly in front of one shop that is currently closed and gestures to the wooden door. "Did you know this is where Dad first met Abraham? Abe had a watch shop here. Beautiful pieces. Dad said he already seemed like a time traveler."

"Did you know him then?"

"Before my time." She smiles at me. "Can I use your MFD?"

I hand the device to her and she dials a number from memory. When the person on the other line picks up, she puts on her most carefree voice. "Hey Soph! You'll never guess where I am!"

She slips into Italian for the rest of the conversation, and I have a hard time following. I pull the earpiece loose from my sunglasses and slip the end into my ear, but by the time I've located the translate option from the menu of apps, she's hung up.

"Good news. She has time to meet. We can head upstairs."

Sophia Laurenzi is a stylishly dressed woman around Mym's age whose well-defined calf muscles are no doubt toned by climbing up and down the numerous staircases of the Uffizi. I'm out of breath by the time we meet her, and I'm quickly reminded that while getting around by time travel may be cool, I'm going to need to make time for some cardio soon. Sophia greets Mym with an enthusiastic hug, and when her attention finds me, she extends a hand for a friendly handshake. "It's wonderful to meet you. I've been wondering who keeps my Mym away from me. You need to share her, you know."

I smile. "I can certainly think of worse places to hang out."

"This old place?" Sophia smirks at me. "I guess it has a few charms." She turns toward Mym. "You have something interesting for me? I know this isn't just a visit for fun."

"I wish it were," Mym says.

Sophia guides us to her office via a long corridor lined with marble statues. Once we're shown into her office, Mym uses the computer system to display an image of the gun in the video. She's used some kind of filter, however, and blurred the figures in the background. It looks like the gun is aimed at a fuzzy wall. The other image is the man in the helmet and his henchmen in masks in the room with the stone walls. This second image is what Sophia stares at the longest.

"Have you seen a gun like this before?" Mym asks, referencing the first screenshot. "Or could you help us narrow down where either image is from?"

Sophia concentrates on the photos in silence for at least twenty seconds before speaking, zooming in on various features. Finally she leans back. She points to the image of the man in the helmet. "Have you been to this place in person?"

"Not yet," I reply. "But we plan to."

"Well, I can tell you that some of the details in this room are interesting. The helmet he's wearing is old. Early first century. Something a Roman gladiator would wear in combat. But the symbols carved on the stones behind him are Etruscan. The wall in the background is going to date to at least 400 BCE. You could almost date this whole room back to the Etruscan Empire."

"Almost?" Mym asks.

Sophia points to a chair in the background that I hadn't even noticed. "If it weren't for that. That chair isn't Etruscan. It's definitely Roman. A really elaborate replica if I had to guess. Or possibly a restoration. The fabric of the cushion could never survive till the modern era looking that bright, and I would expect the wood to be damaged over time. The gold trim would be more tarnished as well. It looks like real gold. It would have belonged to someone wealthy. Is the person in the mask a collector of any kind?"

"Not sure," I reply.

At least now I know what the gladiator Piper mentioned looks like.

"If that chair was original, when would it be from?" I ask. I glance at Mym. I imagine she's thinking what I am. If we are dealing with time travelers, it pays to know all the options.

"Maybe 200 CE? Possibly later. Again, it's hard to say without seeing it in person. But it's a similar age to the gladiator helmet."

I lean forward and study the chair. "You know, I've seen a design like that before, now that you mention it."

"Been traipsing around Ancient Rome?" Sophia jokes. "Lunch with an emperor, perhaps?"

I open my mouth to reply, but notice Mym standing behind her, shaking her head. I know the warning to shut up when I see it. "Maybe I saw it in a movie somewhere."

The other image doesn't get a lot of study. Sophia's hands zoom in briefly on one portion of the gun, then she leaves the image alone. "Muzzle-loading flintlock musket. I'd say the British Long Land Pattern. Dates to around 1775. Prewar, but not by much. It's been repaired by a local gunsmith at least once. Here and here." She points to spots on the barrel and flintlock mechanism.

Sophia has ignored her ringing phone twice during the conversation with us but finally picks it up. "Sorry," she mouths to

Mym. She converses with someone on the other end at a speed that makes me think I wouldn't understand it even if it weren't in Italian.

Mym leans closer and whispers to me. "You have any ideas?"

"Maybe. It's a thin lead, but it might be worth investigating. You know how she said the chair would have to be a replica to look that good in the video? What if it's the real thing?"

"How would that help us?"

"How many time travelers do you think have been that far back in time? If you had to wager a guess, do you think it would be a couple dozen? A hundred? It would be a really long trip to do with chronometers. Probably two hundred stops along the way at minimum. Has to be next to impossible with a Temprovibe. You'd need approval from ASCOTT, and from what I hear, they aren't letting anyone off the Grid without permits, let alone escaped cons. The only way I could see someone getting back that far would be with a time gate."

"You think they are traveling by time gates? I guess it would make sense for staying off the Grid. Not sure where they would find one though," Mym says. "Special events like a chronothon could get one, but those have been disbanded. It would have to be a private owner."

"Right. So it definitely narrows the search for us."

Sophia ends her conversation and hangs up the phone.

"We should let you go," Mym says. "We know you're busy."

Sophia sighs but doesn't argue. The two of them chitchat for a while longer as she leads us toward the exit, making plans to meet up for a cappuccino soon.

A tour group is clogging up the hall we entered by so Sophia takes us on a detour through a contemporary art exhibit to get around them. We walk around a couch that is constructed entirely of broken pencils and through an exhibit featuring giant photos of women with power tools.

Sophia reaches the door and disarms the alarm for us. She swings it open, and the busy sounds of the city beckon.

Mym steps through the doorway and turns around. "You coming, Ben?"

Her voice registers in my mind, but it takes me a moment to respond. "Uh, I think you might want to see this."

Mym walks back to my side, and I move toward a photo on the wall. A group of female welders is precariously balanced on a girder high over a city skyline with sparks flying everywhere as they work. Between the women with the blowtorches and grinding wheels, leaning casually on one of the building's support columns, is a little girl wearing overalls and welding goggles. Her hands are in her pockets, but there is a glint of silver at her left wrist. I can't see her eyes, but she may as well be looking straight at me.

"At least she didn't inherit my issues with heights," I mutter.

Mym follows my gaze. "What are you looking at?"

I point out the girl in the goggles. "I think I just found our daughter."

Mym's mouth falls open. "What on earth . . ."

"I know," I reply. "Let's go get her. We'll make sure she's safe, but then she's definitely grounded."

7

"Time travel is a big help with repetitive chores. With a few hours of work, I've already watered my houseplants for the next six years." -Journal of Dr. Harold Quickly, 1987

"I don't like it. Not even a little bit." I'm staring up at the construction site in early 2075 that the photo of our alternate daughter has led us to. The structure joining the London skyline is still just a steel skeleton at the very top. The rest of the building looks a little more complete, but just barely.

It took a bit of research to locate the construction site the artist used for the photo shoot and to scan social media records for when it was completed. It took a little while longer to convince Sophia to take the image out of the exhibit in Florence for us. I have little doubt that the time travelers we're up against can probably find a version to look at anyway, but any attempt to slow down their hunt for our people is worth it, even if it means an expensive addition to our family art collection.

"You think she's up there yet?" Mym asks.

I study the assembled cars in the parking lot. One is a commercial van with both visible and meta lettering on the side. "She will be soon. Looks like the photographers are already here."

We're still discussing a plan for getting up the building when my MFD starts buzzing in my pocket. I check the display to find an incoming message from Carson.

"We have a tachyon pulse relay around here somewhere?" I ask Mym. "Looks like I'm getting temporal data service." I put the device on video mode and open the call. "Hey, man. You still doing okay?"

Carson is in a car. An urban skyline is whizzing past out the window behind him. "Got you some more details on our Tempus Fugitives. Thought I'd pass them along."

I gaze up at the towering construction site, then turn around and put the earphone from my glasses into my ear, not unhappy about the delay. "What have you got?"

"Interesting bit about the suspected ringleader. Goes by Maxwell Franco. Went away for abducting tourists from a time travel tourism company called Quantum Wanderers. He and a group of buddies would impersonate tour guides, lure travelers on side trips, rob them of their Temprovibes, and then abandon them in distant timestreams. Made quite a haul that way. He was also connected to a string of industrial warehouse thefts, but they never had enough evidence to convict him. He was acquitted on those charges."

"Thefts of what?" I ask.

"Time gates. A whole bunch of them. ASCOTT was storing reclaimed chronothon gates after the races got shut down. They were expecting the tech to show up on the black market, but the gates never resurfaced. Whoever has them is keeping them all to themselves."

"We thought they might be using those to get around."

"Well, they've got chronometers for sure," Carson says. "Not sure they have the gates, but if they do, they'll be tough to track."

"Anything on the other escapees?" I ask.

"I'll send you their files," Carson says. "There was one more thing. The prison gave me the name of the person the escapees were communicating with on the outside. Somebody who goes by the handle of 'TRIK' online. All the correspondence they dug up from

The Way of the All Seeing Eye were linked to this TRIK person. No details on who they are, but they had an interest in busting these guys out."

"We'll keep an eye out," I reply.

"Wish I had more for you," Carson says. "Be safe out there."

"Will do. Thanks, man."

I turn off the display and slip the MFD back into my pocket. I pull the sunglasses from my face as well. The construction site ahead of us seems even more dangerous now.

"Let's get this girl and get out of here," I say. "The sooner we're back on the ground and gone, the better."

Mym tosses me an anchor from her bag. It's a degravitized nail. "From that rooftop in Bruges we visited last year. We should have an exit ready if we get into trouble."

"Good idea." I pull my MFD back out and scan the nail, pulling up the time we logged it, then I put both back into my pocket. "Better safe than sorry."

We find the construction elevator and press the call button. Thankfully it's functional.

The elevator is little more than a rectangular steel cage. I do my best not to look down as it rattles its way up the flimsy-looking scaffolding tower. The correct floor isn't hard to find. A photography crew has taken over the topmost level of the construction site and is bustling about the concrete floor adjusting lights and prepping models. I'm relieved to see that there is at least some safety netting on the side of the building being used for the shot. A number of models are already posing with tools, and it's nice to see that they aren't all of the typical swimsuit model variety. The photographer has included women in all manner of shapes, ages, and walks of life. At least the art world seems to have made some progress since my time.

There's no sign of Piper.

Mym and I are accosted by an assistant of some kind who is sporting blue hair and a shirt collar made of neon feathers. He appraises us skeptically. "Are you from catering? Because the coffee needs refilling." He wags an empty paper cup at me.

"We're from the Department of Time Management," I reply. "Seeing who's wasting ours."

The man frowns at me, tosses his hair out of his eyes, and wanders away.

The shoot site is bustling with activity, but no one else seems to be paying us much attention. We position ourselves where we have an angle on the action. I pull out my MFD to check the arrangement of models in the artwork from the museum. It takes about fifteen minutes till models I recognize are moved into position. It's another ten minutes before the photographer is happy with the lighting. Finally they get under way, posing with blowtorches and grinders.

Then, as quick as thought, she's there.

The little girl in the goggles, directly in the middle of the scene, casually leaning against the girder. She slips her hands into her pockets and the photographer keeps shooting for a few more seconds before realizing what has happened. She finally looks up from her camera, at which point Piper looks directly at me, and smiles. Then she looks to Mym and her smile disappears.

"Watch out!" she shouts.

I turn to see what Piper is looking at and find a huge man wearing a metal helmet looming behind Mym. The Gladiator. He lunges for Mym.

Mym ducks, nimbly dodging the man's arms and scurrying behind me. I swing at him, realizing mid-punch that striking his metal helmet is a stupid move. I open my hand in time and end up just slamming the heel of my palm against his faceplate. It does nothing. The punch he throws, however, connects with the left side of my face, and I stagger sideways from the blow.

The Gladiator moves toward Mym, the sides of his black trench coat flaring out as he walks. "You don't seem to be getting the message! When I said get me the warp clock, I didn't say anything about side trips to London. You're wasting time."

"I don't have it," Mym replies, backing away from him. "I need time to find it."

He takes another step toward her.

"Hey!" I step between him and Mym. "Back off."

I square up with him, but the big man lunges forward and seizes my arm, then pulls me toward him. It happens so fast I barely have time to register it. His fist connects with my face twice before I can get an arm up, but he doesn't let go of me. Stunned from the blows, I teeter, then watch him rear back to hit me again.

My body seems to be reacting in slow motion, while his movements are a blur. How is he so fast? Finally the right synapses connect in my brain and I move, ducking under his arm and twisting in his grip till I'm at his elbow. It's not a great position, but it allows me a moment to recover and send a kick to the big man's knee. He grunts from the blow but doesn't budge. His grip on my arm may as well be a vise.

Around the room, the photography crew is keeping their distance, some dialing phones, but no one is moving to help.

The Gladiator wrenches my arm around and presses on my shoulder. I cry out from the pain. He has my wrist twisted at a hard angle.

"Leave him alone!" The yell comes from my right. Piper is running toward us.

"No! Stay back!" I gasp, waving with my free arm.

Mym is already working to set the chronometer on her wrist, but she's backing away from our attacker.

Smart. Keep some distance. A safe space to jump.

Piper, on the other hand, keeps coming.

The big man in the helmet twists my arm again, and I'm forced to refocus my attention on him. I jab at him with my left, but he evades the blow. He blocks the kick to his groin as well, moving at a speed that seems incongruous with his size. His meaty fist connects with my face again.

"Let him go!"

Something smashes into the man's arm and he releases me. I'm seeing stars as I reel away, but I spot Piper wielding a 2x4.

Smart girl.

I'm reaching for my chronometer even as I stagger. I dig one hand into my pocket and extract the galvanized nail. If I can just jump away, I can come back to this fight with more options. Maybe a shotgun.

I dial my device for the right time, trying to recall the coordinates from memory.

Helmet Head is too fast. He appears right in front of me. He smacks my arm and the nail goes flying out of my hand. I attempt to dodge around him and go after it, but his movements are a blur. As soon as I think of a direction to go, he's there, blocking my path. The only visible parts of the man's face are two bloodshot eyes flicking back and forth in the eyeholes of the helmet. It's almost as though he's not looking at me, but through me. As I watch, a fine mist sprays from around the eyeholes of his helmet directly into his eyes. I recognize the faint floral scent of the performance-enhancing street drug, 4sight. It speeds up users' reaction times almost to the point of them being able to predict the future. No wonder he's so fast.

Then Mym is there. She swings her bag at the Gladiator and smashes him in the head with it, but the contents merely rain around him. She roundhouse kicks him in the ribs and he groans. But then he turns on her. Mym tries to dodge but this time she's not fast enough. He snatches a handful of her shirt. She kicks at him again, but he dodges the blow, then rears back with a fist to punch her in the face.

I barrel into the man at full speed. He lets out a grunt as I hit him, and the force of the blow is enough to make him lose his grip on Mym. The Gladiator stumbles, and we hit the floor together in a heap. He's too fast though. He clamps onto my arm and twists me around in some kind of wrestling maneuver. I find myself facing the wrong direction.

"Let him go!" Piper still has the 2x4 in her hand and is waving it at him. Unfortunately it's far too small to really hurt him. Especially wielded by someone who might weigh sixty-five pounds.

"Looks like we've got the whole Travers family," the Gladiator says, climbing to his feet and dragging me up with him. "Another person you care about?"

"Don't touch her," Mym hisses.

I attempt to free my arm from his grasp, but he violently wrenches it behind my back and forces me to a knee. He's only a few inches taller than me, but his brute strength is incredible.

"You two don't seem to understand how things are working now," he snarls from beneath the helmet. "You do what I say. No questions. You don't, people get hurt." He twists my arm upward, and it feels like it's going to come out of my shoulder socket. I wince and move with the force, trying to keep from tearing anything.

"Stop it!" Piper rushes him, swinging the 2x4. He catches it with his free hand and wrenches it from her grasp in one fluid motion. He hurls the piece of wood away while Piper stands shocked.

The next moment he grabs a handful of her shirt and drags her toward him.

"Hey! Wait. I'll get what you want!" Mym shouts. She has a hand raised. "Just don't hurt them."

"I know you will," the man replies. "Because otherwise you won't be able to live with what I do to them."

I'm desperately searching for solutions to this situation, but I can't see one. My chronometer arm is pinned behind me, and even if I activated it by remote, the Gladiator and Piper would come with me. We might survive, but we could end up fused into whatever was occupying this space hours or days ago. Could be years if the rings on my chronometer have moved. If it was just me I might risk it. But Piper...

Then someone appears behind Mym. Two someones. Now three. The henchmen I saw in the video are popping in right and left.

They are still wearing masks, but I recognize the Hawaiian shirt one of the men had on. They encircle us.

"Go!" I shout to Mym. It's really our best hope right now. If she can find help and come back . . . Mym is wide-eyed, searching my face. She pulls the anchor from her pocket as the thugs close in on her. Then she vanishes.

I breathe a sigh of relief. I don't have time to react further because Helmet Head is tearing at the chronometer on my wrist.

"Hey! Get your hands off that!" I twist and reach for him. "You don't even know how to—"

But then the chronometer is off. Despite the custom lock I've installed on the band, this brute has somehow detached it. He releases my arm.

"Oh shit," I mutter, trying to grab it from him. I can't seem to get my hands on him.

"Dad!" Piper has been snatched by one of the other thugs and is being dragged away.

"Get off me!" she shrieks.

I move toward her but the Gladiator steps in to block me.

This time I'm ready. He swings at me, but right before his fist reaches my face, my fingers find the remote in my pocket. I press the button and he vanishes.

"Didn't see that one coming, did you?" I mutter. "That's what you get for stealing."

I run for the guy holding Piper and his eyes widen. He tries to move faster toward the door to the elevator. Apparently he didn't have an exit jump planned.

Piper is squirming in his grip and reaches one hand in my direction.

I'm almost to them when the Gladiator reappears right in front of me.

He elbows me hard in the gut, taking my breath away.

"Nice try, loser." Next thing I know he has ahold of my collar with both hands, lifting me in the air. "Time to say goodnight."

I don't have time to formulate a response. He pulls me toward him and lowers his helmet—fast—directly into my chin.

He drops me and I stagger backward. The room is swirling, and I just have time to notice it shrinking around me. The horizon gets all wavy. Faces of shocked onlookers and newly installed fire sprinklers spin around in a little dance. Piper is screaming in the arms of her captor. I get one last look at the bloodshot eyes in the metal helmet. Then it's concrete floor, dust, and darkness.

8

"I will admit that there are virtues a time traveler lacks. Patience is typically one of them. It's difficult waiting for the world to turn when Friday night could be a blink away." -Journal of Dr. Harold Quickly, 2002

When I open my eyes, it does no good.

I'm blind.

Well, not blind blind, but definitely blindfolded. Whatever fabric has been tied around my eyes is creating an orange blur. A bandana perhaps?

It smells like road dust and the outdoors here. Salt air and something oily.

The sounds confirm it. Tires on a rough surface. Might be asphalt but it's poorly maintained. Too many bumps.

I do my best to assess what else I know.

My hands are tied behind me. I'm on the floor of a vehicle. Truck bed would be my guess. Electric. There's a faint whine in the air from the motor. No combustion rumble or exhaust fumes. That narrows things down a little.

I attempt to move my legs but find those have been tied too. I'm not gagged, though.

"Hello?" I try to sit up but something mashes me back down. The sole of a boot.

"Stay down," someone rumbles.

"Dad?" Piper's voice chimes in from somewhere nearby.

"Hey," I manage, before getting kicked by the boot again.

"Shut up," the voice commands.

My jaw hurts from my recent knockout. Wherever they've taken me, they must have dragged me here. As we bounce along the rough road to wherever we're headed, I do a mental inventory of the rest of my body. All my major pieces seem to be intact. My wrist is still bare, however. It's pressed against the back of my jacket, and the position of the ropes is a reminder. No chronometer means my options for getting out of this mess have been significantly reduced. My trouser pockets feel empty as well. No phone. No pocketknife.

The truck comes to a stop somewhere dusty, and the tailgate slams down. There's some movement and a shout of greeting from someone outside before two sets of hands reach under my armpits and drag me out of the truck. I'm immediately dropped in the dirt.

There's some more scuffling as someone else is forcibly pulled from the truck. Piper, I would guess, because it only takes one set of crunching footsteps and less dragging. She's deposited next to me.

No one else joins us. No Mym. That's something at least.

"We ready to go?" one of the men asks.

A woman's voice responds. "Front gate is open. Jorge will be waiting on the other side. He's taking these two with him."

"You'd think we had enough hostages by now. We're sending the kid through too?"

"Franco said to keep 'em together. He acts up, we've got her as leverage to keep him in line."

The man grunts, then kicks me again. "You hear that?"

I have enough sense to keep my mouth shut this time.

Someone unties my legs and I'm lifted to my feet. I stretch my ankles and consider my options. Even if I were to run, I can't see anything. God knows what I'd collide with. I'd probably just knock myself out again.

A hand grips my arm and pulls me forward. I get a sudden rush of panic as the vision of the man getting shot with the musket flashes through my brain. I have to remind myself that I'm not in his circumstances. Whatever is tied around my head is just a blindfold. No hood. And while I don't know where I am, I doubt it's colonial times. We did arrive in an electric vehicle.

The facts do little to calm my nerves.

"Where are you taking us?" Piper asks.

"Somewhere far away, kid," a voice replies. "Somewhere even your mommy won't find you."

"You're gonna be sorry," she replies. "You're gonna wish you didn't mess with my dad."

Someone laughs. "You hear that, Sal? You'd better watch out."

The man pulling me along, presumably Sal, chuckles in derision. "I think I'll be okay. What do you think, daddy-o?" My foot catches on his outstretched leg and I crash to the ground. I groan from the impact, not having my arms to break my fall. Luckily I manage to avoid breaking my face.

Several of the voices around us laugh. I count at least four.

"Leave him alone!" Piper shouts.

Sal's voice comes from directly above me. "Don't worry, kid. That's what we're planning to do. Leave you both somewhere nice and alone..." He pulls me to my feet and I work on getting my breath back.

Piper lapses into silence.

We're led for several hundred yards, crossing what might be a small bridge. We climb several sets of steps, but barring some vague changes in sunlight, I couldn't even venture a guess as to where we are. There are some strange smells. Old trash perhaps? I get a whiff of something that smells like an overused bathroom. The scent is stale urine and maybe other worse contributions. Luckily we move on.

"'Bout time you got here. You bring the rest of my supplies?" A voice with a Latin accent greets the others. "I hope you brought the power packs."

"All in the trucks," the woman responds.

"And your heavy-ass scanners," another man with a deep voice adds. "Best be sharing the wealth when this works."

"You get to take these hostages," Sal comments from beside me. "They take priority for now. As soon as we get the call from Franco, then we can proceed with the rest of TRIK's plans. That's the deal."

"Don't like playing no games with this TRIK dude," the deep voice says. "He's the real deal. We fail at what he wants, who knows what he does to us."

"Franco says he can handle him," the woman says. "Just do your jobs."

The trucks are off-loaded. There is a lot of moving of equipment and dragging of things. Piper and I are sat on a low wall or barrier of some kind and left alone while this is going on, but I sense someone is watching us nearby.

"Can you see anything?" I whisper.

Piper is to my left and scoots a little closer till her arm is against mine. "I can see a little, but it's just the end of my nose."

I get the impression she's moving her head around and trying to see beneath the edge of her blindfold. "Try not to attract attention," I say. "You have any idea if they took my phone?"

"Yeah. The one who tied you up took it."

"The Gladiator?"

"No. It was another one. The one with the flower shirt on."

I recall the Hawaiian shirt one of the thugs had been wearing. He was stocky. Not tall, but muscular. Couldn't tell much else in the mask. I don't recall hearing his voice.

"That's too bad," I mutter. "What else did you see before they blindfolded you?"

"They jumped us somewhere new before they put us in the trucks. A garage, I think. I couldn't see outside though."

"What else is in the trucks?"

"Guns."

"That's not good," I reply.

"And a helicopter."

"A helicopter?"

"Hey! Shut up over there. I will knock you out if I have to," the man with the Latin accent says. "It'll just make my life that much easier. And make your brain that much stupider."

I slump into a position that I hope will appear submissive. I have a feeling I'll be needing all my brain cells if I'm going to get out of this.

Piper stays close. After a few minutes someone calls our guardian to help with something, and Piper dares to whisper again. "Dad?"

I hesitate a moment. "Yeah?"

"Do you think Mom will find us?"

I have no way to physically reassure her so I whisper back. "I know she won't stop trying till she does." After a lapse of silence I whisper again. "You know I'm not your actual dad, right? If you came back and changed things, the odds that I'm him are kind of . . . well . . . slim. There are factors involved that would change from you doing something like that."

"I know how it works," Piper says. "I know how they make babies. I'm not a little kid, you know."

I can't see her face to make out her expression, but she sounds indignant.

"Sorry. I don't really know when we—when your parents explain the details . . ."

"I know all about sex. It's when you kiss someone with no clothes on. I've seen it on TV. It's how people get babies and why you shouldn't ever kiss boys without clothes on till you are a grown up. That's easy."

I try to think of an appropriate response. "I'm sure your parents will be happy to hear that."

Working slowly, I attempt to loosen the bonds around my wrist. Whoever tied me up knew what they were doing. My wrists don't budge.

"I know you're not him exactly," Piper says. "But my dad's in trouble. You'll help me save him, right?"

I recall the man from the video. The me who was older. Was that him? I still don't know which one of me was under that hood when he was shot. Could that have been Piper's dad? What does that mean for me if it wasn't?

I can feel the warmth of her back pressed into my shoulder. She's turned herself to lean against me.

"I'm going to do everything I can, okay?"

"You promise?"

"I promise," I say.

"We'll think our way out of this?"

"What do you mean?" I ask.

"That's what you always tell me. To think my way out of problems. And if you can't think your way out, then talk your way out. But always think first."

"Sounds like a plan. We'll see what we can do."

Piper's fingers find mine, and she grabs hold of the ones she can reach. I clench her fingers in mine. We stay that way till Jorge comes to get us.

"Okay, on your feet. Hope you're ready for a ride."

We are guided onto some kind of vehicle, but I can't make out what. It has a flat floor and no top. The electric motors whir loudly behind us as we begin to move, but the ride is smooth. A few of the other voices shout goodbyes to Jorge. They apparently aren't coming with us. I'm still trying to figure out what we're riding on when the wave of color hits us. It lights up my vision in a whirl of brilliance that's unmistakable, even wearing a blindfold. We've passed through a time gate.

The squealing of the metal wheels finally gives away what we're riding. It's some kind of train car.

As the car rolls to a stop, we rock forward and the motors shut off. It's hot here. The sun is bright. Its light and heat penetrate the blindfold to warm my face. There's a subtle breeze bearing the scent of evergreen trees. Some shuffling and clunking ensues as someone walks past, and the time gate is shut down.

After a few minutes, a hand grabs at my face and pulls the blindfold loose. Jorge is staring back at me. His wide face is sparsely decorated with a thin mustache and an attempt at a beard. His black hair is loose and shaggy, and he's wearing a broad hat for the sun.

"You two will walk from here. I can't tow you around no more. Don't fall off a cliff or nothin'."

I blink in the sunlight. We are surrounded by evergreen trees. The rails we're perched on stretch into the distance but stop perhaps a quarter mile away with a wooden barricade. Train tracks. I turn around to find that an enormous time gate has been rigged up behind us, but the train tracks don't extend past the gate. This track is a dead end.

Jorge pulls the blindfold from Piper's face as well, and I'm able to get a better look at her. Her eyes are bright like Mym's, and her face, while currently dirty, seems full of youthful optimism. She doesn't seem discouraged by our circumstances. She looks up and meets my gaze, then scans the area around us.

"Where are we?" she asks.

"You don't recognize it?" Jorge says. "This is your native land. At least it might be one day. Right now it's still part of Mexico."

I study the mountains in the distance and the long hills. "Is this California?"

"Good guess, guero," Jorge says. "You got it."

Birdsong is resounding through the trees. We don't seem to be near any sort of civilization.

"What are we doing here?" I ask.

Jorge reaches into his pocket and pulls something out. He holds out his hand. On his palm is a stone about the size of a walnut. An unmistakable metallic vein runs through the center of the stone. Gold.

"We're here to get rich," Jorge says. "Well, I am anyway. You're here as a bargaining chip."

Voices emanate from the woods, and I turn to find a group of young Native Americans emerging from the tree line. A few of them are wearing western clothing, and several are carrying sifting pans. One is holding a pickaxe. They linger near the trees, watching us from a distance.

"Wait a minute . . . you brought us back to the California gold rush?" I ask as Jorge puts away his ore.

Jorge shakes his head. "Nope. Gold rush isn't for another ten years. We're here early. We've got a few things to change."

9

"A clock is a valuable possession, not only as a means of telling time, but also as something to ignore on particularly beautiful days." -Journal of Dr. Harold Quickly, 2002.

"I'm going to untie your hands for one reason and one reason only. I ain't gonna be helping you take a piss." Jorge waves a long knife at me. "But you try to do some stupid shit? Guess who gets hurt?" He aims the knife at Piper. "We clear?"

"Crystal," I say. "You won't get any trouble from me."

I suspect I'm lying, but if it gets my hands untied I'm good with it. He cuts the ropes and I rub my wrists. What sort of trouble I get into remains to be seen.

"You go do any business you need to do over in the woods there. Then you come on back." He keeps a firm grip on Piper's shoulder with one hand, while still holding the knife with the other. I don't have a choice but to comply.

I take my time at the edge of the woods, scanning the trees and looking for anything that might help us. All I see is a few deer droppings and a lot of poison oak. Jorge was right about one thing, it's going to be hard for Mym to find us. An unlicensed time gate jump to the early 1800s? Rural Northern California before it even became a state? Records here will be spotty to say the least. Nobody even knew how to govern this land till after the gold rush. A decade beforehand this was all just Native American land and a few sparsely populated white settlements. I reluctantly wander back up the hill to the train tracks and Jorge.

"Which timestream are we in?"

"I'm sure you'd love to know," Jorge replies. He gestures for me to come closer and zip ties my hands. This time they are in front of my body at least. He then clips a locking carabiner and a long piece of cable around my wrists. The other end gets locked to the flatbed rail car. He considers his work for a moment, then, seemingly satisfied, turns to Piper. "Okay. Same deal, okay? You do your business, then you come right back or your dad here pays the price. Got it?" He aims the knife at me for emphasis.

Piper nods and looks at me, then she turns back to Jorge. "Where's the toilet paper?"

"You don't get no toilet paper," Jorge says. "You gotta squat."

"What if I need to go number two?"

Jorge sighs, then moves to one of the cases loaded atop the train car. He rummages through several before finally returning with a roll of toilet paper. "Okay, here you go. Don't use too much. That's hard to get around here."

She doesn't say anything but turns and heads for the woods. She picks her way slowly through the trees.

"Don't go so far!" Jorge shouts.

"I don't want you to look!" Piper shouts back. "That's gross!"

Jorge looks at me, then shakes his head. "My old lady wanted more kids. I told her she's crazy."

"You leave them behind for this job?" I ask.

Jorge appraises the cargo. "Nah, she left me first. But she's going to regret it when she finds out I'm a millionaire." He starts unpacking some of the gear. One crate appears to be full of metal detectors.

"You're going to mine this land? All of it? One guy with all the gold in California? How do you plan to manage that?"

"Won't be just me, guero. I got a whole army here. This is Washo Indian land. More tribes to the west. They're all going to be in on it. We get that gold, we hide it away. Ain't gonna be no gold rush around here for the white folks. We're gonna rewrite American history."

"You're going to talk hundreds of Native Americans into doing your bidding? What do they get out of it?"

Jorge grins. "I'm from the future, holmes. I got everything they need."

My eye catches movement in the trees on the far side of the grove. Piper is coming *down* the hill, flitting from tree to tree and making her way toward the time gate.

"Hey, what's that mountain range right there?" I blurt out, pointing away from Piper and across the valley.

Jorge looks that direction. "That's Lake Tahoe that way. Sierra Nevadas." He considers the view. "But maybe not no more. I think maybe that's going to be Lake Jorge now." He grins at me. "Maybe Lake *King* Jorge. We'll see." His gaze lowers to the trees. "Where's that kid got to?" He cups his hands. "Hey! Chiquita! Hurry it up!" I glance over my shoulder to where Piper is fiddling with the time gate. She has the control panel open and seems to be meddling with something.

"You know how kids are," I say. "Love to take their time."

"Well, I ain't got all day," Jorge says. He checks notifications on his phone. "Once I get the call, it's game on."

"What call?"

"The one that says we got what we want. The one when your old lady gives up the goods."

I frown. "What happens then? You let us go?"

"Sure thing, guero. We'll let you go." Jorge laughs. "If you can find your way home from here, be my guest. But don't be looking to me for no favors. I'll be busy getting rich."

He turns around and looks at the time gate. My heart jolts in my chest, but I relax when I see that Piper is no longer there. Jorge goes on with his preparations. A few minutes later, Piper emerges from the woods down the hill, still carrying the roll of toilet paper. She has wisely torn some squares off and let the end of the roll dangle free. She politely hands it back to Jorge.

"Took you long enough," he says.

"There's nowhere to wash my hands."

"That's your problem, kid," Jorge says.

She holds her hands out again to be retied. "Yours too."

Jorge stares at them skeptically, then reties her wrists while trying to avoid touching her hands.

Once Piper's hands are retied, he attaches her to the train car the way he did with me, then gestures to the group of Native Americans lingering near the edge of the woods. They follow him back up the hill to help unload the gear.

There are two train cars linked together. The one we're attached to is a flatbed mostly piled with waterproof crates and racks of cylindrical power cells. The second is a standard boxcar, and when Jorge gets the doors open and extends a ramp from it, I'm surprised to find it holds a fleet of electric dirt bikes. I had assumed these would be shocking to the locals, but I'm wrong. This is clearly not the first time Jorge has visited, because the dirt bikes are met with raucous cheering.

As the bikes are rolled down the ramp, several of the natives take turns hopping on and starting them up. Before long, the young men are racing around the grove. The gleeful joyriding continues until one man takes a turn too sharply and topples off his bike. Jorge shouts at them in a language I don't recognize, and they reluctantly put away the bikes and get on with unloading.

Piper and I retreat to the shade near the base of the boxcar. She gets close to me and whispers, "Do you have Breadcrumbs?"

"What?"

"Can you leave bread crumbs when they take us somewhere?"

"Where would I get bread right now?" I ask.

Piper sighs. "No, the app. Breadcrumbs. Do you have it?"

"Oh. They took my phone, remember?"

"But they didn't take your glasses."

I reach into the inner pocket of my jacket and find that I do indeed still have my sunglasses. The left lens has been cracked, likely as a result of my fall, but the interior of the lenses still powers on.

"It should be in your apps menu," Piper says. "Do you see it?"

I don my sunglasses and toggle through various apps. Sure enough, the Breadcrumbs app is available. The GPS is inoperative, but the app says it's still capable of mapping my movements over the current terrain. It offers a generic map to be filled in. I turn the app on. A slice of bread character pops up in my vision and waves, then relegates itself to the upper corner of my lenses next to the power meter. My lenses are still three quarters of the way charged so I'm grateful for that.

I stash the glasses away again when I hear footsteps.

Jorge and two other men are toting weapons now. These are no Old West revolvers. They appear to be something akin to an AR-15 rifle. I don't know who they are defending themselves against, but I'm happy the guns aren't aimed at me.

"Time to mount up."

When Jorge detaches us from the train car, we are led around the back to an all-terrain vehicle fitted with knobby tires and a massive antenna. It's powered by six of the cylindrical power packs and has a gun mounted on top. Jorge clearly isn't messing around.

Jorge secures Piper in the back seat of the ATV, then locks my wrist to the passenger seat rail. He doesn't bother to buckle me in though. I'll be toast if we roll over.

The ATV has a small trailer attached to the back that bounces along behind us as we head downhill. The group stays mainly to an overgrown dirt track that weaves its way among the pines and ultimately leads us to a stream. The ATV and dirt bikes alternate between the bank and splashing through the stream itself, depending on whichever offers a clearer path. Before long, our caravan of historical oddities arrives at a broader branch of river with a long stretch of gravel bank. We aren't the only ones here.

All along the riverbank, locals of every age are using sifting pans and plucking bits of gold from the river. Men, women, and even toddlers are going about their work. The real spectacle is the camp that has been set up along the riverbank. An area of trees has been cleared and now holds an array of solar panels perched at a jaunty angle to catch the late afternoon sun. A number of other structures have been erected in the area as well. These are round huts made of vertical wooden planks lashed together. I notice all the doors are facing east.

The camp is crowded. Kids run to greet Jorge after he parks the vehicle, and Piper and I get our fair share of curious looks. Jorge leaves us in the ATV and goes to converse with an older, native man who looks like he may be the leader of the group, a chief perhaps. I turn around and address Piper, happy to finally have a moment alone. "What were you doing at the time gate? You think you can work it?"

"It's a bunch of preset destinations. Most of them are used up already, but there are a couple left. I think we could use it to jump to a different time than we came from. Maybe even a different place."

"How long do you think it would take to get it up and running?"

"I don't know." She shrugs.

"Crap."

Jorge walks back over and unlocks us from the ATV. He hands us off to a pair of young men who lead us to one of the huts. We are tied to a structural pole of the interior wall and then promptly abandoned. A few minutes later, an old, mostly toothless woman is led in and sat down on a cot across from us, presumably to watch us. She smiles benignly and waits. The young men exit again and their voices recede into the distance.

After several minutes of awkward silence, the old woman rises from her chair, extracts a pipe from a little bag hidden under her skirt, and shuffles over to the fire. She selects a smoldering twig from the edge of the fire, then uses it to light her pipe. After several long draws, she shuffles back to her chair and settles into it. I'm not sure what's in the pipe, put it doesn't seem to be helping her stay alert. After a few minutes she's staring off into space in a sort of languid stupor.

I turn to Piper and whisper, "You have anything near you we could use to whittle at these zip ties? I'm not sure this lady is even looking at us."

The old woman has the same expression on her face as when she first sat down, but the hazy color of her eyes makes me wonder if she can even see across the room. Piper pulls back the edges of the rugs we're sitting on and probes the hard-packed earth beneath us. After a few minutes of searching, she comes up with a jagged little stone. With my eyes still on the old woman, I instruct Piper to whittle at the zip ties around my wrists. It takes some effort, but she's able to saw through the thick plastic of one of the ties. When one of my wrists is free, I'm able to make short work of the other bonds. I get Piper free as well.

"Okay. That was easier than I expected," I say. I watch the woman on the cot for any sign of alarm, but she is just smiling in our direction. Her eyelids seem a little droopier than before. I think she may be falling asleep. Still seated, I begin slowly inching my way toward the doorway.

When I reach the wooden door, I nudge it with my elbow, but it doesn't open. Peering through a crack, I see that someone has secured a leather thong around the handle. Piper finds another chink in the wall and whispers, "They're down by the river. I think they're weighing the gold."

I get to my feet and work my way around the perimeter of the hut, searching for another way out. "Keep an eye on them. If anyone heads this way, you let me know, okay?"

"Okay."

The boards making up the walls of the hut are all securely fastened. Short of an axe, I don't see how we can make it out. Finally my eyes fall on the hole in the ceiling where smoke from the nearly extinguished cooking fire is drifting lazily up into the twilight.

"Hey, how good are you at climbing?"

Piper looks back to me and then up at the hole in the ceiling.

"If I give you a boost, do you think you could make it up there?"

She looks skeptical but walks over to me. "You promise you won't drop me?"

"Not on purpose." I glance at the old woman who appears to be fast asleep now. "I think it's our best shot."

"What if they see me?"

"Try to peek your head up, then climb down the back side of the hut. If you come around the side away from the river to open the door, they shouldn't see much." I reach into a pile of blankets similar to the one the old woman has wrapped around her. "And if you disguise yourself, maybe no one will notice."

"What do we do once we're out?" Piper asks.

"One step at a time," I reply. "You get us out, I'll figure out a way to get us back to the time gate."

Piper steps closer, and I go down on one knee to get her onto my back. I get her positioned atop my shoulders, holding her knees, then carefully get to my feet. Piper clutches at my head desperately as I wobble, but once I'm balanced she relaxes her grip.

"See if you can reach it," I say.

She stretches for the roof but can't quite touch. She uses the top of my head to balance and gets one foot on my shoulder, then the other. I grip her ankles as she stands.

"Got it!" she says as her hands grasp the blackened wood at the edge of the opening. I push her feet as high as I can until she can get her elbows and then one knee up through the opening. She scrambles out the hole with what I hope is not enough noise to attract attention.

A fair amount of dust has fallen from the ceiling and is drifting down around the old woman like a descending fog. She coughs once in her drowsed state. Piper sticks her head back into the hole and whispers, "Okay, I think I can do it." I toss one of the blankets up to her and she catches it, then disappears from view.

I listen to the scrapes and thumps of Piper moving down the slope of the back wall, then catch little glimpses of movement through the chinks in the boards as she works her way around to the door. The leather thong seems to give her some trouble. She's still working at it when suddenly she freezes. The next thing I know, she disappears.

"Piper?" I whisper through the crack. "Are you out there?"

There are voices outside but not hers. A group of women walk by chatting to one another and shepherding a half-dozen tiny children along in front of them. I wait patiently for them to pass. A minute later, Piper is back, her fingers working frantically over the leather.

Something snaps and I spin around to find the old woman standing directly behind me. My heart jolts in my chest. I'm terrified that she might suddenly sound an alarm, but instead, the old woman grins a toothless smile at me and holds out her arms, offering me a blanket.

I hesitate briefly, then accept the blanket from her. "Um, thank you." I don't know what the Washoe word for grandma is, but I'm fairly certain she's a good one, even if she's stoned. I turn around again when Piper swings the door open. I throw the blanket over my head, stoop to a more average height for a native, then follow Piper out the door. I give the old woman one last wave before we flee.

The sun is down behind the mountains. The Ponderosa pines cast deep shadows as I lead Piper into the safety of the woods. We won't get far on foot. I know that much. I circle us around to the edge of the riverbank where Jorge and his accomplices have parked the dirt bikes. The ATV is closest to the water, but several of the bikes have been propped up against trees at the edge of the woods. I creep towards the nearest one, Piper close on my heels.

"Wait right here," I instruct her when we've reached the closest bike. "I'm going to see if I can buy us some time." I look over the controls of the bike, then inch forward.

I duck and crawl on hands and knees to the second-closest bike. I reach behind the seat and unclip the power pack. The cylindrical tube slides up and out at an angle, and I lay it in the gravel next to the rear tire.

Jorge and the rest of the villagers still seem absorbed in the activity near the water. I creep forward and reach the next bike. The power pack slides out without resistance. I repeat this several more times. A couple of the bikes are too far down the beach to reach without being seen, but there's a chance I could disable the ATV too. I creep forward again, keeping the vehicle squarely between me and the group at the waterside. When I reach it, I double-check that I'm still unnoticed before unclipping the first power cell. I'm about to pull it loose when a loud ringing emanates from the back of the ATV.

"Shit!" I drop to my knees behind one of the knobby rear tires and try to contort myself into as small a shape as possible. Should I run for it? I peer beneath the ATV at the crowd at the river. Jorge is looking my way, along with another dozen faces.

What now?

The ATV keeps ringing. I wrap the blanket closely around me and crawl as fast as I can back to the nearest dirt bike. I've left an obvious trail in the sand, but I'm praying no one has spotted me as I position myself behind the bike. Jorge and several others approach the back of the ATV, and Jorge pulls a handset from what I now recognize to be a portable tachyon pulse transmitter.

He sets the handset to his ear. "Bueno." He listens for a moment, then grins. "She already caved, huh? Okay, I guess el jefe was right. We're home free!" He slaps the back of the ATV. "Orale, we got this shit done, vato." He listens again then nods at the phone. "Yeah, yeah. I'll be ready. What do you want me to do with the hostages?" He looks away toward the hut where Piper and I had been tied up. "Okay. Tell Franco it's done."

He slams the handset back in its cradle and whoops to the sky. "We got it made!" He turns to the men who have followed him and says something in their native language. They smile in agreement, then head up the beach toward the huts. I'm watching Jorge through the spokes of the rear wheel, hoping he'll follow his men, but he's now staring past the wheel of the ATV to the lines in the sand I've made from crawling away. His hand goes to the knife at his hip as he steps closer.

He stops when he reaches the dirt bike and finds me staring back at him from behind it.

I'm caught.

10

"Visiting your ancestors is a tricky business. In some you may find kindred spirits, but you may discover that others lived lives best confined to their photographs." -Journal of Dr. Harold Quickly, 1945

"Hi, Jorge," I say.

"What the hell?" Jorge pulls the knife as I rise from behind the dirt bike. Capitalizing on his momentary confusion, I hurl the heavy blanket over him and kick the bike over. The maneuver sends Jorge sprawling to the sand beneath it. I turn and sprint for the trees.

Jorge is sputtering and yelling behind me when I reach the working motorcycle. Piper is ready. I pull the bike away from the tree and straddle it, my fingers flying over the controls to get the motor on. Thankfully someone has disabled the owner authentication software. Sometimes it pays to steal from thieves.

Piper climbs onto the bike behind me, wrapping her arms around my waist. "You know how to drive this, right?"

"Just hang on!" I shout, and gun the throttle. The motorcycle leaps into action.

The burst of energy from the bike is nearly silent but highly effective. We rocket away from the river, bouncing up and over small rises in the terrain. There's shouting from the village and, a few moments later, a rat-a-tat-tat of gunfire. Wherever the bullets hit, it's thankfully not close enough for us to see. I get the impression someone might be firing blindly into the trees.

There's no clutch on the electric motorbike. That's one less thing to worry about, but I have plenty enough on my mind at the moment.

"Where are we going?" I shout to Piper.

She fishes in my jacket pockets with one hand and finds my sunglasses for me. I don them with my left hand while still keeping the throttle going with my right. A few bumps later I've got them on my face and can make out the virtual breadcrumbs scattered through the woods. I'm off course.

We tear through the underbrush as I work the bike steadily uphill.

The lack of noise coming from the bike would help if I were trying to lose pursuit in any other scenario. But I have no delusions about the men who will be after us. They'll know where we're headed immediately. The real downside of the quiet bikes is that I won't hear my pursuers until they're almost on us. I hope that temporarily disabling a few of the bikes may have bought us a few extra moments of confusion, but they won't be far behind. Not only do I need to outrun the bikes, I need to outrun their guns.

It's only a few minutes later when I hear the shots. Climbing an especially steep hillside, our pace has slowed enough for the first of our pursuers to spot us. It's one of the locals. He attempts to shoot as he rides, but the bullets spray wide.

My heartbeat accelerates with my bike as I crank the throttle open, giving the electric motor as much juice as it can handle. Piper squeezes me tightly, as if trying to make us smaller targets by her efforts. We reach the top of the hill without being hit, and I'm able to make up some distance on the shooter. I fly downhill and into the glade with the train tracks. There is no one near the time gate, but it also has no cover. We'll be sitting ducks while Piper tries to get the gate open. I skid the motorbike to a stop and help Piper off.

"Get the gate open as fast as you can. I need to see if I can slow these guys down."

"We have to go together!" Piper shouts. "I need you!"

"I'm coming. Don't worry. Just get that thing open to a time that looks safe. I'll make it."

She dashes toward the gate controls as I speed away. I've got thirty seconds at most till the next rider will make the glade. It doesn't give me a lot of options. I tear toward the edge of the woods that's south and slightly uphill from where the rider will arrive. I scan the low boughs of trees and the fallen logs at their bases till I find what I'm looking for. A branch of a fallen tree is dry enough for me to snap it off. I strip the excess twigs quickly, crafting myself a makeshift lance. It's primitive, but it's all I've got.

I hold the long stick against my body with my left arm and brace it on the handlebars. That's all the prep time I get because my quarry is flying into the glade. His eyes and gun sights are fixed on the time gate. I twist the throttle and burst out of the woods to intercept him.

I don't know if the man on the bike is exclusively looking to shoot me, if he's conserving ammo, or if he's just hoping to get closer and improve his aim, but he isn't firing at Piper yet. I'm grateful for that. I close the gap on him from an angle just outside his peripheral vision. The high grass whips my legs as I ride. I have a slight advantage since I'm racing downhill. The extra speed is enough that I'm on him just as he reaches the midpoint of the glade. He's begun looking side-to-side now, aware that I'm not at the gate. He spots me just as I'm bearing down on him. He shouts, and, luckily for me, he opts to use the throttle and not the gun. He puts on an extra burst of speed, just enough to avoid our collision, but not enough to avoid my real goal.

I ram my makeshift lance through the spokes of the bike's rear wheel.

The wood explodes into shards and splinters all around me as the stick impacts the frame of the bike and is pulverized by its forward momentum. It does the job. The back wheel of his bike locks up, sending the machine into an aggressive skid. Coming unbalanced, the rider loses control of the front end of the bike as well. He flies through the air as the motorbike tumbles, then he thuds to the grass and rolls over several times before coming to a stop.

I turn my bike around and am quick to get to his fallen gun before he can get to his feet. I scoop up the rifle, then race away a dozen yards to put myself between him and Piper's position. The young man gets blearily to his feet, and his eyes widen when he sees me with the gun. I fire a couple of warning shots into the grass, but it's unnecessary. He's already running for the cover of the woods in the direction he came.

I'm smiling from my success, but my smile vanishes when I see what's beyond him. Several more riders are pouring out of the woods, and directly behind them is Jorge in the ATV. He isn't the one driving but is standing up, strapped into a harness so he can man the gun turret atop the machine.

That's not good.

I raise the rifle for half a second, considering taking a shot, but I'll never stop them all. The thud thud thud of bullets kicking up dirt around me jolts me out of my indecision, and I drop the gun, wrenching on the bike's throttle instead and launching myself toward the time gate.

Piper is standing, waving her arms at me. The gate is illuminated, a swirl of vibrant colors washing across the opening.

"Go! I'm right behind you!" I shout, launching over the railway tracks and spitting gravel with the bike's rear wheel as I make the turn. Piper vanishes through the time gate as bullets ricochet off the train cars. I don't bother to slow down till my front wheel is through the blinding brilliance of the doorway. When I clamp the front brake and stomp the pedal for the rear wheel, I send the bike into a skid. It's still not enough to stop me from hitting a mining car on the other side of the time gate. As my front wheel hits the car and sends me flying over the handlebars, I get a strange flash of clarity as if time has slowed. I fall through the air seemingly in slow motion. Then I crash into the pile of ore and go straight through the mining car's wall.

I'm lying dazed on the ground wondering vaguely if I'm going to be paralyzed, when Piper appears overhead. She dashes up, out of breath, and looks me over. I'm partially buried with what I expected to be ore, but if so, they're the softest, lightest rocks ever discovered. Piper picks up one of the stones and squeezes it. It crumbles in her hand.

"They're Styrofoam." She drops the stone and picks up another one, then tosses it away too. "It's all fake."

I climb gingerly off the floor and have a look at what she's talking about.

The cavern or mine we've arrived in is, in fact, fake. The metal mining car I collided with wasn't metal at all. The motorbike has caved in an entire side and is lying partially atop one end, while my ignominious crash landing has flattened the other side, simultaneously spilling its cargo of phony ore. The car itself appears to be made of a now-misshapen plastic, and even the walls around us are clearly only pretending to be stone. Someone has airbrushed more polystyrene or plastic to fit the look.

"Where on earth are we?" I mutter. I look back at the time gate we came through. Piper has already shut it off, but the hardware still adorns a fake tunnel wall with a painting of a mineshaft on it. I'm reminded of the cartoon tunnel depictions Wile E. Coyote would paint on boulders in his attempts to stop the Roadrunner.

"We good on keeping them from coming through after us?" I ask.

Piper nods. "I took the first spot on the list. If they come through, it has to be a lot of years from now."

"Good girl," I say, rubbing my neck and straightening up. "Where'd you learn to operate a time gate? Your mom teach you that?"

"No. You did," Piper replies. "You said I should understand how things work so I don't have to count on other people to fix my problems for me."

I rub my fingers over my sore chin. "Yeah. That sounds like something I'd say. I guess I need to add time gate operation to my to-do list, huh?"

Piper smiles. "You do if you want to teach your kid someday."

"Well, I'll concentrate on surviving till then," I mutter. "Let's see if we can figure out where in the heck we are." I pick my way over the Styrofoam and plastic rubble, then move along the narrow rail tracks

The Warp Clock 71

toward sunlight at the far end of the tunnel. "What year did the gate say this was?"

"2120," Piper replies.

"Did it list a timestream?"

"Yeah, but it didn't match any of the Central Streams."

"That's never a good sign. We could be anywhere."

The narrow rails lead us to a junction of more rails that head off to the left. More mining cars and fake scenery line the sides of the tracks. Abandoned pickaxes and gleaming veins of gold decorate the mine walls. I turn right and head toward the daylight. That's when we encounter the next set of rail cars. They aren't mining cars, however. They're seats.

The two cars are linked together by a coupler, and in total, offer a comfortable padded ride to at least a dozen riders. Lap bars ratchet down to keep the riders secure. This place isn't a mine. It's an amusement park ride.

I study the ride cars for another few seconds, then follow the rails back to a boarding station. Another set of cars sits beside a platform. Metal handrails wind their way back and forth to guide customers to the ride in an orderly fashion. But there are no riders in sight. The amusement ride sits quiet and abandoned. Bits of trash line the tracks, and someone's long lost shoe sits in the middle of the loading platform. The ride cars themselves have been tagged with colorful graffiti.

The ride is surrounded by fake mountains complete with miner shacks, artificial trees, and a few old-timey mining implements.

"Is this Disneyland?" Piper asks, her voice full of wonder.

"I sure hope not," I say. "I have a feeling this isn't quite the 'happiest place on earth' anymore."

I lead the way out the ride's entrance and turn around when we reach the sign. A dilapidated board reads, "Old Sutter's Mill." Then a smaller sign exclaims, "There be gold in them thar hills!" and below that, "Riders must be this tall to board." The red arrow is sun faded and barely legible.

I take a few steps down the wide, paved sidewalk and look up to find the twisting steel rails and latticed frame of a wooden roller coaster. Abandoned snack carts and overturned trash bins line the walkway. I walk to the nearest bin and stoop to grab a mostly deteriorated color map.

"Welcome to Yesteryear Adventure Park" it proudly declares in moldy bubble lettering. "Where history comes to life!" It lists destinations like Frontier Town and Liberty Village, but most of the map is missing.

I let the paper slip from my fingers, back to the pile of trash it came from.

I glance up to the dingy brown sky and look for any sign of aircraft or movement. There isn't so much as a bird.

The place is deathly quiet.

"You think we can get home from here?" Piper asks. She slips her hand into mine and holds on to my arm.

I consider the twisting walkway and the abandoned amusements. "We definitely aren't going to need more than the day pass."

I spot a sign that says "EXIT" on a post near a brick bathroom and tow Piper that way. "Come on. We'll see where this place really is." She follows me down a twisting path that says "Employees Only" till we reach a broad wall plastered with stucco to make it look like adobe. A steel door stands partially ajar in the wall. A sign on the door reads "Emergency Exit Only." When we reach it, I swing the door open to view the parking lot beyond. My breath catches in my throat.

I step through the doorway to take in the view.

The world outside is gone.

11

"I'm frequently reminded of the scale of time, and that despite my being a time traveler, the earth will spend far more days without my company than with it. That is as it should be. Cosmic insignificance does wonders to keep an ego in check." -Journal of Dr. Harold Quickly, 2218.

"Are we going to die here?"

Piper is staring out at the vast parking lot awash with sand and rotting cars. There are a few lifeless trees in the barren lane dividers, but otherwise, the view is eerie and desolate. Deteriorating buildings dot the horizon, and I spot what looks to be a partially collapsed freeway overpass. Nothing is moving except the drifts of sand that exchange occasional particles in the breeze.

"I wouldn't get too attached to this place," I say. "We're going to find a way out of here."

I approach a few of the cars in the parking lot. Tires have rotted on most of them, and none look like they could be inspired to move. I manage to pry the door open on one sand-covered vehicle, but when I look inside, there are no operator controls. Whatever automated system made these things run is no longer in use. I mash a few of the emergency mode buttons, but nothing happens. I leave the door open as I walk back to Piper. She has her arms across her body, hugging herself. She seems to be studying the ground.

"What are you looking at?" I ask.

"There are no tracks," she replies. "In the dirt. If someone else got out this way, they would have left tracks, right?"

"Hard to say. It's pretty breezy out here. Might have been covered up."

"Well, I don't think my dad would go this way. I think he'd think of something better."

I put my sunglasses into binocular mode and scan the parking lot. "I think I agree with you there. Don't see much of anything worth heading for this direction." The crack in the left lens cuts a scar across the landscape. It seems fitting. I take the sunglasses back off and switch them to sleep mode, then tuck them into my jacket. "Come on. Let's have another look around inside. There has to be something worth finding in there."

"You think my dad is here somewhere?"

I think of the video, but try to ignore the possibility that I know exactly where he is. I could still be wrong.

"Wouldn't hurt to look."

The winding path back to the pedestrian walkway seems shorter this time. We reemerge into the dusty artificial landscape of the Gold Rush era. I pick a direction and lead Piper along an avenue of Old West façades. There are saloons and boarding houses, and even banks to deposit your treasure. Piper walks over to the building and picks up a golden rock that has spilled from a broken window display. She holds it up. "Is this real?"

"It's fool's gold," I reply. "Not completely worthless, but pretty close."

Piper puts the shiny rock in her pocket and half-skips her way back over to me. She doesn't seem daunted by our predicament yet. I have to admire that.

My own feet are beginning to drag a little. The adrenaline of the motorbike chase has worn off, and my energy has ebbed with it. It's only midday here, but I've been awake for what feels like a long time.

"Keep an eye out for a coffee cart. That's some treasure I wouldn't mind discovering," I say.

Piper scrunches up her nose. "Coffee is gross. I want an ice cream." She's looking at a cart that offers frozen treats. She dashes over to the rusty cooler and opens the lid. Her face falls when she looks inside. She closes the lid with disgust.

"No joy?" I ask.

"There's just dead bugs in there."

"Let's hope those don't end up being dinner."

"Ewwww," she says. "That's super gross."

I smile at her. "Let's keep going. We're going to figure this place out. I want to know why a time gate would lead here. Doesn't make much sense, but there has to be a reason."

Piper catches up to me again. We pass over a bridge and a dried-up, plastic riverbed. The Lewis and Clark Wild River Rapids has a sign that suggests the wait time to be forty-five minutes. We move on and find a sign made of wooden arrows pointing different directions. Each arrow is labeled with a time period like "1860s" or "Early 20th Century." I opt to head that direction and we approach a raised archway. The archway sign reads "European Theatre." Above that is a replica of an inline engine fighter plane with red, white, and blue roundels on each wing. The aircraft is banked in a turn and has two angry looking gun barrels protruding from the wings.

"Seems a bit intense for a kids park, don't you think?" I ask.

Piper shrugs.

We move through the archway and find ourselves overlooking a re-creation of a WWII battlefield. A tank with a Nazi swastika and one with a Soviet star are facing off with one another. Farther along we encounter an American bomber plane with a pin-up girl painted on the nose. It is accompanied by a P-51 Mustang that once must have been a shiny aluminum. Now all of the aircraft are badly corroded and missing pieces.

A steel roller coaster loops overhead. Dogfight Over London. The sign features a British Spitfire in pursuit of a German Messerschmitt Bf. 109. Despite the deadly reality of the theme, the illustrations and descriptions are depicted with a sort of cheerful theatricality. The aircraft are cartoonish and there is no gunfire to be seen. The park has managed to inject fun into world war history. It makes me wonder what timestream we're in. I don't think it would pass the political correctness standards of my own time.

Piper wanders over to a children's carousel. In addition to the standard horses, riders can climb aboard seats fashioned as planes, motorcycles, and even miniature tanks.

Piper studies the ride, then steps up and walks to a motorcycle. "You think one day I'll learn to ride a motorcycle like you do?"

"I don't see why not." I look around the park trying to figure out our next move.

Piper swings a leg over the motorcycle and places her hands on the handgrips. But as she does, the ride moves. The entire carousel jolts and rotates amid a squealing of rusted steel.

Piper shrieks.

I rush onto the platform and snatch her off the motorcycle as it rises several feet into the air.

I jump off the carousel and deposit Piper back on the ground as it grinds to a halt.

"Oh my God," Piper exclaims. "Did I almost die?"

The ride has stopped as suddenly as it started, and other than a bit of dust lingering in the air, it has gone back to appearing lifeless.

"I guess this place still has power."

"It tried to kill me," Piper says.

"I'm not sure about that, but we should definitely stay off the rides from now on." I cast a suspicious glance at the array of solar panels behind the ride. "Not sure what brought it to life though . . ."

Piper is staring hard at the carousel and frowning.

"Come on. Let's keep going." I spot a snack stand advertising Cracker Jack and candied apples. The food is long gone, but there is a map preserved on the interior of the glass. Unlike its counterparts I found on the ground, this one is whole and legible. Piper and I move in to take a closer look at the full scope of the Yesteryear Adventure Park.

It seems that if we so choose, we can experience historical time periods varying from the time of the Vikings through the Twentieth Century. While most of the park has devoted itself to American history, there are sections showcasing selected events from world history as well. The French Revolution has a corner, and one can even traverse a section of the Great Wall of China, inexplicably passing the Great Pyramids of Egypt along the way, before stopping by the Coliseum in Rome.

My eye catches on a section of the park labeled "Independence Corner." The attractions list the Liberty Bell, a Delaware River Crossing Adventure, and Paul Revere's Wild Ride.

"That's where we came from," Piper says, pointing out the Frontier section of the park and the California Gold Rush attraction. Her finger hovers over the Sutter's Mill Mine Ride. "Right there."

I lean closer and notice a little symbol next to the name. The symbol looks like an hour and a minute hand. The clock hands are positioned directly over the spot we came out of the time gate.

Curious, I scan the legend, but the description says, "Popular attraction. Possibility of longer than normal wait times." It doesn't say anything about the fact that there is an unlicensed time gate hidden in the tunnel. I run my finger over the symbol, noting its appearance in several other locations in the park.

I find the door to the vending cart unlocked, so I go inside and rip the laminated map from the window.

"Are you allowed to do that?" Piper says.

"This doesn't count as vandalism," I reply. "Whoever abandoned this place obviously didn't want it. This is probably the property of some bank at this point anyway, but I'm guessing they won't care either."

"Because they're all dead?"

I glance at Piper's worried face, then the vacant, dusty sky. "Maybe. But let's hope they just moved."

I lead us around the corner to an attraction called "Allied Invasion."

It's a self-driving vehicle ride. A few amphibious trucks made up to look like troop carriers have been left at various stages of a course that involved motoring through a lake and along a beach before roaming up and down some hills and back. I climb over a railing and head for the rear of the course where the vehicles pass through another tunnel.

"Where are you going?" Piper asks.

"I want to investigate something."

Walking across the dry lakebed with Piper on my heels, I cross the beach to the hillside where the track enters the tunnel.

I put on my sunglasses and flip them to low-light mode. It's not as good as real night-vision goggles, but it helps a little. I'm able to make out more of the tunnel details. I step inside and work my way through the darkness.

"This is creepy," Piper says. "I don't like it."

"Just stay close. If anything is living in here, we'll try not to wake it up."

The track makes a few bends past re-creations of underground German bunkers before leading to a tunnel exit. The fake blast doors to the bunker are hanging off their hinges, but the hardware around the edges looks familiar. Some of the façade of the wall has fallen away, revealing bundles of wiring and several elaborate temporal field emitters.

"Bingo."

"Another time gate?" Piper asks.

I shove some debris out of the way and search for the control panel. "Whoever ran this park must have had a little side business going on. Some sort of time travel junction. I'm guessing these might be ASCOTT's missing time gates."

"Where do you think it goes?" Piper asks.

I locate the control panel for the gate hidden behind a faux boulder. I depress the power button and the display screen comes to life. "You want to show me how to use this thing?" I ask.

Piper stands next to me and points out the various operations of the control box. It seems, like at the previous time gate, that we have limited options on places to jump to, but there are multiple gates listed as possible exits. The majority of the preprogrammed time slots have been used up, but there are still a few in the mid 20th Century.

"It's looking like 1941 is our best bet." I say. "If we can get there, we'll still be almost sixty years away from the millennium, but it's closer to home. At least we'll be out of this depressing theme park."

"It doesn't show states or countries. Someone deleted the names." Piper is scrolling through various data fields for our target destination. "We won't even know where we're going."

"I'm not a big fan of that, but even if there are more time gates in this park, I don't see any other time periods closer to home on this list." I scan the map of the theme park, my eyes lingering on Independence Corner. "Nowhere I want to be, anyway."

"What about my dad?" Piper says. "We still need to find him."

"I think your dad would want you somewhere safe first. If we end up in a stream where we can contact other time travelers, we may be able to reach your grandfather or someone who can pick you up."

"I don't want to get picked up!" Piper says. "I need to save my dad." She lowers her voice. "You told me you'd help."

"I will help. But without chronometers and no idea where we are, we have slim chances at finding him. We need help. You agree we don't have a lot of options here, right?"

She crosses her arms but doesn't speak.

"Let's try this gate, and if for some reason we can't find any help in the 1940s, then we can always jump back, okay?"

Piper seems to be weighing the options. "You think maybe they took him through this gate? Like they took us through the other one?"

"Could be," I say.

"Okay. I'll do it then." Piper uncrosses her arms and studies the array of temporal field emitters. "He would do it for me."

I punch up our mystery destination and power on the emitters. A multicolored wave of light illuminates the tunnel and connects the space between the tunnel walls. The colors wash from side to side and swirl around before settling into a consistent pattern of oscillations.

"I'll go first and make sure it's safe," I say. "Wait maybe thirty seconds, then follow me through, okay?"

"Okay." She glances back the way we came. "What if someone comes while you're gone?"

"Then come find me." I grab her by the shoulder. "Don't worry. I'll see you on the other side."

I adjust my sunglasses to compensate for the increased light, then step quickly through the time gate.

The floor is wobbling.

I've stepped into a narrow space neatly decorated with carpet and a few armchairs. The rocking from side to side is accompanied by a clickety-clack noise that is now recognizable.

I'm on a train.

Okay. That doesn't seem bad. I move to one of the small windows in the cabin and roll up the shade. Wooded hills are rolling by out the window. A mountain range in the distance is topped with snow. A few cattle are grazing lazily in a field. One lifts its head and stares idly at the train as it rolls past.

"Are we on a Harry Potter ride?"

I turn around to find Piper standing near the back wall of the cabin.

"There's no way that was thirty seconds," I say.

"It was on my end. You probably just forgot to set the exit timing right."

I glance at the time gate hardware that's been haphazardly secured to the wall. "That does sound like something I'd forget."

"Where are we?" Piper asks.

"I don't know. Stay here for a minute and let me look around." I walk to the door and open it a crack, listening for activity in the corridor. Piper is watching me intently. I hold my finger to my lips and slide the door open a little farther, then I slip outside.

The windows are dressed with elegant curtains. Wherever we're headed, we appear to be traveling in style. The pleasant view of the countryside helps a little with the nervousness of trespassing. I move forward. There are muffled voices in some of the other cabins. I pass a couple of closed compartment doors and consider knocking on one, but I opt to look for a ticket agent or some kind of rail official who might be able to tell me where the next stop is. I reach the end of the car and spot someone in uniform stationed between our car and the next. His back is to me but his starched collar protrudes above his jacket. He's standing stiffly at attention.

I've almost reached the door when footsteps sound on the carpet behind me. I turn to find Piper running a hand along the windowsill, moving toward me with the half-skipping walk she seems to like.

"I thought you were going to wait in the cabin."

"I didn't want to miss seeing Hogwarts."

"I don't know where we're headed, but I doubt it's there."

Turning around, I reach for the door handle.

The man stationed outside has a red and white armband wrapped around his bicep. It gives me a moment's pause. A placard near the doorframe reads: *Führersonderzug Amerika*. My sunglasses automatically supply a translation option and a definition that hovers in midair. As soon as I read the words I spin around.

"Get back to the gate! Right now!"

"Why?" Piper says.

"Because this is no Harry Potter Ride. We just boarded Adolf Hitler's train!"

12

"Death doesn't frighten me. I fear living a life unworthy of the many opportunities I've been gifted. That, and bears." -Journal of Dr. Harold Quickly, 1910.

We're halfway down the corridor when one of the compartment doors opens, and two soldiers step into the hall. My breath catches.

Both men are wearing Nazi uniforms, and one has a pistol holstered at his waist. I grab Piper and bring her to a stop, while frantically pulling up a German translation menu on my sunglasses.

The man in front of us has short, stiff hair that stabs from under his hat. He looks us up and down and states something in German. Only a few words register in the translation app. " . . . doing in . . . car."

I smile while skimming a list of common German phrases. "Um. Wo ist die Toilette?" I continue smiling while gesturing to Piper.

Piper gets the message and crosses her knees in an urgent need sort of way.

The second man whispers something to his companion, narrowing his eyes at me. I get the impression that my accent wasn't very passable.

That and the fact that Piper and I are wearing clothes that are clearly from another time.

The man reaches for his gun.

I push Piper behind me and prepare to charge him, just as a tremendous boom resonates from outside the car. The man with the gun wobbles, then regains his balance, but he turns his attention immediately to the window. There's another sound. A sort of whump whump whump noise. Wait, is that a . . .

The windows beyond the Nazis explode inward, and bullets rip through the wall of the train. I spin and flatten Piper to the floor as a hail of lead rips through the doors of the passenger compartments.

The gunfire tears through the train, moving forward, and it rains debris on us as it passes overhead. Then it moves on. I definitely recognize the sound now. A helicopter.

I lift my head to check Piper. She's wide-eyed but seems to be unhurt. I spin around to find that one of the men in the hall has vanished, disappeared through the open doorway of their compartment. Only his shoe is visible now, toe pointing skyward. The other man uncovers his head, then gets to his knees. Our eyes meet and he reaches for his pistol on the floor. I'm to my feet quicker and send an instinctive kick to his skull. His head rocks back, then he slumps to the floor. I snatch up the pistol and look out the gaping hole in the wall where the bullets have demolished the window. Outside, I spot what looks to be an Apache attack helicopter pummeling the train with its chain gun.

"Holy shit." I grab Piper by the arm. "Come on!"

Piper steps gingerly over the Nazi's prone body.

I drag her down the hallway looking for the larger compartment we came from.

"You kicked that man. You kicked him right in the face."

"He had it coming."

"And you said shit. My dad says not to say that."

I find the compartment door and fight to get it open. Gunfire has erupted from other parts of the train. It sounds like the Nazis are firing back.

"I thought you were going to talk to him. Think your way out, or talk your way out. That's what you always say."

"I'm adding an addendum to that rule," I say, finally getting the door open. "If you can't think your way out, or talk your way out, then you have to fight your way out. And if it's Nazis, you can skip right to that one."

I pull Piper to the wall where the time gate was mounted, but my heart immediately sinks. The machine gun has done its work here too. Several of the temporal field emitters are dangling by strands of wire, and the power cables to the portable power pack have been nicked and exposed by bullets. One bullet has even struck the power cells themselves. A gaping hole in one cell is leaking a viscous gel.

"Son of a b-"

"That's another word he says not to say."

I put my hands to my head.

"Can you fix it?" Piper asks.

"Definitely not." I spin around and check the compartment for any other options. Think, Ben. Think. Whoever came through here had to have a plan. They wouldn't have left this gate here and vulnerable if they still needed it. "There's another way out," I say.

"There is?"

"Definitely. We just need to find it." I check the pistol in my hand. It's a model I've seen before, a Luger, but I've never fired one. I fiddle with it and try to figure out the cocking mechanism. I manage to eject a bullet by accident. Piper picks it up for me.

She hands it back. "Who are you going to shoot?"

"Hopefully no one, but better to have it and not need it than the other way around. Come on. We need to find the other time travelers here. Someone has a plan and we don't want to be left behind. Not here."

Out in the hallway, the man is still prone on the floor. I opt to head the other direction toward the rear of the car. The sliding door to the next car opens easily enough. I try to ignore the smear of blood on the railing where someone must have previously been standing.

The car behind us seems to have gotten much of the same

treatment ours has. Someone is shouting, however, and when I walk to the edge of the train and look to the rear, I spot several rifle barrels protruding from windows.

Not going that way.

I locate the safety lever on the Luger and set it before tucking the gun into the waistband of my jeans. "Stay right here for just a second," I say. "I'm going to have a quick look up top."

There is a ladder extending from the rear platform to the top of the car, and I gingerly put a foot on it. The rocking of the train gives me pause, but I shove the fear down as I get a grip on the rails. Falling off a train is probably the least of my worries right now.

I take each step slowly but finally reach the top rung. The cold wind whips my hair, and I have to squint as I look around. We're near the back of the train. There are a few cars behind us, but the last is not a passenger car, it's armed with what look to be anti-aircraft guns. A few remaining soldiers are struggling to get one aimed, but it seems they have only been designed to hit targets high overhead. The armored walls of the car limit the movement of the barrel. I turn and locate the attack helicopter. It's wisely staying low to the ground, only having to deal with occasional pistol and rifle fire from a few windows of cars. That is minimal now, as the initial attack seems to have done its job well. The helicopter continues to strafe cars, but as we round a bend in the tracks, I notice one car hasn't taken any damage.

It's several cars up from us, midway down the train. There are multiple men in Nazi uniforms atop it and dangling from the sides. But far from being in danger, it seems the helicopter is protecting them. The men are working at speed, attempting to attach some sort of contraption to the frame of the train. They've fixed a crate of power cells to the roof and have wires running to all four corners. What the hell are they up to?

I climb back down the ladder to Piper.

"Are we screwed?" Piper asks.

I put a hand on her shoulder. "Not just yet. I think I found the other time travelers. We just need to get up there." I pull the door of the train car back open.

"Will they be happy to see us?"

"I'm guessing not."

We work our way back through the hallway. I notice with some concern that the officer I kicked in the face is no longer there.

I pause and remove the Luger from my waistband, then flip off the safety.

Piper glides along behind me. "What if they kick us off the train? Are we going to have to live in Germany?"

"Shhh." I put my finger to my lips. "Let's not give them a chance."

The other officer we met earlier has not moved and won't be moving again. I block the view of the doorway as best I can as we pass. Piper keeps her eyes forward. There are a few vague noises from some other compartments, but I lack the courage to open them. I'm not excited about anything I would find.

When we reach the forward door, the guard is gone. I peek out the window and scan the car ahead of us. The door to the next car has been left partly open. I gently open ours and admit the rushing noise and wind.

"Stay behind me, okay?" I say.

Piper grabs onto the back of my jacket.

There is a little walkway made for navigating the junction. We teeter across it until we have reached the rear platform of the next car. The half-open doorway reveals broken glass on the floor and a few spent shell casings. Someone in here has a gun.

I push the door open a little farther to squeeze through and take a step inside. My shoe crunches glass. A pop pop pop erupts from the corridor and three bullets strike the wood paneling to my left, showering me with tiny splinters.

"Shit. Back up." I push Piper back out the door to the platform and fire a couple of shots blindly down the hallway just to let whoever's firing know that I have a gun too.

I shrink behind the metal wall outside the doorway and block Piper into the corner. Her back is to the wind, and some of her hair has come undone from her braid and is flying around her head.

"Why are they shooting at us?" She yells over the noise of the wheels.

"I think they're probably shooting at everybody," I say. "I wouldn't take it personally."

"There's a man out there." Piper points along the outside of the train. We're making a bend to the right, making that side of the train more visible ahead. I lean into the wind to see what she's looking at. She's noticed the men two cars up rigging the cables to the sides of the train. Blue sparks of electricity have begun flashing from the corners of the car. I now recognize the contraption they are attaching.

"That looks like a portable gravitizer. I think they may be trying to gravitize that entire train car! They must have rigged another time gate somewhere on this track."

"Like maybe that bridge?" Piper points farther down the track. Perhaps a mile and a half away, an old stone bridge spans the tracks. I can't make out much from this distance, but when I zoom in with my sunglasses, I spot figures manning the bridge. They appear to be German soldiers, but when I scan beneath the bridge I spot one of the electric dirt bikes stashed in the bushes.

"Shit," I mutter. "That's definitely the gate. We need to move."

The full danger of the situation begins to dawn on me. They are only gravitizing one car. That's all that's going to make the transition through the gate. I don't like imagining what will happen to this train when one of its cars suddenly goes missing while moving. But even if the train doesn't immediately derail and kill us, if we don't make it through the gate before they shut it down, we'll be stuck in Nazi Germany for the duration of the war. Neither option sounds good. But there are two cars of angry Nazis between us and the soon-to-be-gravitized passenger car. And we're running out of time.

I poke my head toward the doorway of the car in front of me. I toss a piece of broken glass into the corridor. The action is immediately met with frantic gunfire.

"That decides that," I say. "We're going to have to go over."

Piper is watching the bridge drawing nearer. "I don't like this."

She squeezes close to me as a roaring blast of air passes over. The

Apache gunship swoops overhead and races across the fields beyond. It makes a tight, banking turn and comes back around to rain more fire on the rear of the train. The sound of the chain gun makes me cringe.

"Come on! We gotta run for it." I climb up the ladder a little, then wait for Piper to follow. "Just hold on tightly. Hands on the sides so you never have to let go completely. You can do it." Part of me feels like I'm encouraging myself. This plan is crazy.

When I reach the roof of the train, I don't see anyone else on top. The men who had affixed the gravitizer to the train car have climbed down. I scramble onto the roof, then turn around and watch for the gunship. The pilot definitely sees me. The blades dip, and the helicopter races forward from its position at the rear of the train. It banks to the side and slides alongside the train, keeping its gun barrels aimed at the cars.

Shit.

"Keep your head down!" I shout to Piper as she reaches the top of the ladder.

When it reaches my position, the helicopter hovers while keeping pace with the train. I have a clear view of a woman in a flight helmet in the pilot's seat. She yanks on the collective and climbs, bringing the gun barrel up to the height of the roof. I stand and stare at her. Ignoring my shouts, Piper climbs up next to me and takes my hand.

The woman keeps the chain gun aimed at us for another long second, then the nose lifts and she falls away, banking the aircraft back toward the rear of the train.

"I think we just got very lucky," I shout to Piper.

She holds a hand up and points past me. "They're doing it!"

I spin around to find that the train car two ahead of ours is glowing with an electric blue light. The roof crackles with static and electricity arcs along the ladder, even leaping the gaps between rungs and flashing brightly as the energy courses throughout the train car. Beyond the glowing car, the stone bridge is rapidly approaching.

"Come on! We've got to hurry!" I grab Piper's hand, and we race along the top of the train, running as fast as we dare across the curved and rocking rooftop. We reach the first gap and are confronted with the divide between cars. Fortunately the gap is narrow and is easily crossed. I step across the divide but am immediately startled by gunfire. Several holes appear in the roof in front of me, and I stumble backward, falling over and nearly plummeting into the gap between train cars as several more shots pierce the roof. I roll over and leap back to the car I just came from where Piper is cowering in fear.

"Good God!" I collapse to the roof next to her and check my lower body for damage. My heart is hammering but I don't seem to have been hit.

"We can't cross that!" Piper yells.

The front of the train is almost to the bridge. We've reached the last straight stretch of track and are barreling right for it. The men on the bridge have scrambled to the ground and activated the time gate. The space beneath the span of the bridge lights up with the familiar swirling colors of the temporal field.

Even if the engineer braked completely, the train would never stop in time. Something tells me that whoever was at the controls is either dead or has been otherwise convinced to abandon his post.

"We have to get across. There's no other way!" I help Piper to her feet. I pull the Luger from my waistband. "I have a few shots left. I'm going to cover you. When I start shooting into the car, you run like hell, okay?"

"What about you?" Piper screams back over the noise of the wind.

"Don't worry about me. You just run. And don't look back till you're through that gate! We have to do it now. Get ready!"

Piper stares into my face with wide eyes, but to her credit, she nods and turns toward the approaching bridge. The front of the train has already passed beneath the span. The cars behind it are plummeting through the light and onward down the tracks.

"Okay!" I aim the pistol at the area where the bullets exited the roof and squeeze off the first round. "Go!" I fire four more rounds in quick succession as Piper sprints forward. She's quickly past the point where the bullets had come from and is now running the length of the car at full speed. I leap across the gap myself and continue shooting through the floor as I go. The gun goes silent with a sickening click as I empty the last of the magazine. Bullets rip through the roof behind me as I run. I toss the Luger aside and pump my arms as I sprint along the top of the train car. The front of the next train car has already reached the bridge. It's being swallowed by the light. Piper is already across, waving her arms from the center of the car. Then she vanishes. I stretch my legs as far as they'll go as I run. There are perhaps fifteen feet of gravitized car left on this side of the bridge.

Ten.

Five.

I shout as I reach the end of my car and leap.

Zero.

13

"I've failed to time travel far more times than I've succeeded. That's the paradox of invention. Our greatest achievements are birthed like a phoenix from the ashes of disappointment." -Journal of Doctor Harold Quickly, 1996.

The colors dazzle my eyes in a blinding swirl of brilliance, then I'm falling.

I hit the roof of the train car off balance, then tumble, rolling to a stop with arms splayed to arrest my momentum. The train car is braking too. The rails squeal and complain as the wheels slide along them, objecting to this sudden hulk of metal from another time.

We've made the jump.

Piper is on her hands and knees a few yards farther along the roof of the car. She's looking around at our new environment.

Only it isn't new at all. We're back in the 1830s. The train car is braking along the solitary stretch of track we left behind in the pre-gold-rush time. Jorge and his band of Native American youths are waiting alongside the tracks. Some are on the dirt bikes, some are on foot, but all of them are armed. Jorge stares up at me as we roll by, then he grins.

We haven't escaped after all.

I walk the few yards to Piper and help her to her feet. She's searching my face. "What do we do now?"

"I don't know. Let's not make any rash decisions till we see what we're up against here."

A thundering rumble erupts from behind us as the Apache attack helicopter roars through the time gate. The gate has been widened for our arrival, but it's still a tight squeeze. The nose of the aircraft is almost scraping the ground. The pilot manages to clear the tracks and then soars overhead, but the end of the tail rotor catches the frame of the time gate, sending a shower of sparks into the air. The young men in the clearing duck and cower for a moment, then several of them cheer as the helicopter circles the field. The pilot puts the aircraft into a hover and settles into a corner of the clearing.

Our train car finally comes to a stop several hundred yards from the time gate. The men on motorbikes zip along the ground to circle it as more men climb off the car. It seems several people have been clinging to the side of the train and now drop into the grass.

"Hot damn!" a man below me shouts. "Now that was some fun." He immediately starts stripping out of his Nazi uniform and flings the jacket to the ground. He rips off his shirt to reveal he's wearing a Hawaiian shirt underneath. He greets Jorge with a handshake that becomes a hug. They clap each other on the back.

The time gate is toast. A couple of men are observing the damage from the helicopter. The tail rotor has severed the conduit bridging the emitters. There's no going back that way now.

"You got my gold for me yet, Ramirez?" One of the other men from the train heist walks over to Jorge for a handshake. He's heavily tattooed on both forearms.

"All in the works, güey." Jorge reaches into his pocket and tosses a rock to him.

The man turns the gold ore over in his hands. "Oh hell yeah."

I guide Piper to the back of the train car and begin climbing down the ladder. Two native men with guns rush to the back of the train to cover me with their weapons. I recognize one of them as the guy I knocked off the motorbike. Once I reach the ground, I hold up my hands. "Good to see you again too."

Piper hesitates at the top of the ladder as Jorge and his two companions walk over.

"Took yourself a little detour, eh, guero?"

"He got away?" the man in the Hawaiian shirt asks.

"Not far enough," I reply.

"That's okay," Jorge says. "You saved me a week of feeding your ass while you were gone." He pushes me against the train car, then glances up the ladder. "You come on down, chiquita. Daddy here needs to learn a lesson."

"You're not going to touch her," I say.

"You think you're giving the orders now?" His fist flies forward and strikes me in the gut. I groan from the impact and double over.

He keeps his fist raised and is about to hit me again when Piper shouts, "Leave him alone!"

Jorge looks up to find Piper at the top of the car peering down. He reaches behind his back and pulls out his long knife. "Get down now, little girl. Unless you want Daddy losing pieces." He takes a few steps back so he can watch her. I can't see Piper's reaction, but a few seconds later her red Converse sneakers appear on the rungs of the ladder. She carefully makes her way down, casting occasional looks behind her and then to me.

I straighten up and try to look reassuring.

When she reaches the ground, Piper turns and backs up against me.

Jorge steps forward to reach for her, but I grab her first and shove her behind me, blocking his path. "No way."

"You want to get cut, guero? 'Cause that's how this is going to go."

My blood is boiling.

"You're pretty tough when you have an advantage," I say. "If I had a chronometer right now you'd be in a world of hurt."

"A chronometer?" Jorge cocks his head. "What, like one of these?" He reaches into his pocket, then holds up a stainless steel chronometer that looks vaguely familiar. "You go right ahead, bro." He tosses it to me and I catch it. "You think that will save you?"

My fingers find the dials instinctually. Tune for a time we'd arrive at night. I grab Piper's hand and depress the pin.

Nothing happens.

"Boss man has the warp clock now," Jorge says. "Good luck getting anywhere with that paperweight."

I mutter curses at the lifeless chronometer. We were wrong. These criminals aren't trying to use the chronometers themselves. They've shut them all off in favor of the time gates, knowing no one can find them that way.

"So let's see how tough you are," Jorge says. "You got what you wanted." He waves the knife at me.

"We've got bigger fish, Ramirez." A woman's voice comes from around the side of the train, and I turn to see the pilot walking up in her jumpsuit. I recognize her as the same woman Mym and I faced off against at Dr. Quickly's funeral. She seems to have recovered well from the kick Mym gave her. Her tight afro has been teased out farther, and she looks more in her element here. She walks confidently. Probably the confidence you get from having a heavily armed gunship at your disposal. "Franco wants them alive, remember?" She walks up and stands next to the other men. "He has special plans." She locks eyes with me, but unlike our encounter at the funeral, her gaze isn't aggressive. She seems to be studying me closely. Why is she sticking up for me?

"Son-in-law here needs a reminder to obey the rules," Jorge says. "I'm thinking maybe his little girl loses an ear."

"We didn't come here for this, man," Hawaiian Shirt Guy says. "We came to deliver the goods and get paid. Let's get this nut cracked already."

Jorge eyes me with disdain. He lowers the knife. "I'll deal with you later, puto."

The man with the arm tattoos climbs the steps of the train car and enters. When he comes back, he's guiding a battered and disheveled looking man in a Nazi uniform. The man is handcuffed and blindfolded, but his distinctive mustache clues me in to his identity. That and the stream of German curses coming out of his mouth. He shouts at the world around him, raging at his captivity. He is guided to the edge of the steps, then the man behind him plants a foot on his lower back and kicks.

Adolf Hitler lands in a heap in the grass.

"Shit, Sal. You'd think he would know how to get off his own train by now." Hawaiian Shirt Guy laughs and walks over to study the groaning man in the grass.

"Let's get him roped up," Sal responds. "These two also. The sooner we get them secured, the sooner we can relax."

Jorge shouts to some of the natives, and they bring rope to tie us up with. For the third time today I find myself being bound. Hitler is back on his feet and cursing. Piper looks downcast.

"Don't worry, kiddo. We're going to get out of this."

She looks up but seems unconvinced.

As we are led past the pilot, I catch her eye. "Thank you."

She doesn't reply, but she gives me a nod.

That's twice now she's chosen not to harm us. Not exactly an ally, but I'll take what we can get.

We're led across the clearing, and more of the Native Americans join us. They seem fascinated by the mustached man and his litany of swearing.

I'm not sure why, but I always thought Adolf Hitler would be short. Perhaps I'd assumed his Napoleonic, world-conquering tendencies stemmed from some physical insecurity. But it's not the case. As he is led through the woods ahead of me, I try to process that I am looking at one of the most despised killers in modern history. I've met some terrible people in my life, but the extent of his atrocities makes every scumbag I've ever met seem tame.

I address Piper next to me. "Whatever happens here, make sure you stay well away from that man."

"Well, duh," Piper replies.

I stare at her for a moment, then nod. "Yeah, I guess that kind of goes without saying."

We are being guarded by several of the young natives, but the man they called Sal is only a few paces behind us.

"Why kidnap him?" I ask, pointing with my bound hands toward Hitler. "The Nazis have something you want too?"

Sal considers me briefly then spits into the bushes. "We just had to take him out of the equation. That's done. The rest is for shits and giggles."

I consider what he's saying. Taking Hitler out of history isn't an original idea. Time travelers have been trying it since time travel first went public, but the results don't always turn out well.

"You know sometimes killing Hitler makes Germany win World War II, right? Some people think his instability is what makes them lose."

"Not my problem," Sal says. "Boss man says take him out, we take him out."

"You mean the Gladiator dude? Is he your boss?"

Sal chuckles. "Nah. I mean the big boss. Ol' Franco just thinks he's the boss."

I still have a lot of questions, but at least I'm getting a few things sorted. Apparently this Franco guy is the Gladiator. Still not sure who this big boss is though.

"Hope your boss knows what he's doing," I say. "Looks like you're making some big changes to history."

"You better believe he does," Sal says. "And don't worry. We're just getting started."

By the time we reach the camp, the sun is down and my body is ready to give up on me. My eyes have begun to droop even while walking. I'm not only exhausted, but I stink to the high heavens. I can't even begin to count the amount of hours I've been awake. Fortunately it doesn't seem like we're moving again tonight.

The young natives argue with one another about what to do with us but, somewhat inexplicably, Piper and I get tossed back into the same hut we escaped from the last time. The little old lady who was watching us is still there, sitting on the bed and shelling acorns. Apparently the hut belongs to her family, and she has nowhere else to go. We aren't left to our own devices this time, however. My wrists get securely bound to a support pole of the hut, and I'm forced to sit with my legs wrapped around it and pinned underneath me. It's a unique position I've seen employed before, but I've previously only seen it done by high school friends goofing around, mostly torturing underclassmen. I wisely avoided participating in the past, but now I remember why. With my left leg around the pole, and my right leg and foot wrapped rather painfully over my other ankle and squashed beneath me, I wouldn't be able to escape even if my hands weren't bound.

Thankfully Piper avoids enduring this treatment for long simply by having skinny legs. As soon as our captors exit the hut, she's able to finagle her feet out from under herself and sit. She's still tied to a pole but infinitely more comfortable.

"I'm getting hungry," she declares from her position at the neighboring roof support. "And I miss Mom. I bet she'd know how to get out of this."

I think of the stricken look on Mym's face the moment before she jumped away in London. Where is she? She's probably worried sick.

"Where's your mom right now?" I ask, attempting to shift my weight and ease the uncomfortable pressure on my ankle.

"She's still at home. I don't think she knows I'm gone."

"What? How did you manage that?"

Piper splays her legs out in front of her and wags her feet back and forth in a manner I currently envy. "I didn't tell her I was leaving. I knew she wouldn't let me go. I thought I'd be home before she ever noticed I was gone."

I consider what she's saying. I've heard several time travelers bemoan the near impossibility of keeping track of their kids once they become capable of time travel. It's rare that any would travel on their own so young. I imagine it's far more rare that they end up trapped in the 1800s with Adolf Hitler. Leave it to my kid to be the prodigy when it comes to running away.

"You must have wanted to get away pretty badly," I say. "You couldn't just tell your mom where you were headed?"

"She wouldn't have let me," Piper replies. "I ran away to find you because you were supposed to come get me and you didn't. I knew you must be in trouble and that you needed my help. She said you were probably just forgetful and lost track of which week I was supposed to visit."

"Visit? Where was I that you had to come visit? Don't we all live in the same spot in the future?"

"Not anymore," Piper says. "Not since you and mom split up."

I thought the sitting position I was in was painful enough already, but her statement hits me right in the gut. I temporarily forget my physical discomfort in the wave of thoughts that overwhelm me. Mym and I are split up? What the hell kind of future is she from?

I study the little girl on the floor across from me. She's an anomaly; the results of a life lived in an alternate future. But throughout this long and absurdly surreal day, she's proven herself brave, capable, and unflinchingly positive. What could be wrong with my future self that I've screwed up parenting so badly?

It seems insensitive to ask but I can't help myself.

"What happened? I know it's kind of not my business, but in a way I guess it is. Do you know why your parents split up?"

Piper looks at her hands and fidgets with a loose end of rope between her fingertips. "I think it's maybe my fault. I think it's different now than it used to be because I'm there."

"Stop. There's no way that's the reason."

Piper looks up at me. "You don't know that. You weren't there. That's the whole problem." She pivots angrily around the pole, putting her back to me.

"Hey. Piper. That's not what I meant. I'm not saying you're wrong, I'm just saying that there's got to be more to it than that. Heck, I've only known you for a day, and I already think you're really cool. Your dad has to be your biggest fan ever." I wince as I try to get circulation back to my foot. "We're going to find him, okay? Then he can tell you himself."

Piper keeps staring at the far wall. "That's what you said before, but now we're right back where we started."

I try to pull myself upward on the pole to release my feet but to no avail. I grunt. "If it helps any, I don't think we're exactly back where we started." I slump back onto my bent ankle. "I think I'm considerably worse off."

Piper turns and glares at me.

"That was a joke," I say. "That's how I deal with adversity when I'm out of ideas."

"Mom would have ideas," Piper mutters.

"Yeah. You're probably right about that."

My legs are growing uncomfortable to the point of consistent pain. I'm not going to be able to keep my weight off my ankle much longer. When my arms give out sometime soon, I'm likely going to tear a muscle.

Darkness has fallen outside. Someone is laughing down by the river. I hiss through my teeth as I try to find a way to ease the pain in my legs. I look up to adjust myself and find the old toothless woman standing next to me. She seems to be listening more than watching. She walks around behind me. I hold my breath, trying not to annoy her further with my gasping, but finally I have to exhale. My arms are shaking as I struggle to keep myself upright. The woman cocks her head, peers through the darkness, then gives my shoe a swift kick. My foot slides out from underneath my butt, and I'm finally able to fall back and free my leg. I twist my other leg from around the pole and collapse onto my side in relief.

The woman grunts, then says something in her own language before puttering back over to her bed.

"Thank you," I whisper.

She lies down and rolls over to face away from me.

I slump all the way to the floor. My wrists are still bound around the pole, but I can finally relax. Piper is lying down now too. She watches me for a little, then rolls onto her back to stare upward at the few stars we can make out through the hole in the ceiling. The last lucid thoughts I have before drifting off to sleep are that she looks a lot like her mother, and that we're both still a long way from home.

14

"A time period can become home as easily as any physical location. And the bonds that keep us there are identical: love, duty, and the hope for a better future." -Journal of Dr. Harold Quickly, 2112

I've had some bad nights of sleep before. Uncomfortable. Restless. But I can honestly say I've never had a tied-to-a-pole-in-the-1800s level of bad night's sleep. When I wake up, my back and neck are stiff, and I have aches in muscles I wasn't even aware I had.

I'm rousted by several of the native youths at sunrise, then permitted to stretch my legs and go about the business of my morning under careful supervision. Going to the bathroom in the woods is an activity not improved by company. Especially when that company is dudes with guns. I do get a chance to splash myself in the river and wash away some of the sweat and stink from my previous day of futile activities. That is the highlight of my day so far.

Piper is likewise being kept under supervision, but I get the impression it's more of a formality. The disappointed expressions of the young men assigned to guard her clearly indicate that they wish they had been given something more important to do.

The women of the tribe have made some sort of porridge for breakfast, possibly out of acorns, and they gave some to Piper. She's gracious enough to share a little with me. It's pretty terrible, but appreciated. I feel like I could eat about anything at this point. After eating, we're tied up again near a stand of trees while we wait for the group to finish setting up the next time gate.

"Which one is that one again?" I ask Piper for probably the third time.

"That one's Sal." She points with bound hands toward the man with the plentiful arm tattoos. He's unloading electrical equipment from a crate and hardwiring it into the power cells near the solar array.

"And we decided that one is Jimmy," I say, watching the guy in the Hawaiian shirt curse at a lock on one of the crates.

Figuring out the names of our captors has been the most entertainment we've managed this morning.

Hitler has quieted down overnight. He's no longer blindfolded, and the environment he's found himself in is no doubt a shock. He's tied up on the far side of the little beach watching the activity in the camp. He doesn't look too pleased about his circumstances. The helicopter pilot is guarding him. She has a camp chair set up nearby and a rifle laid across her lap, but her feet are up on a crate and she seems to be giving herself a manicure with a knife. Apparently she doesn't find guarding the Führer especially taxing.

"Did you figure out her name?" I ask.

"That one's Vanessa," Piper says.

She's obviously been listening a lot more attentively to conversations than I have.

"Why haven't they let us go yet?" Piper asks.

"What?"

"Mom gave them what they wanted. You heard them say so. If they have what they want, then why haven't they let us go?"

"I'm not sure it's going to be that simple."

"I think they should do what they said they would."

The question gets me wondering what they do intend to do with us. And with Hitler. If they were just removing him from history, a strategically placed bullet would have sufficed. They obviously have additional plans beyond screwing up history. I'm curious as to what they might be.

We're one step closer to finding out when Sal and Jimmy get the new time gate working. With the old gate damaged by the helicopter tail rotor, it looks like they opted to set up a new one instead of attempting repairs. Sal is apparently the tech guy of the operation. It doesn't take him long to have the temporal field emitters tuned and pulsing with light.

Jorge shows up with several more of his Native American friends but not to accompany us. Apparently he's staying behind to work on his mining project. I've managed to avoid eye contact with him all morning, but when we're untied from our tree and marched to the time gate, we are led right past him. He tilts his head back and appraises me. "You're lucky, cabron. You get to leave again. But I think maybe you won't like where you're headed."

I know better than to respond. He looks at Piper. "You better keep your dad in line today, chiquita. Or he won't last long."

Piper glares at him but likewise stays silent.

He never asks for his deactivated chronometer back.

The others are packed up, and apparently Hitler is coming too. He studies the time gate with wonder, but goes back to cursing his captors when they shove him toward it. He squirms and tries to get away, but Jimmy and Sal manhandle him through the gateway in short order. They vanish into the ether.

Vanessa gestures for us to get going. She addresses Jorge as we move. "We'll be back for the shipments. Don't be forgetting that gold gets split lots of ways."

"Six months," Jorge says. "I'll have you swimming in it by then."

"Happy to hear it." Vanessa hoists one of the power packs to haul along with her. "And don't let these locals eff up my chopper. I'm coming back for her, pronto."

"Ain't nobody gonna mess with your bird," Jorge says. "They call you 'The Monster Rider.' I think you scare them shitless."

"Damn straight," Vanessa says. "That's a wise attitude." She fist bumps Jorge, then picks up her rifle and looks at me. "Okay, we've got a lot of time to cross. Let's get moving."

Piper and I are led to the time gate. I can't see the destination on the display screen, but once we are through, I immediately recognize where we are. We're back in Yesteryear Adventure Park.

Despite our delay on the other side of the time gate, we emerge moments after the others. Hitler looks flabbergasted. He's staring with wide eyes at the change in scenery. He spins around several times, trying to process what he is looking at and how we've gotten here. There is an edge of wonder in his eyes though too. It makes me hope these guys are planning to keep him carefully detained. The last thing we need is a time traveling Hitler running amok in history.

We're in a different section of the park than we were before. We didn't exit the mine ride but rather a different doorway in the Frontier section of the park. The room we enter is drafty and bare with only a few rusting tools left strewn around the floor. When we make it out of the dilapidated building, we find that it was the façade of the blacksmith shop. We are led out of the Frontier village via a different route than Piper and I took, over another bridge and onward to the other end of the World History section.

We pass beneath a gate in the Great Wall of China that is flying tattered remains of various flags. There are a few decrepit animatronic guards atop the wall, staring lifelessly into the distance for signs of invaders.

Once inside the wall, we pass pagodas and pavilions of various shapes and sizes. There is a dragon themed roller coaster spiraling through a long-forgotten garden. Most of the plants are now brittle twigs, but I notice one determined vine still climbing its way up a wall, reaching for the supports of the roller coaster. It makes me wonder if in a different climate it might one day wrap itself over the entirety of the ride. Would that be a plant's greatest aspiration?

A toddler's version of the roller coaster is set up near the garden with mild undulating rises and comforting lap bars. As we walk past the ride, one of the cars clunks and moves a few inches.

Jimmy jumps.

"What the hell?" He spins to aim his rifle at the ride as if to threaten it into submission. When nothing else happens, he slowly lowers his gun and we move on. I look behind us a couple of times, and when I glance up at the now-receding battlements of the Great Wall, I catch one of the animatronic soldiers watching us.

Weren't they all facing the other direction before?

We've only made it to the next building when we hear the music. A tinny and metallic sound is emanating from a speaker somewhere. Instrumental Chinese music.

"I thought this place was supposed to be empty," Sal said.

Vanessa mocks him. "What's the matter, Sal? Afraid of ghosts? It's just old systems left in the sun too long."

Another group of animatronic figures is ahead of us to the left—a group of six traditional Chinese dancers with ribbons and parasols.

Piper walks a little closer to me.

As we maneuver past, one of the dancers pivots and locks her eyes on Piper. Then she begins to move—an eerie sort of swaying. She is joined by one dancer after another. After a few moments, all six of the animatronic dancers are jolting and swaying. The music has stopped so the only sounds are their stiff and rusty parts scraping and grinding as they attempt to perform for us. The dancers all bear smiles, but several of the faces have deteriorated from being outdoors. One of the dancers has a wasp's nest in her mouth. As she moves her mouth to attempt to sing, the angry wasps begin climbing out of various holes in her face.

"Oh, hell no," Jimmy says. He lifts his rifle and starts shooting dancers.

Piper cringes and hides behind me.

"Hey! You're wasting ammo!" Vanessa shouts. "Get it together. They're just dolls."

Jimmy raises his gun, smoke wafting from the barrel. The dancer with the wasp's nest is now missing most of her head.

I catch Hitler smiling.

"Let's get the hell out of here," Sal says.

But the weirdness doesn't stop there. The farther we walk, the more the park comes alive. Music begins playing in entryways, lights flicker along walkways, and occasional robotic voices beckon us toward rides and concessions.

"This place is really creeping me out. Let's hustle to the gate and get gone," Jimmy says.

The next time gate is hidden in the park's version of the Coliseum. The amphitheater's arched doorways permit us inside, and we climb a series of ramps past rows of stadium seats. The seats have been modeled to resemble stone steps, but consistent with theme park style, the stonework is all fake. This Coliseum is steel and concrete with more foam and plastic for façades, but I have to admit they've done a decent job. I imagine that whenever it was in operation, the arena would have been quite a spectacle.

It seems Hitler has finally found a place he recognizes. He spouts something in German I don't understand. Sal just hustles him along.

"Let me guess. This gate leads to our metal-headed friend," I say to Vanessa. "You guys draw straws for who had to wear that helmet or did he lose a different bet?"

"Franco was dressing like a gladiator long before I met him," Vanessa says. "He says it gives him an edge."

"I smelled the 4sight. His *edge* is all chemically induced."

"Kicked your ass, didn't he?"

"That what you go for in a guy? Thick skull?"

"What makes you think I go for guys?" Vanessa asks. "I'll tell you what. When a man says he has a way out of prison *and* a boatload of time gates, you don't care what he likes to wear on his head. Now stop yapping."

I lapse into silence while I look around. There are a lot of passageways here. Enough to get lost in? Until now there haven't been many escape opportunities. But even if Piper and I were to make a run for it, there isn't anywhere to go. If we successfully eluded our captors here, there is still nothing but desolation outside the park. Whatever timestream we're in, it's nowhere we want to stay long. I'll have to hope for something better at the next stop.

If I could find out which of these assholes has the warp clock, then maybe we'd be talking. Jorge's deactivated chronometer is in the pocket of my jacket. If I could figure out how to turn it back on . . . well, then there would be the issue of finding an anchor from another timestream, and any of a long list of other problems to solve. But one thing at a time.

Sal has activated the time gate. Multi-colored brilliance illuminates a doorway down a corridor. The colors oscillate and swirl, making strange and beautiful patterns across the floor.

"Are we going to Italy?" Piper asks. "I like Italy."

"Your guess is as good as mine," I reply.

"They have the best gelato there," she says. "You think they might let us get some?"

"Do we not take you out for gelato in St. Pete in the future?" I ask. "Is that what's wrong with me as a parent?"

Piper wrinkles her nose. "It's okay there. But in Italy it's better."

"Didn't know I'd raise such a gelato snob . . ."

"Hey. Shut up back there," Jimmy says. "Gate's set. Get on through." He waves us forward. "You keep your mouths shut, you'll live longer."

Piper falls in behind me.

"I'll go through first. You follow. Got it?" Jimmy says. He waves a pistol at me. "No funny business on either end. I don't want to shoot either of yas. But I will if I have to."

"We won't make trouble as long as we get gelato," I say.

"What?" Jimmy balks at the comment.

"Nothing," I reply. "Just a joke."

"It's how he deals with stress," Piper adds helpfully.

"Just get your asses through, or I'll really give you something to stress about." Jimmy glances at Sal and once Sal gives him a nod, steps through the gate.

Sal resets something on the control panel, then waves us forward. "You two can go together. Get out of the way on the other side if you want to live."

I know that drill. I'm not excited to be fused to a rifle, or to a part of Vanessa when she follows us. Clearing away from a time gate makes surviving a trip a lot easier. I take a breath, then walk on through.

The air is dusty and hot. Sound assaults my ears as soon as I'm through. Cheering. Screaming. Metal on metal. Drums are beating rhythmically somewhere overhead. We're below the stadium now. A stadium anyway. There is a window on one side of the corridor looking out over broad expanses of countryside, so I don't think it's the Coliseum anymore.

I take a few steps, pulling Piper with me. Her head swivels, processing the ceiling above and the thunderous applause that erupts from beyond the corridor. Jimmy gestures for us to keep moving, and we pass a barred doorway leading to the heart of the arena. The shouting and chanting is louder out there.

Vanessa and Sal appear through the time gate separately, but then Sal shuts the gate back down.

Definitely not the Coliseum. It's too small. Even with the limited view of corridors from my perspective, there's no way this would match up. When we're led onward, my suspicion is confirmed. We follow Jimmy and Adolf Hitler up a set of stairs to a platform overlooking the arena. Wide, sail-shaped sunshades protect patrons in numerous rows of seats.

It looks like we are in the past. At least it seems so, but some of the spectators are wearing sunglasses. Others have bags of popcorn and bottles of beer. There is a chariot racing around the arena below us at high speed, and a man with a lance on a horse. He's not Roman. He's wearing medieval armor and a shield. It's an exhibition or a Renaissance fair. It would almost make sense if I weren't standing on a balcony next to Adolf Hitler.

In a raised section of seats to our right, I spot the Gladiator seated in a high-backed chair. It's the first time I'm seeing him without his helmet on. It's sitting next to him on a stand. He looks about how I imagined. He's got a square jaw, a buzz cut, and a glare that's all business. Beside him is a man I'm surprised I recognize. As we are led over to them, I gape at the balding time traveler I last recall seeing in a toga outside Ancient Rome. He's in less formal robes today and he's wearing boat shoes.

Octavius Theophilus Graccus. It was the name he went by at the time, anyway. The former chronothon facilitator glances over and spots us approaching. His eyes widen at the sight of me.

"Ben? Benjamin Travers?" He gets out of his seat and comes rushing over. He ignores my bound wrists and grasps me by the shoulders. "What a wonderful surprise!"

"Hello, Phil," I reply. "It's been a long time."

"Has it?" Phil replies. "It's so hard to know these days." He looks down at Piper and leans toward her. "And you brought a little friend."

I take a step sideways to block Piper from him, and Phil bumps his forehead into my shoulder. He straightens up and rubs his head. He looks at me, offended. "I'm just saying hello. No need to be alarmed."

"Talk to me then, Phil. Where the hell are we?"

"What? This?" He turns to the spectacle below us. The armored knight makes a charge and successfully knocks the charioteer from his chariot, hurling him to the dust. The crowd erupts into raucous applause. The charioteer doesn't look like he'll be getting back up. Phil winks at me and sweeps his arm across the view of the arena. "This is the Circus Nefarious! The place where evil men come to die."

15

"It is a gift that we are unable to stop time completely. We must all pay for life one second at a time. If this spending could be stopped, we might become misers and fear to live at all." -Journal of Dr. Harold Quickly, 2025

"You made a *Celebrity Deathmatch*?" I ask, recalling the old Claymation MTV show. "But with real people. That's horrifying."

"I don't know what you're talking about," Phil replies. "We've merely created a spectacle for time travelers to flock to. A place where we can enjoy the great villains of history meeting their timely ends." He grins at me.

I glance back to find that Jimmy and Vanessa have handed off their other prisoner. Adolph Hitler is being led away down the corridor. He's back to cursing loudly.

I'm not sure which to be more disgusted by, the idea of completely altering history at a whim, or the brutality I've just witnessed in the arena. "Who's that?" I say, pointing to the knight on horseback.

"John Hawkwood. Mercenary. Cuts quite the gallant figure, doesn't he? Tends to play the role of hero here, but make no mistake, he's a brutal man. If you stay for the events this afternoon, you'll see him face off against Attila the Hun! That should be very exciting."

"You can't do this," Piper says. She's crept up behind me and has clearly been listening. "You can't just take people from time and move them around. It's wrong."

"Wrong for whom, my dear?" Phil says. He rests his entwined fingers on his ample belly. "Wouldn't you say that the timestreams these villains were plucked from would be better off?"

"You can't possibly know that," I argue. "You could be making things worse!"

"Well, thankfully it's not up to me," Phil replies. "We only do as we're told."

"By who? Him?" I gesture to Franco in the chair beyond him. The Gladiator seems engrossed in another matchup that's just beginning. A mustached man wearing a bowler hat is being dragged out from a gate in the wall and forced toward the middle of the arena. Onlookers are whooping and hollering.

"Not to disparage Mr. Franco, but we get our orders from a higher intelligence now," Phil says.

"The prisoners do not require explanations of our business, Graccus," the Gladiator rumbles, apparently overhearing us despite the noise from the crowd.

Phil turns toward him. "You'll have to forgive me. Not everyday I meet someone from the glory days. Did you know Benjamin here competed in a chronothon? We met in Rome. He did quite well." He turns back to me. "Weren't you awarded first place?"

I don't have an opportunity to respond because the Gladiator rises from his chair and picks up his helmet. He's now wearing a leather breastplate and has abandoned his modern clothing altogether. He steps over and appraises me. "Chronothon champion. You must think you're a big hero."

I glare at him but don't take the bait.

"The only thing chronothons have been good for is providing us with our supply of time gates," he says.

"You stole these gates from chronothons?"

Phil knits his fingers together as I glare at him. "I *may* have let some people know where ASCOTT was storing the gates after they were confiscated. It's not exactly my fault if they left them inadequately secured..."

"We are putting them to better use," the Gladiator says. "Out here, away from the coddling of ASCOTT and the regulations of the Central Streams, heroes are defined by their actions, not made-up games. We don't need sanctioning now, or the rules of old men in lab coats."

"We wouldn't be here if it weren't for some of those old men," I say.

"The Quickly family is a different matter," the Gladiator replies. "But we're done with their ways too. We have a new mentor now."

"You all keep talking about this great intelligence you're following. I heard about your prison chats and crazy A.I. church. Whoever is running it is obviously playing you for suckers. You think if they are really that smart, they would organize this nonsense?" I gesture to the arena. The man who has been forced to the center is now stumbling around with a brown bottle in his hand. He looks disoriented.

"This is my arena," the Gladiator says. "No one made me do this. It's my reward for services rendered."

"Who have you got out there now?" Phil asks. He reaches into a pocket and removes a wrinkled program. "Oh it's H. H. Holmes, the serial killer. His weapon of choice was apparently chloroform and piano wire. Can't say that will serve him very well. Wonder who he's drawn for competition."

Another gate opens in the wall and a man rides out on horseback. He has an elaborate helmet and pointed beard and is carrying a curved sword.

"Who is that?" Piper asks.

"Oh my. Poor luck there," Phil says, scratching out something on his program. I notice it has bid amounts listed near matchups. "He's drawn Genghis Khan. Very bad luck. Khan's been winning all day. I rather think he enjoys this."

The man on horseback locates Holmes in the center of the arena and urges his horse into a run. He swings his sword once, as if warming up his wrist, then bears down in the saddle and focuses on his target. H.

H. Holmes makes a break for the wall. He's running full out, but he doesn't stand a chance. The Mongol is on him in seconds.

I pull Piper aside and make her look away. "You won't want to see this." I duck down with her and have her focus on me. There's nothing I can do about the sickening sounds from the arena or the shouting of the crowd, but I pull her closer anyway. "Don't let this scare you, okay?"

When the cheering has died down, I look up to find the Gladiator watching me. He's scowling.

"Get him below till I've made arrangements for them," he barks.

I'm hauled to my feet by guards that appear out of nowhere. The men shove me roughly toward the corridor. In a matter of moments, I'm being dragged away. Piper tries to follow but is restrained by the Gladiator. He grips the back of her hair. She squirms and shrieks but to no avail.

"Get your damned hands off her!" I shout before the wind gets knocked out of me by one of the guards' fists. I shove the guard away from me, attempting to get back to Piper, but the other guard wraps me in a bear hug from behind. The first guard pulls a baton and brandishes it at me.

I make eye contact with Vanessa, who simply shakes her head. I bite back my anger and stop resisting. Getting brained by the guard with the baton isn't going to help the situation.

"I'll get us out of this, Piper. I promise!"

I'm dragged backward toward the corridor.

"No! Dad! Wait!" Her shouts continue as I'm dragged away. I grit my teeth and try not to think of what might happen to her on her own in the company of these men. For several dozen yards, I can still hear her shouting, even over the noise from the crowd outside.

"She's just a kid," I say, pleading with my nameless captors. "Don't hurt her." I have a hard time knowing if they even understand me. Are they locals? Are these more time travelers? I'm so confused about how I even got into this mess, but now all I can think about is how it's getting worse.

I'm forced down a flight of steps into the bowels of the arena. We pass several chambers including one that looks like an armory before proceeding through a set of locked doors. It's dark down here. The passage is smoky and dimly lit with torches. My stomach tightens at the sight of blood on the floor. Blood and what might be a human finger. The mystery appendage is on the floor near a table that looks like it may have been used for medical treatment. Wads of bandages, used cutting implements, and several bottles of murky liquid still adorn the tabletop.

I'm hauled past the table and down a corridor lined with cells. The barred chambers are occupied by a variety of morose-looking individuals. Some are sleeping, a few are pacing their cells, and several are hanging on the bars slinging what I assume to be curses at the guards. The curses are in a colorful variety of languages from Chinese to Spanish, to strange tongues I've never heard involving clicking. I spot Adolf Hitler with a sour expression on his face, sharing a cell with an Asian man I vaguely recognize from my history studies. I'm ninety percent certain he's Pol Pot, but the lighting isn't the best.

The guards stop at the gate of a cell occupied by a single man lounging on a cot. He's dressed in an elaborate black coat trimmed with red. His narrow face and sunken eyes follow my movements as I'm shoved into the cell. The bars clunk solidly behind me as the guards lock me in. They retreat without a word and disappear back down the corridor.

"Hey," I manage, addressing my new cellmate. His mustache twitches slightly but he doesn't get off the cot. I look around the dingy cell, finding nothing remotely pleasant about it, then turn back to the door.

I need to get out of here.

Despite having been a captive for over a day, I still have a fair amount of my possessions left. My sunglasses are still in my jacket pocket, as well as the broken chronometer. I wish I still had my phone or pocketknife, but those were a no-brainer for getting confiscated. My pen was also stolen, but I guess that's to be expected too. I pull the sunglasses out again, however, and power them on. Perhaps there is a lock picking tutorial somewhere in the menu of apps? I'm cycling through the index when I hear the voice.

"Benjamin? Is that you?"

I lift the glasses from my face and look around. "Hello?"

"Ben! Over here!"

I locate the face behind the bars the same moment my mind registers the voice. It's coming from a cell across the hallway and a couple doors down. "Abe? Oh man! It's good to see you! Are you okay?"

Abraham Manembo is about the last person I'd expected to find down here, but if there is any time for a friendly face, now seems like a good one.

"I'm okay," Abraham replies, pressing himself up against the bars to see me better. "Where's Mym?"

I glance down the corridor, noting several faces at the bars listening in.

"You don't have to worry too much about them," Abraham says. "At least most of them. Only a few know English. Be careful of the one behind you though. He has a mean streak."

I glance behind me to the cot and my reclining cellmate. He has his arms behind his head but is watching me with curiosity.

"Who is he?" I ask. "Anyone I need to worry about?"

"That's Vlad III," Abraham says. "Or Vlad Dracula as some called him."

"Vlad the Impaler?" I ask. "Holy shit." I turn and look again, mostly to make sure the man is not currently in the act of murdering me from behind. "Just how many of these creeps have they got in this place?"

"The numbers seem to be dwindling today," Abraham says, "now that the festivities have started."

"They're a bunch of loons with this," I say. "An arena full of the worst people in history? With time travelers as spectators? I can't help but assume they didn't think this one through all the way."

"ASCOTT would be most displeased with tourists making this kind of excursion," Abraham says.

"I doubt many of these tourists will be seeing the Central Streams again," I say. I recall what Carson had said about the Gladiator's previous line of work—kidnapping and abandoning time travel tourists. It seems he's gone right back to it after his escape.

"How did they get you?" Abraham asks.

I give him the abbreviated version and fill him in about Piper.

"You mean they have her up there right now?" Abraham asks.

"Until I can get her back. You have any ideas on getting out of here?"

"None that I haven't tried already."

Abraham's features are hard to make out in the dim light. From what I can tell, he looks exhausted, possibly bruised as well. My fingers find the chronometer in my pocket. "Did they make you tell them about the warp clock? Did they hurt you?"

"Only as much as can be expected," Abraham says. "I didn't have much choice. Once they got the device, I knew it was only a matter of time till they'd figure it out. It would have been worse if they had broken it in their attempts. As it is now, there's still a chance we could salvage this. We just need to get it back."

"Any idea where they're keeping it?"

"No. Not anymore. I doubt it's here. They have someone higher up. Someone directing their efforts."

"I heard the name," I say. "They called him TRIK. Sounds like whoever he is, he's the one who sprung them from Rookwood Penitentiary. You haven't seen him?"

"Not that I know of," Abraham replies. "You don't see much from a prison cell."

"If we do somehow get our hands on the warp clock, how do we get it back on?" I ask.

Abraham grips the bars. "It's not difficult. With the training you've had working on chronometers, I'm confident you could operate it, but until we find it, we won't be getting any help. The chronometers our people have will only work in limited capacities. Even Harry would have trouble getting from time to time now. I wouldn't expect a rescue."

"Wait, you mean there's still a way for chronometers to function? I thought the warp clock totally disabled them."

"It has disabled their temporal tuning," Abraham explains. "It's impossible to jump from timestream to timestream. The frequencies won't modulate properly. But there would still be some limited functions in a timestream you already occupy."

"Like what kinds of functions?" I ask, my mind starting to race with possibilities.

"I'll be sure to give you a lesson in temporal frequency modulation if we ever get out of here, but right now I'm afraid the discussion wouldn't be very relevant."

"Might be more relevant than you think," I say. I pull the chronometer from my pocket and flash it at him before hiding it away again.

Abraham straightens up. "You have one?" He lowers his voice a little. "Here? That's incredible!"

"They seemed to think they're just dead weight now," I reply. "The cons that had them are just throwing them away."

"That may work in our favor," Abraham says.

Someone shouts something from down the corridor. They sound mad. They try again in broken English. "American. Shut up!"

I ignore them and focus on Abe. "How do I get it to work?"

"It's going to be difficult," Abe says. "You'll have to get it open and detach the power supply. Once you set the time interval you want on the face and reattach the power supply, you'll have a set increment to jump. You can travel forward or backward but only in this stream. Problem is, you won't be able to change the time increment without taking it back apart again. The settings dials won't work like normal."

"So what do you pick for an interval?" I ask.

"Hard to say. Any idea how much power it has left?"

I shake my head. "No idea."

"Better stick to something short then. You won't get far around here anyway. It's a long way from anywhere, at least temporally speaking. There won't be an easy escape by chronometer."

"I'll figure out a way," I say. "I have to. Piper is counting on me." I take the chronometer from my pocket and study the small screws of the backplate. I don't have any way to get them out right now. "I'll get us all out of here," I say.

"You don't worry about me," Abraham says. "It will be hard enough sneaking away with two, let alone three. You get that little girl away from this place, and find a way to call for help. When you get the warp clock back, you can bring the cavalry down on this place and come back for me."

"You can't expect me to leave you here," I say.

"This is time travel we're dealing with, Ben. You won't leave me for long. You can find a way back in time to help me."

"Assuming I can get out of this cell."

Abraham looks as though he's going to speak, but then his eyes flit down the corridor. He puts a finger to his lips.

A few moments later, I hear what he's worried about. The guards are back.

"Looks like you get to skip the line," one of the guards says as he reaches my cell. I guess he does know English. "Back up," he adds, shooing me away from the bars. "The boss must be excited to see your match-up. Bumped the whole afternoon agenda."

"Match-up?" I say. "What are you talking about?" He gets the gate open. The other guard marches in and pulls me from the cell.

"Everyone gets a match-up sooner or later. It's your turn. You're headed into the arena."

16

"Throughout time, no matter the century, people believe they are the pinnacle of historical knowledge and modern science. None are. As a man of science myself it's a humbling reminder that every truth I hold may one day be proven wrong." -Journal of Dr. Harold Quickly. 1615

"You get to choose a weapon."

The guards have guided me to the armory under close supervision. Two bulky men in armor have joined us in the room, and a moment later Vanessa walks in.

"I can handle this one, boys. I'll see that he gets sorted out."

The two burly guards share a glance, but when Vanessa continues to stare them down, they exit.

"You have something to do with this?" I ask. "Why I'm getting tossed into the arena?"

"You have yourself to blame for that. You shouldn't have upset Franco. He was planning to let you live. None of us wanted to kill you. Except maybe Jorge. Now that's going to be more difficult."

"You could still let me out of here. I know you don't want me dead. You could have taken me out on top of that train but you didn't."

Vanessa narrows her eyes. "I had my reasons. You think I'm the sort of person who shoots a man right in front of his daughter?"

"Apparently not. But what good is saving me if you let me die now? Help me again."

"I'm trying," Vanessa hisses. "But there's no letting you go. That little girl is in trouble now, and you're the only chance she's got."

"What are they doing with her?"

Vanessa tilts her head toward a grated window that's admitting dusty light and the sounds of the crowd high above us. "She'll be out there too."

"What? You've got to be kidding me!" I say. "With the tyrants and killers greatest hits collection?" I move to the table of weapons and angrily sort through options. "It's psychopath city around here." I inspect the rusty armor and dented helmets. There are some bows and quivers of arrows and a few swords. Vanessa adjusts her grip on her rifle as I pick up a dinged blade.

"You're going to have to be smart out there. Franco will have some game in mind. He likes a story to his events. If you're lucky, you'll be playing the role of a hero. I tried to talk him into that. Some of the people in the audience might recognize you and see you that way."

"I *might* be playing a hero? That's how you plan to save Piper?"

"I have limited influence here. This is Franco's world. I'm doing what I can."

"You're a real saint," I say.

"You want to be dead? That's fine. I can let you figure this out on your own." Vanessa spins on her heel and makes for the door again.

"No! Wait." I hold up a hand. "I do need help. I'm sorry."

Vanessa turns around slowly.

"I need to know what I'm up against, and how to get Piper back."

"Listen, that little girl is the only reason I'm down here. That and because..."

"Because what?"

"It's nothing. Look, whacking tyrants from history is one thing—Hitler and the rest of this bunch would have had me dead in short order in their time, so I'm not going to shed tears there—but orphaning little girls is something else entirely," Vanessa says. "I know she isn't even really your kid, so if I help keep you alive, you'd better do right by her. I'm risking my neck for this."

"I intend to get her home safely if I can," I reply. "As soon as I find her real dad."

Vanessa looks away quickly.

"What?" I ask. "You know what happens to him? Do you know if he's alive?" I don't ask the follow-up question. Whether she knows which version of me has been shot.

She looks back at the table. "Listen, I think you might be up against animals. I heard roaring in the pens this morning."

"Roaring? Shit." I pick up the bow and search around for the arrows.

"Take the spear. Everyone with a bow has been dying today. Unless you think you're Robin Hood."

"Is he here somewhere? Can I get him on my team?"

Vanessa rolls her eyes. "Just pick two items, okay? You only get to have two."

I look at the table of weapons and realize I'm not especially adept at any of them. "I need a screwdriver."

"What?" Vanessa says.

"A screwdriver. A small one. Has to be a number one tip or smaller. Preferably the kind you might use on eyeglasses."

"That's not a weapon. Take the shield and the spear. That's your best bet."

Footsteps sound in the hall. The guards are coming back.

"Screwdriver. That's what I want." I cross my arms.

Vanessa glares at me and puts a hand to her hip. "You're being an idiot. Come on and hurry up. They want you up there." She casts a quick glance toward the doorway, but then she reaches into the pocket of her trousers and extracts a stainless steel multi-tool. She tosses it to me. "You happy now?"

The multi-tool has several screwdriver options.

I knew a pilot would have tools. I slide over to the weapons table as the guards appear in the doorway. I grab the dented circular shield and a wood-handled spear. The shield looks like someone jumped up and down on it, but it feels solid.

The guards aim their rifles at me.

"Selection time's up. Get a move on," one of the men says.

As I move past Vanessa, she grips my arm and whispers though tight lips. "1958. It's an option on the time gate. If you survive the arena, she'll be safer there."

I nod to her, then make my way back into the corridor.

The guards usher me onward.

The straps on the shield are frayed and worn and it takes me a few attempts to get it fitted over my forearm. It's heavy. The spear is likewise heavy but at least it seems well balanced.

I'm guided to a metal gate that leads to a ramp. The steady incline ends with a second gate at the upper end. One of the guards gestures with the barrel of his gun. "Go stand up there. When the gate opens, you fight." He doesn't bother with any additional instructions, but merely slams the door, locking it behind me and trapping me in the ramped corridor. I have no choice but to walk up to the exit.

Fight. I feel like I've received a death sentence.

I reach the crack in the gate and attempt to peer through. I can't see much, just a stretch of sand, then a barricade of some kind. Where is Piper?

Vanessa's words come back to me. Roaring.

I take a step back from the gate. No use getting eaten instantly.

I set the spear against the wall, pull my newly acquired multi-tool from my pocket and flip out the screwdriver attachments. It has pliers and a knife as well, which may come in handy. I palm the tool in the same hand I'm using for the shield, then dig around in my pocket for the chronometer.

Someone is speaking outside. A loudspeaker. It's muffled by the door but I make out a few words. Dangerous. Heroic. Heartbreak. Then a sympathetic "Awww" sound coming from the crowd. They must think this is a show. All some kind of act. Who in their right mind would come to see real people getting mauled or killed in an arena?

I get the chronometer into my shield hand and have just started unscrewing the grounding plate screws when the gate groans. I take a step back as someone lifts a locking pin from the top of the doors. They are swung open via ropes and sunlight streams into my corridor.

"... but will he find and save her before she is discovered?"

I catch the last snippet of someone's voice as I pocket the chronometer.

"Let's hear it for our heroic warrior from the far reaches of time, Benjamin Travers!"

The crowd erupts into applause. I put away the multi-tool and pick up my spear, then cautiously take a step forward.

This doesn't look good.

The arena has changed since I last saw it. Instead of an open oval like a racetrack, someone has dragged various barriers and barricades out. It reminds me of a paintball course. There are stacks of logs and bales of hay. An electric bulldozer is parked in the corner, a leftover from the rearranging. Franco is clearly not a purist with his recreations. There's no sign of Piper.

"Get to the middle!" someone from the stands shouts. I look up to find several people in the crowd pointing and encouraging me onward. I take a few steps in that direction.

"Hurry up!" someone shouts.

I break into a cautious jog. Are they really trying to help, or are they going to get me killed? Not sure arena death matches are a time for polling the audience. But what choice do I have?

I stay within shouting distance of the wall and call up to the crowd. "Where is she?"

"That way!" a woman shouts. She points toward the center.

"Hurry! You're gonna be too late!" her companion adds.

I cut left and veer around a barrier made from leafy tree limbs. These obstructions are laid out in a particular pattern. As random as they seem, the positioning is deliberate. It's a maze.

"And now entering the arena from the north ... he's merciless, he's unforgiving—he once beat his own son so badly he gave him brain damage ... I give you the first Tsar of Russia—Ivan the Terrible!"

A cascade of booing sweeps through the crowd. I pivot in place to get a sense of the sun. Which way is north? I get my bearings and keep moving toward the center of the arena. The twists and turns are disorienting. I have to be almost there.

"The lions are certainly looking hungry," the announcer says.

Oh shit. There are lions already in here somewhere? I cast a quick glance behind me.

Piper screams.

The sound pierces the air ahead of me. She's close. The far side of the next barrier.

I run. When I round the pile of timber in my way, I skid to a halt.

Not good.

Piper is up a tree. Well, a tree house. Sort of. It's a shoddy-looking structure that looks more likely to collapse than anything. Someone has shored up one side of a precarious wooden platform with a tree trunk, but it's no longer alive. The whole thing looks like something you'd find in a backyard jungle gym—if you were a terrible parent with no regard for safety.

"Help me!" Piper yells. She's clinging to a part of the tree house structure near the very top. One of her hands is secured to the post with rope. She's prying at the knots with her other hand. "Help!"

"I'm here!" I shout back.

Piper glances my way and looks down.

"Dad!"

Then I see why she was screaming.

A lion has found its way to the base of the far side of the tree house. It's heard my shouting and is now eyeing me.

The big cat is golden and beautiful and utterly terrifying. It looks pissed.

It's clear now that it's a lioness. I'm pretty sure that's worse. The lioness lifts her head to look back at Piper and stretches upward, testing the strength of the tree house supports. The movement is almost lazy, the way a house cat might stretch up the back of a couch. Only this cat's claws and teeth are deadly.

That little girl will not die here.

The thought rushes through my brain. Not like this. Not without a fight.

I slam the spear into the edge of my shield and then repeat it, making as much noise as possible.

"Hey! Get away!" I have no idea if my shooing motion with the spear and shield are remotely a good idea, but it seems to work. The lioness drops to all fours and hunkers down in the dirt. I hoist the spear in the air, then bang the shield a few more times as I walk forward.

The lioness leans, then freezes halfway out of her crouch. She's indecisive.

"From the south gate, I would like you to witness the most hated man of the Twentieth Century, the monster himself—Adolf Hitler!"

The crowd erupts again, this time into fierce booing. I don't take my eyes off the cat.

"Get away! Get!" I bang the shield again and the lioness snarls at me, but she retreats. She slinks beyond the next barricade, her tail swishing.

I've done it! At least for now.

I drop the spear. I need my hands. The shield will have to go too. There's no way I'm getting up the rungs of the tree house ladder with it still on my arm. I recall watching Captain America perform all manner of feats with a shield in the movies, including slinging it effortlessly onto his back and still performing acrobatic stunts. That's some brand of Hollywood bullshit because no matter how hard I try, the only time the shield is out of my way is when I leave it on the ground.

I clamber up the makeshift tree house fast, only pausing once as the structure sways. I ignore my screaming internal alarm sirens and force myself up to the platform. Piper is wide-eyed. Once I'm to her she looks back to the barricade where we last saw the lioness. "I'm scared."

"I know you are, kiddo. So am I. But we're getting out of here." I pull the multi-tool from my pocket and extract the knife blade, using it to cut Piper free. Once she's loose, she clings to my waist.

"And from the west gate, I give you our reigning champion of today's events. The Mongol conqueror and warlord of warlords, Genghis Khan!"

This time people are screaming with excitement. The noise of hooves on dirt is quickly drowned out. Apparently this murderous man has won them over with his exploits.

Whatever game is afoot, I'd rather not play. I drop to one knee and extract the chronometer from my pocket. I get to work on the screws on the backing plate.

"What are you doing?" Piper asks.

"I've got a plan. I'm going to get us out of here. Keep watch for me."

Snarling and yowling erupts from an area to the south.

"Oh! It looks like Ivan the Terrible has been discovered!" The announcer sounds excited by the prospects. "Let's see how he does against his fearsome new opponents."

The screws on the chronometer take what feels like an eternity to remove, but I know in reality it's less than a minute. People in the stands can see me from their seats, but I doubt any have a clear view of what I'm up to. I do my best to conceal the chronometer behind my hands in case any of them have binocular lenses.

A shout of collective surprise goes up from the crowd.

"Oh my," the announcer says. "Well, I guess that does it for Ivan. That's a point for the lion pride."

Shit. I study the part of the maze that people seem to be watching, but I can't make anything out from here. I'd better hurry.

"Dad?"

"Yeah?" I keep my focus on the chronometer. I get the backing plate free and search carefully for the power cell connection. It's a powerful device, and it won't do to damage it in the process.

"Dad!"

I look up this time. Piper is looking over the edge of the platform. I follow her gaze and find the source of her worry. The lioness is back.

Or rather, another lioness is back. I'd swear this one is bigger.

Piper retreats from the edge of the platform. The cat circles the tree house, sniffing the air and eyeing us in a fashion that I can't help but think is a hungry expression. She seems to be focused on Piper.

"You stay close to me," I say. "And keep your eyes on her. I think they are less likely to confront head on while you are watching them."

I'm pretty sure I'm not lying. Haven't I heard that somewhere?

"Do lions eat people?" Piper asks. "Are they going to eat us?"

"They prefer antelope," I say. "You aren't an antelope, are you?" I finally locate the power cell. What had Abe said? Was it set the time you want first and then disconnect it, or was it the other way around?

"It looks like things are getting interesting for Benjamin Travers and his young companion. The other members of the pride seem to have located them. Will this spell the end for the heroic time traveler?" I look up as the announcer says my name.

The announcer must have cameras in here somewhere. He knows we're in trouble.

"There are two now," Piper says.

"What?" But I don't need her to say anything else. It's true. The second lioness has entered our section of the maze from the north. She stretches up one support post, but this animal doesn't hesitate long. She crouches, twitches her tail, and leaps. Razor sharp claws find purchase in the wood of the platform. The big cat is now only feet away from me, ears flat and muscles straining. Her rear paws scrabble to find a grip on the post below, and for a single horrifying second, she begins to pull herself up.

Then the post gives way.

With a jolt and a shudder, the thick beam holding up one corner of the tree house fails. It crashes to the dirt below us. The lioness releases her grip, dropping nimbly to four paws before retreating from the creaking structure. But she doesn't go far.

My relief at the lion's fall is immediately subverted by the swaying of the platform. I shove the chronometer and multi-tool into my pockets and snatch up Piper, pulling her to me. She shrieks as the platform sways the opposite direction. There are only three support posts remaining, and every one of them is in motion.

My breath is caught in my throat. Piper's grip on my jacket tightens. The crowd sends up a collective gasp as a second support pole comes apart beneath us. My last thought is that I never would have expected my day to end like this...

The platform tips and gravity seizes us.

We fall.

17

"It's easy to get nostalgic about the past. Just remember that those citizens of yesterday were dreaming of a better future. You still have the opportunity to prove them right." -Journal of Dr. Harold Quickly.

I don't hate heights. I hate the ground.

As I hit the dirt, my legs buckle under me and I roll. Piper sprawls next to me, along with a pile of splintered timber. The collapsing tree house raises a cloud of dust around us with continuing thuds of falling boards.

I can't see the lions.

"Time to go!" I say, scrambling to my feet and helping Piper to hers. She winces as she stands, then teeters against me.

"Ow! Ow ow ow." She lifts her foot and clutches at my arm.

"Is it your ankle?"

She nods, a pained expression across her face.

That's going to be trouble. We had little to no chance of outrunning lions as it was, but now we'll be sitting ducks.

I frantically search the rubble where I left my weapons. Piper coughs from the dust.

The collapse of the tower seems to have startled the lionesses away, but I can't imagine it's for long.

I locate the shield and drag it out from under some plywood. The shaft of the spear is beneath it.

Turning to Piper, I shrug out of my jacket. "Here, put this on." Leather won't help much against lion claws, but I have another idea.

Piper doesn't argue. She slips her arms through the oversized jacket. "It's too big."

"That's because I want you to get as big as possible." I crouch and move her around to my back. "Get on my shoulders, like we did to escape from the hut."

Piper limps closer and climbs onto my back. I position her legs over my shoulders, and she grips the top of my head to hold on.

"When these lions come back we're going to be huge, okay? I want you to wave your arms and get as big as possible. We're going to be the biggest, scariest thing they've ever seen."

I get a grip on the shield and spear and use them to keep my balance as I stand. I teeter slightly as Piper gets situated, but it seems to work.

I have a choice to make. It's not a pleasant one.

I need to get the chronometer apart, but I'm currently holding the spear with one hand and the shield in the other.

I need more hands.

"I'm going to give you the spear, okay?" I hold the handle up. "Use both hands. If anything tries to hurt us, you stab it."

"What if I miss?"

"It's okay. I've got a plan."

My plan is currently in several pieces in my pocket, but I retrieve the partially disassembled chronometer as I walk us carefully away from the wreckage of the tree house. I head toward the edge of the arena. As the dust clears, I have a better view of the stands. People aren't even watching. Many of them are on phones or viewing tablets. The entire crowd erupts into cheering, however, and a few look up to catch the action on the far side of the arena. Most stay focused on their devices. That's when I realize they are seeing the action there too.

"Hey!" I shout toward the nearest group of spectators. "Help us!"

One middle-aged man looks up and seems surprised to see us. He points toward the north end of the arena. "There's a safe place. If you get in, you can survive."

A safe place. I start to turn north.

"But it's only going to fit one!"

The melodic voice of the announcer comes on over the speakers again. "We've got a new threat from the south. Looks like . . . yes, that's a pack of grey wolves. Can our contenders survive this new danger? Only one competitor will claim the safety of the cage."

The sound of hooves makes me turn. Genghis Khan flies past a set of barricades to our left, his horse at a full gallop.

I swear under my breath.

With Piper on my shoulders I can't move very quickly. I stagger onward, retrieving the multi-tool from my pocket and studying the innards of the chronometer. I've had training on these, but I never thought I'd be doing repairs like this . . .

"Dad?" Piper sounds worried. She pivots the spear to our left. I turn to see several wolves go loping past on the trail of the Mongol and his horse. They disappear past the barricades without noticing us.

"Stay ready," I whisper.

I locate the power cell for the chronometer and pry the terminal loose. No time to waste now. I turn the chronometer over in my palm and study the rings. We need a destination time.

"Dad!" This time Piper doesn't bother with subtlety. Her knee bangs into the side of my face as she pivots on my shoulders. I spin to find the problem behind us.

One of the wolves has tracked us down.

Shit.

Piper hoists the spear, keeping it in front of us. "That's it," I say. "Wave that thing around."

I position the shield across my body, peering over the top of it. The wolf is lean and hungry-looking, a thin body with long legs and protruding hips. It hasn't bared its teeth, however. It's frozen in place, analyzing us.

"Get away!" I shout. I flail my one free arm and take a step toward it. "Get!"

The wolf retreats a few steps but doesn't go far.

"Get away!" Piper repeats. The wolf snarls at us and Piper shrieks.

"It's okay," I say. "Just keep your eyes on him." My mind flashes to every wolf encounter I've ever seen in the movies and the hours of nature documentaries I've watched over the years. If we can deal with them one at a time, we might have a chance.

I glance back at my chronometer. Destination. We need an anchor first. Everything around us has been lifted and bulldozed into place in the last few hours. I have no idea where any of it will be in the hours to come either. I don't want to use a wall of the arena. Won't be much of an escape if we don't get out of here.

A guttural roar echoes off the arena walls.

"Oh! It looks like the wolf pack has discovered the lion pride!" the announcer says, and the crowd murmurs its delight. A wolf yelps in the distance, and the wolf near us perks its ears up. It skirts us cautiously, then runs to join its pack.

"We did it!" Piper shouts.

"Good job, kiddo," I say, turning north again. "Now let's find a way out of here."

I'm hoping the distraction of the lions will keep the wolves occupied long enough to find this safe place the spectator was talking about. I keep my eyes open for anchors as I move, working my way out and around the barricades, away from the last place I saw the wolves.

It doesn't take long to find what the spectator was referring to. The shouting gives it away.

Adolf Hitler and Genghis Khan are at a standoff.

The Führer has found himself a crossbow, but it looks like he only has one shot left. Genghis Khan has ditched his horse and is lingering on the opposite side of a ladder that leads up to another platform. This platform has a small cage affixed to the top. It looks secure enough to protect someone from the lions and high enough to be safe from wolves. But it's just an open cage. No protection from arrows or swords or spears.

Safe place my ass.

Hitler glances our way but keeps the crossbow aimed at the Mongol. I don't blame him. I doubt a man with a nine-year-old girl on his shoulders is his biggest threat. Genghis Khan is holding a wooden shield and has it raised toward Hitler. He's still armed with a sword as well. He doesn't look worried. I get the impression it's not the first time he's faced arrows, but he's keeping his distance just the same. He's suffering from the same issue I had before. Climbing the ladder to the cage means putting something down, and that will leave him exposed.

The crowd is getting excited. The occasional shouting from the stands has morphed into a steady roar.

This can't last long.

"What do we do?" Piper asks.

I crouch and let her slide off my back. She doesn't look ready to relinquish her grip on the spear, so I let her keep it. I have a decision to make. I need an anchor. The solution dawns on me and makes me marvel at my own stupidity. It's been right in front of my face. The shield. It was lying face-up in the armory when I walked in. If I can jump us back...

I do some estimating in my head. How long have I been in here? I back away from the safe zone slowly. If I can get to a wall, maybe one of the spectators can tell me. I can also get out of range of the crossbow. I keep myself between Piper and Hitler as we move. "Come on. I have an idea."

But we don't get far.

"Dad!" Piper yanks on my shirt.

The wolves are back.

This time there are more of them.

A snarling alpha male is creeping toward us. His black fur is raised on his shoulders and his teeth are bared. I get a wave of chills up my back just looking at him. I grab Piper by the hand and pull her away. She's still limping.

I'm not the only one who's seen the threat, and these aren't the only wolves. The pack has separated and is entering the safe zone from multiple angles. Hitler is forced to retreat. He looks worried now. With only one arrow and this many targets, I would be too.

It's time to make a decision. Trust the humans or face the wolves.

If it was anyone other than these two it might be an easier choice.

"Can I get back on your shoulders?" Piper says.

"We're not staying," I say as we inch closer to the Mongol and the ladder to the cage.

Genghis Khan checks the position of the wolves, considers Hitler, then tosses his shield aside and lunges for the ladder.

"Nein!" Hitler shouts, waving the crossbow at him. Khan ignores the threat and plants his foot on the bottom rung. Hitler rushes forward and the wolves close in behind him. Not wanting to be the first ones eaten, I pull Piper toward the ladder as well. That's when Hitler swings the crossbow toward us and fires the bolt. I barely have time to get the shield up before the arrowhead imbeds itself in the metal just above my arm. I stumble back from the impact. Hitler hurls the entire crossbow at me, narrowly missing us, then lunges for Khan. The two men grapple at the base of the ladder, pushing back and forth. Hitler somehow manages to wrest the sword away from Khan, forcing the Mongol away, then spins and starts climbing the ladder.

Piper screams as Genghis Khan grabs hold of the spear in her hands and tries to yank it away from her. She holds on tightly, but before I can stop him, Khan flings her sideways into the path of the wolves. Piper tumbles to the dirt in a heap. The Mongol hoists the spear, aims, then hurls it toward me. I get the shield up, but this time nothing hits me. The spear flies overhead and Hitler grunts as he reaches for the shaft in his back, then plummets from the ladder.

The wolves lunge for Piper.

I barrel through Khan on my way to her. He is caught off guard and the edge of the shield hits him in the chin. He goes over backward, hitting his head in the process.

A wolf has Piper by the bottom of her shoe. It's the ankle she twisted earlier, and she's shrieking in pain and terror. I swing the shield and shout as I rush forward, forcing the wolf to release her, but it only retreats a few feet. The pack is closing in. They're getting bolder. I pull Piper to her feet and she clutches me by the waist. I cover her with the shield and half drag her toward the ladder. Hitler is writhing on the ground attempting to get up. The spear has come loose and is lying at the base of the ladder. As soon as we are close enough, I scoop up Piper and deposit her on the first rung. "You have to climb."

"I can't!" There are tears in her eyes.

"You have to. You can do this." I swing the shield around to keep the wolves at bay. Piper begins to climb.

Khan is getting back up. He gets to his knees and puts a hand to his head. Then he realizes his danger. The wolves are under the platform now, snarling and nipping at him, trying to get a piece of him between their teeth. He rushes for me but I spin to block him with the shield.

I'm facing the same choice he did before. Fight or climb. I snatch up the spear and then hurl it at him. It doesn't hit him at the right angle to do any damage, but he ducks anyway and the shaft at least ricochets off his head. It buys me enough time to clamber onto the ladder. With the shield on one arm, I'm forced to basically climb one-handed, but I'm winning the only contest that matters right now. Don't be the last one up.

I make it several rungs then look down to find Hitler and Khan grappling again, fighting for position on the ladder.

Piper has reached the top and scrambles up onto the platform.

I make it perhaps halfway up when I feel the hand on my ankle. I look down to find Khan yanking on it. His face is red and furious. He's working desperately to climb up after me and pull me from the rungs. Hitler is attempting to climb behind him but there is no room. The wolves close in and one of them leaps for his legs. The first wolf misses, but then the black-furred alpha emerges from the pack and leaps, burying his fangs into the dictator's thigh. Hitler screams and scrabbles to grab ahold of Khan, but the Mongol yanks his foot free and kicks him. The wolf pulls Hitler from the ladder.

I cringe at the horrifying sounds that follow and keep climbing. Piper is at the top of the platform, her arms wrapped around the bars of the cage, but her eyes are closed. I don't blame her. I scramble up to join her. The cage is too small to fit both of us and the shield. "Get in and lock the door," I say, gesturing for her to climb inside.

Her bright eyes find mine and she shakes her head.

"Please. I need your help." I hold the shield out to her while reaching for the chronometer in my pocket. "We'll use this as an anchor. I'm going to get us back to this morning."

Piper takes the shield. Hitler's crossbow bolt is still protruding from one side.

Khan reaches the top of the ladder. He shrieks something at me in a language I don't understand, but I really don't care what he's saying. I pull the multi-tool from my pocket and select both the screwdriver and the knife.

"Lock the cage, Piper. I won't let him hurt you."

I set the chronometer dials quickly, then plug the power cell back in.

There is a very small ledge surrounding the cage. If Khan stays on the ladder, or if he hangs out calmly, we should all be able to survive the wolves.

Unfortunately it doesn't seem like he's the calm type. He shouts at me, waving one arm and gesturing to the cage. I have no idea what he's saying. He repeats himself and gestures again.

"He says there can only be one," Piper says.

She has pulled my sunglasses from my jacket and is now wearing them. She must be running the translation app.

"He says the game won't end till there's one. He says he'll kill me because you won't. As a favor."

"How do you say, 'Go to hell' in Mongolian?" I ask.

Khan gets the idea. He narrows his eyes and starts to ascend to the platform. I haven't got the chronometer finished, but there's no time. I set the multi-tool and the chronometer inside the cage. "I need you to screw that back together. Screws are in the jacket pocket. Anything happens to me, you make the jump, okay?"

Piper looks like she's about to cry. "Come inside. Come inside!" she shrieks. But there's no room.

"It's okay. We've got this," I say. "Just put it together."

Then Khan is up.

I go for the quick finish. With one hand gripping the cage bars, I kick for his midsection, looking to knock him from the tower. He's too fast and grabs my leg. He rams a fist toward me, narrowly missing my groin and hitting me in the thigh. He scrambles upward, using my body as his ladder, all fists, sweat, and cursing. I land a right hook to the side of his head, but then he's too close, pressed up against me and trying to wrench me from the bars. He's crazy. If I let go now, we'll both go over. But he doesn't seem to care.

Having one fewer hands is a huge disadvantage. His fists and hands keep alternating. Grasping here. Punching there. I've never had to fight like this before. I pry at his throat with my forearm. He's hissing and spitting and now my fingers are slipping from the bars. He's somehow managed to wedge himself under my arm and is prying my body away from the cage with his strong, compact frame. My height advantage does me no good. In fact, it's a liability. I realize, possibly too late, that I'm losing this fight.

"Aaagh!" Khan lunges and sinks his teeth into the hand I'm grasping the cage with. I slam my other fist into his midsection, then his back, but he doesn't stop. I have no choice but to release my grip on the bars before he rips my thumb off.

He knew exactly what he was doing. I teeter on the ledge. His foot flashes out and kicks me in the shin, dislodging me. The world spins and my brain gives me a view of the arena in slow motion. Rows of observers under a clear blue sky. Long drop to the arena floor. Ravenous wolves.

Ladder.

I wrap my arms around the rungs before they disappear. My body slams into the ladder.

My wind is knocked out of me but I haven't fallen. Not yet.

Genghis Khan now looms over me, grinning. He says something I don't understand, but lifts his boot to kick me in the face. I understand that completely.

The noise of the strike is quiet but distinct.

Khan's face suddenly changes. He wavers, half-attempts to put the foot down but can't. He winces as he pivots, revealing the crossbow bolt wedged into his hip. Piper is backing away, looking tiny in my oversized jacket and sunglasses. Bits of feather from the arrow's fletching drift away from her fingertips. Khan is turning on her, his face a mask of rage, but it's all the distraction I need. I grab his lame leg by the ankle and pull. The Mongol ruler teeters, arms waving wildly, but then gravity wins.

The crowd in the arena holds its collective breath.

Khan tumbles past me and hits the ground hard. I don't watch the rest.

I scramble onto the platform and wrap Piper in my arms.

"You said I could skip straight to fighting if it's Nazis. Was he a Nazi?"

"Close enough," I say. "Good girl." I kiss her on the head and usher her back to our shield. Even with the fight, she's managed to get all the screws started in the back plate of the chronometer. They aren't tight but it's close enough.

The announcer is saying something over the loudspeaker. People are cheering.

The game is apparently finished but I don't care. We aren't staying. I mash the shield to the floor of the platform and squat atop it.

I snap the chronometer to my wrist, set the timer mechanism to five seconds, then grab Piper by the wrist. My chronometer hand extends for the shield. Piper wraps her other arm around my shoulders.

Three.

Two.

One.

We blink.

T he past is dark. At least it seems that way a lot of the time for me. I've jumped us twelve hours. It's the middle of the night in the armory. A dwindling torch near the doorway is the only light to illuminate our arrival.

A crunching noise follows our jump, and the previously rounded shield buckles under our weight.

I waver but keep my balance.

Piper stays silent as we gingerly climb off the table full of weapons. She tests out her ankle.

"Can you walk on it?" I ask.

"I think so." She takes a few careful steps.

I adjust the position of my now dented shield on the table, trying to remember how it looked when I found it. I'll be picking it out later today with Vanessa.

Vanessa. The way out.

I rub my forehead, trying to recall her exact words. "Come on," I tell Piper. "We need to get to the gate."

I lead us into the hallway but have to pause. I can't see much of anything beyond the small ring of torchlight.

"I can see," Piper whispers. She's still wearing the sunglasses. Low light vision comes standard.

She leads the way down the hall while holding my hand. She's limping a little, but it seems like the injury isn't serious. Either way, she hasn't let me out of reach since the tower. Her fingers are still tightly clenched to mine.

I look back once as we walk.

Abraham is still down here, sleeping in his cell somewhere. There's nothing I can do about it right now. Without him being there later to instruct me on the chronometer, I'd never escape. No way I can change that now and not affect the timeline. We'll have to come back for him later, preferably with reinforcements.

The time gate is still where we last saw it. Well, we haven't even come through it yet. That gives me pause, thinking of the events that the me who comes through later will have to deal with. I don't envy his day.

"Can you get it powered on?" I ask Piper.

She releases her grip on my hand and moves to the control panel. She gets the access door open and starts punching in commands.

"Look for a destination in 1958. She said we might be safer there."

"Who did?" Piper turns on the destination menu.

"Vanes—"

The time gate suddenly illuminates. The colored streams of light blast from the emitters and meet in the middle, warping into the temporal field.

"Whoa!" Piper says.

"What happened?" I say.

"I didn't do that," Piper blurts out.

I take a step back just in time. A huge figure steps through the gate. Broad shoulders, muscled arms. That terrifying metal helmet. The Gladiator. He's holding a sword this time.

I back away a few more feet. Piper shrinks against the wall.

"Did you think I wouldn't find you? Did you think you could really escape?" Franco's voice resonates inside the helmet. "This is *my* world! My world and my rules. You are here to do as I say, and you survive at my will." He steps toward me and I put my hands up.

"Whoa whoa whoa." I get down to a knee. "We don't want trouble. I'm sorry. I promise we won't try to escape anymore. Just please don't hurt us." I fiddle with the chronometer on my wrist and slip it off. I hold it aloft to him and keep my head down. "Please, take it. Just don't hurt us anymore."

He looms over me, his sheer bulk making the room seem smaller by comparison. He snatches the chronometer from my hand. "Your life is mine now, Travers. You are right to kneel in—"

The Gladiator vanishes.

I pick a little dust out of my eyelashes and then get slowly to my feet. I brush the dirt off my knees, then locate Piper in the corner.

"So, I'm going to give you a little dad knowledge right now. These bad guys? They always fall for the timer trick. Like clockwork." I hold out my hand and smile. Piper rushes over. She wraps me in a hug again. "Okay." I pat her shoulder. "I just switched the directional slider on the chronometer to forward, so now that he's holding onto it for the next twelve hours, we're going to need to use your time gate skills again. You think you can find us 1958 on that thing?"

Piper nods.

"Okay. Let's get out of here."

18

"Throughout life there are two kinds of people: Those who tempt you to become a lesser version of yourself, and those who will inspire you to greatness. Choose carefully to whom you will give your time." -Journal of Dr. Harold Quickly 2010

Time gates are a leap of faith.

With my usual method of time travel—chronometers—I'm at least assured that some diligence has gone into planning an arrival location and time. There has been research involved and often photographic proof that the destination is safe for arrival, all conducted by experienced time travelers that I trust.

Those were the days.

I'm currently stepping through a stolen time gate hot-wired by criminals and reprogrammed for timestreams so far out in the multiverse that they don't even show up on the charts. I can only take small comfort in the fact that my guidance has come from the least murderous of the ex-convicts involved. But I've known her for less than a day, and during that time she's mostly been holding me hostage.

I could be stepping into a war zone. Or a volcano.

Or . . . a theme park.

As the brilliant colors of the transition dissipate from my vision, my senses attempt to process my new but semi-familiar surroundings. Piper and I have arrived in the back corner of some sort of dressing room. It could be a costume shop or perhaps we're backstage at a play. The racks of extravagant outfits and strange furry masks are cute and friendly-looking, and the noises coming from beyond the closed door are distinctly cheerful as well—laughter, and high-pitched chatter, the kind that only comes from one segment of the population. Children.

"Are we safe now?" Piper asks.

I look down at the little girl who has so bravely managed this ordeal so far. Somewhere in her question is a desperation—a hope that our trials will be over.

I wish they were too.

I turn and face the time gate. It's been anchored to a wall but is concealed by artwork. The structure around it resembles a medieval castle gate. It appears to be mobile, a set piece for a play or production perhaps.

"Let's get this thing disconnected somehow," I say, running my hands along the surface near the temporal field emitters. "We don't want Helmet Head coming after us."

"I think you can just unplug it," Piper says.

I lean around the back of the gate and discover that it's plugged into a 220 volt outlet in the wall. I pull the plug from the socket and let the cord dangle, then look back at Piper. "You remind me of your mom, you know that? Glad you got her brains."

Piper is still swimming in my leather coat. She shifts the sunglasses up to her head and smiles. "But she says I got your guts."

"Even more than mine," I say. "You're way braver than I was at your age." She grins and I reach for her hand. "Come on. Let's see where the heck we are."

"I smell popcorn," she says.

"Yeah. Me too."

We slip out of the dressing room past a stage door with a cartoon teddy bear on it. A few yards down the hallway there is a poster for a show featuring dancing animatronic bears in medieval costumes. It looks like a ridiculous premise, but judging by the applause and laughter coming from the auditorium, we're witnessing a smash hit.

An exit sign on a doorway beckons.

I push my way through it with Piper on my heels.

We emerge into pleasant and sunny daylight. A cool breeze is wafting down the sidewalk, bearing the scent of delicious fried and sugary things. I recognize a logo on one of the nearby signs. True to my suspicions, we're back in Yesteryear Adventure Park, but this time the park is alive.

"It's happy now," Piper says, observing the bustling atmosphere. A quartet of young boys races past with a string of paper tickets in their hands. They've got shirts tucked into their high-waisted shorts and socks up to their knees.

Piper shrugs out of my jacket and hands it back to me, but she lowers the sunglasses back over her eyes, clearly not caring that they are too large for her face. "They have food."

I don my jacket again, then follow her gaze across the pedestrian walkway to a snack stand. Customers are walking away with corn dogs, soda bottles, and tiny, delicious-smelling packets of French fries. My stomach growls immediately. I don't know where we are or what our next step should be, but food seems like a good place to start.

"Can we get something?" Piper peers up at me and grasps my hand. I get the impression it's not the first time she's employed the tactic.

I'm woefully aware that I have no money. I don't even have a chronometer to use to resolve my problems. Looking at Piper, it's clear I have an obligation regardless. She's been running on a partial bowl of acorn porridge, and I don't even have a good sense of how long ago that was. Having her pass out from exhaustion would be unlikely to earn me any dad points.

"I want you to stay right here, okay? Don't move from this spot. I'm going to see what I can do."

"Okay."

I stride across the walkway and join the short line. The near proximity to the food isn't helping my brain think any clearer. What am I supposed to do, steal something?

The cashier at the snack stand is a burly man in an apron and paper crown. His pimply teenage coworker hands a basket of fries to a waiting patron, then vanishes back to the grill. The cashier eyes my dirty clothes and scuffed jacket as I walk up. I can almost smell the judgment over the scent of the fries.

"Hi," I say.

"What'll it be?" the man asks.

"Uh, do you have any free samples?"

"Samples?"

"Yeah. Like to see what's good? I've got my daughter back there and she's really hungry, but her mom has my wallet. We can't find her at the moment. I thought maybe we could have a sample till she gets here?" I gesture toward Piper, who is waiting patiently on the far side of the walkway, face obscured by the oversized sunglasses. She seems to be staring into space.

The cashier sighs. "Look, mac, I got people linin' up here all day. You want something or you don't. It ain't a soup kitchen."

"I know. I know. I just don't have any money on me at the moment." I try to look like a sympathetic case, but it's clear he's not having it. Someone behind me in line clears their throat.

"I got people waiting here," the cashier says. "I'm gonna need you to step aside."

"Okay, wait a minute." I hold up a hand. "I've got something you might want." I dig in my pocket and find the multi-tool. "You look like a handy guy. You ever see one of these?"

The cashier finally looks interested as I fold out the pliers and show him the other features.

He leans across the counter to have a closer look.

I let him hold the multi-tool.

"It's worth quite a bit," I add. "Hard to come by." He turns it over in his hands approvingly. My growling stomach is feeling hopeful. "I use it all the time. My daughter and I just had the knife out a bit ago . . . to . . ." I turn to gesture to Piper, but freeze.

Piper is gone.

I spin around to search the other side of the line, then take a few steps away from the snack stand.

"Hey. You staying in line, or what?" The comment comes from a teenage boy with his gum-chewing girlfriend on his arm. She blows a slow bubble in my direction.

Where on earth did she go?

I take a few more steps away from the snack stand, and then I spot her. She's running away, headed along the walkway toward the exit of the medieval zone. Her untidy braid is bouncing on her back as she flees.

What the heck?

"Piper!" I cup my hands and shout, then take off after her.

"Hey buddy! You forgot your knife," the cashier shouts, but I don't have time to turn around. Piper has already disappeared between the faux rock walls of the exit arch. I barrel past surprised patrons holding cotton candy and Cracker Jack, then race across the drawbridge making up the exit from this section of the park. I catch a quick glimpse of Piper climbing a twisting pathway ahead, leading toward another section of the park—Independence Corner.

As she rushes onward, I can only guess what's happening. Did something startle her? Did she see something I didn't and get scared? She's not running like she's scared. It seems like she's running toward something. I shout after her as she vanishes into Liberty Village, a theme park hamlet made up to look like a colonial town. We rush past a teacup ride that threatens to dunk riders in the harbor before whisking them away again amid cheerful fife music. A sign reads, "You're Invited to Our Boston Tea Party."

By the time we've passed Paul Revere's Wild Ride, I'm almost caught up. Piper is forced to stop, searching to find her way. She's looking for something specific. I notice she's grabbed a park map similar to ones we studied before.

"Piper! Wait up!" I call.

She sees me coming and starts to run again.

Surprised, I put on some extra speed and finally catch her by the arm just before she reaches a wooden footbridge.

"Hey! What's going on?"

Piper spins and flails at my arm. "Let me go!"

People are staring but I hold on to her.

"What are you—"

"You lied to me!" she shouts. "You knew! You knew this whole time!" Her face is streaked with tears.

"Knew what?" I'm as baffled as I've ever been. "Just calm down, okay? What's going on?"

"I don't want to calm down!" Piper yells. "You lied to me! You told me you didn't know where he was, but you did know. You knew it from the beginning!"

The situation dawns on me. The sunglasses. She found the video.

"What happens at the end?" she demands. "Do you know? You do, don't you!"

"The end of what?"

She flings her hand out and shakes the sunglasses at me. "With this! The power died. Right when I could see him. What happens? Did you know? Why did you lie to me?"

"Hey, hold up, okay? I've been in the same mess as you all day. I've been trying to find him too."

"No you weren't," Piper argues. "If you knew he was here you should have come here first. You should have told me!"

I don't have an argument for that. She's right. I did have a suspicion that her father was in the colonial time, but I didn't want to believe it was this timeline. More precisely, I wanted to avoid a scenario where the other me in the video was me. Actual me.

"I'm sorry I didn't tell you about the video," I say. "But I didn't know for sure. I wasn't positive it was him."

"That's my dad. I saw him," Piper says. "You have to tell me what happens. Does he get out at the end? They had a bag. They put it over his head..."

She watched almost to the end. She must not have seen the shooting, but she's probably figuring it out. Nothing good usually comes from being led places blindfolded by thugs, no matter the century. Today has been proof of that.

"I have to find him. I have to get him back." Piper waves the map. It's an earlier version, a 1958 version, no glossy paper or fancy colors, but it must still have the clock symbols. Time travelers have definitely been here. She turns and continues to search for her destination. When she finds what she's looking for, she keeps going, half-walking, half-running as I try to keep up.

"We can't keep jumping into places where we know these guys are," I say. "We need reinforcements."

"We need to save my dad!" Piper shouts.

A married couple walking past pull their little boy a bit closer to them as they skirt around us. Apparently we're causing a scene.

"There's another gate," Piper says. "It's in there." She points to a building made up to look like a pub. The sign on the door reads "Green Dragon Tavern."

"Well, what do you know about that . . ." I mutter.

"What?" Piper says.

"Nothing. I've just been there before. Not that one, but the real one. They put a time gate in there?"

"I have to go get him," Piper says, and marches toward the pub.

The Tavern is just a façade. The door does open, but there is only a small space inside.

Children have carved their names on the support beams for the structure, but even the graffiti looks milder in the 1950s. It's almost charming. Several bundles of wires have been mounted to the structure. To the untrained eye, they look like the electrical wiring for the tavern window lights and signs, but the reality is much more complicated.

Piper discovers the time gate control panel mounted beneath a fuse box for the lights. It doesn't appear to have been there long. She reaches for the controls.

"Whoa whoa whoa," I say, grabbing her by the arm. "Not like this. Not yet."

Piper glares at me. "You said you'd help me save him. You promised."

I sigh and squat so I am below her eye level. "Listen to me, kiddo. You can't go in there. Not this time. It's not safe."

"If it's not safe then we *have* to go get him," Piper argues.

"That's not how this works. Not for kids."

"I'm not a little kid," Piper says. "I'm almost ten."

"And that seems old to you. I get that. But if I take you knowingly into danger when there is a better option available, that makes me a really bad dad. You'll be safer if you stay here."

"You said you aren't even my dad," Piper says. "I told you I know how it works. You don't have to keep me safe, but we still have to save him."

"Not we," I say. "Not this time."

Piper stares at me, her sky-blue eyes searching mine. "But we have to."

"I'm going to go," I say. "I'll find your dad and I'll bring him back."

"You said that before. You promised me, but you lied. I don't believe you."

"Look, I'm going to go in there." I say. "And I'm going to find him. And you are going to stay safe. Because the only way I'm going to be able to convince him to come with me is if he knows you are somewhere out of danger. If I put you in danger, well, then he's not going to like me very much, and I wouldn't blame him."

Piper seems to be considering this. "Who will work the time gate on the other side?"

"I feel like I have the hang of it now," I say. "And besides, if I have your dad with me, he can do it, right?"

Piper nods. She seems to be searching for any holes in my logic. No doubt another trait she's inherited from Mym.

"I just need you to stay here, okay? If I'm going to succeed, I need to know you are safe."

"I'll be safe," Piper replies. "It's okay here. It's nice."

"I'm glad you think so," I say. "I know you're hungry, and you're probably tired, but we can still get out of this. We just need to find a way to contact your mom and get her here. If we can figure out any connections between this 1958 and one of ours from the Central Streams, maybe we can make contact. I don't know. But we can figure something out. We just need to find the warp clock..."

"After you save my dad."

I study the little girl in front of me. She's as determined a person as I've ever met. It makes me wonder how he did it. What wonders did he conjure to make her love him with such devotion? Will my own children love me that much?

I stand up and face the gate.

"If for some reason I don't come back, I want you to find a police officer. Tell them that your dad is missing and make them keep you safe. But don't come after me. Understand?"

"How long do I wait?" Piper says.

"At least till whatever the next exit interval on the gate is," I say. "Or until you can't wait any longer. But I'm going to make sure you aren't alone, okay? Your dad is going to walk back out of this gate."

"Okay."

"Does it say where we are now? I just need to know the coordinates to jump back to."

Piper powers on the gate, then pulls up the destination identifiers for where we are currently. It's no stream I've ever heard of, but I memorize the coordinates anyway.

I don't have any weapons. I've honestly got nothing going for me right now other than sheer willpower. There's no telling what's going to be on the other side of the gate.

We locate a cluster of destination coordinates that were used last. They are grouped closely together. A menu on the control panel shows temporal data, and one of the options shows timestream signatures from people who have made jumps through the gate. I'm not a hundred percent sure, but one of them looks a lot like my own temporal signature. If that's not Piper's dad, I don't know what else to choose.

I opt for the time slot a few hours after he went through. It's my best bet.

Once the temporal field stabilizes, I turn to Piper one more time.

"You've done really great today. I know your dad is going to be super proud of you when I tell him."

"I guess you did pretty good too," she replies.

I lean over and give her a hug.

When I straighten up again, there's nothing left to be done. The time gate is open, and the question of my destiny is lingering in the ether. I recall the image of the musket—the smoke and the blast. On the other side of this gate, someone is going to get shot, and either way it's one of me. Another leap of faith. Will I survive this one?

I know there is only one way to find out.

I step through the gate.

19

"It's a strange feeling to know a time traveler is nowhere to be found in the universe at a present moment, but to have faith that they'll be back one day."
–Journal of Dr. Harold Quickly, 2087

I've never respected colonial times very much.

I suppose it was mostly the fashion. A three-cornered hat? Buckles on shoes? Who thought these were good choices? I need buttons on the calves of breeches about as much as I need another hole in me somewhere.

And the powdered wigs are just ridiculous. I don't know how I'm expected to take a man seriously with that on his head.

But nobody asked me.

They also didn't consult me when setting up this time gate. The barn I've wandered into smells of bovine flatulence and hay dust. I wish I could say that was the worst of it.

The two men with rifles standing guard at the gate don't look happy to see me at all. One of them is wearing a wig.

"Who the hell are you?" the man in the wig says.

It is apparently a rhetorical question as his companion immediately raises his gun. It doesn't look very colonial. "Get on the ground."

I put my hands up and kneel. Today really isn't my day.

"Just passing through, fellas. You really don't have to trouble yourselves." I attempt a smile.

"Franco said we were only getting one hostage to manage," the man with the gun says. He's black, broad-chested and dressed in simple laborer's clothing. "What's with sending us another one?"

His companion in the wig moves around behind me and grumbles as he checks my pockets and waistband for weapons. "He always seems to think we'll just jump whenever he says. Would've been nice to get a heads up."

"Actually Franco said to send his love," I comment. "He gets a little busy hosting his festival of fiends all day, but he wanted to pass along a hug."

"Shut up," the man with the rifle says. "We don't need your lip. You don't zip it, we'll knock your ass out."

Friendly bunch.

"It's like he thinks we have nothing else to do all day but babysit his hostages. And I'll bet he still wants the job done at the same time." Wig guy looks at me. "Take off that jacket."

"What?"

"Take it off. We can't have you seen in these clothes. Nobody is going to believe you're a British spy wearing that."

"Because I'm not a British spy?" I offer.

They still don't want my opinion.

I'm forced to strip out of my jacket and shirt and don a loose-sleeved bit of ridiculousness that must be what passes for a shirt around here. It laces up at the collar. Not that I can lace anything once they tie my hands. I'm getting really tired of being tied up.

"Where are we?" I ask. The coordinates on the time gate had given a year—1777—but I couldn't decipher the physical location.

Wig For Brains doesn't answer. He walks behind me and begins addressing someone else. That's when I notice the other prisoner. He's wearing a shirt similar to mine, but there's a bag over his head.

"You villains will meet a merciless end," the man says. "You do a disservice to God and to your country by laying hands on me!"

"Figure the country will do just fine without you, turncoat." The man in the wig guides the prisoner over to the time gate.

"I have never betrayed our new country's cause," the man argues.

"Doesn't mean you won't," his captor replies. The time gate gets reactivated and the man in the wig sets the coordinates. "Don't suspect you're gonna like this destination much, but maybe you'll do okay, being a war hero and all." The temporal emitters connect across the doorway and stabilize. The prisoner blusters a bit more, but there's nothing he can do. He's shoved unceremoniously through the gate and vanishes.

The man in the wig shuts the time gate down, then turns back to me. "One less villain in history."

"Turncoat..." I reply. "Benedict Arnold?"

My captor smiles. "I see you paid attention in school."

"Not for all of it, but enough to know that Benedict Arnold did the American Revolution a fair amount of good too. Do you guys have any idea what the repercussions of removing him from history will do?"

"Don't have to know," the man replies. "Not my job. I wasn't one of the guys that paid much attention in school, you know what I mean? But I know an opportunity when I see it."

"You could be changing everything," I argue. "You have no idea what you're doing."

"Don't care," he replies. "Only care that I get what I was promised. The planning shit is up to the boss."

The boss.

I still have no idea who this TRIK character is or what he's up to.

"Whoever your boss is, he's going to screw up a lot of timelines. Who knows what he's creating? It could be catastrophic."

"Why don't you shut your mouth?" This time it's the big guy with the gun speaking. "Ain't none of your business. Once your old lady gives up the goods, none of your friends will be able to mess with us. After that, we don't care what the boss does."

Interesting. I've jumped into a part of the timeline prior to them knowing Mym has already given up the warp clock. It's coming, but they haven't gotten the call yet. They must have a tachyon pulse transmitter somewhere if they are going to communicate about it. Maybe there's a way I can use it to call for help.

"Let's get going," Wig Guy says, "before we lose the daylight."

I'm not great at riding horses. I'm even less great with my hands tied in front of me. At least I'm not obligated to do any steering as my horse is being led along behind the others.

I try to get my bearings as we ride. We're out in the countryside. The weather is blustery and cool, with red and gold leaves drifting down in a lazy sort of rain from the trees overhead. I'm grateful they haven't blindfolded me because otherwise I'd have no idea how to get back to the time gate. I'd also be missing what is inarguably a magnificent vista. My two captors have lapsed into silence as we trot along. Perhaps even they are feeling reverence for the incredible view.

I don't know for sure which state I'm in. If they came here to abduct Benedict Arnold, then it narrows it down. Connecticut? I suspect it's somewhere in New England at least.

My captors don't seem especially worried about my presence. They look back to check on me periodically, but they don't seem concerned that I'll fall from my horse and try to run for it.

One advantage of being earlier in the collective timeline, these two won't have heard about any of my previous escape attempts. They seem to be handling this hostage-taking thing rather casually. That may work to my advantage.

I need a plan. The bad news is, these guys aren't my main problem. My main issue is time itself. If the other me they have hostage is Piper's dad, I already saw the video of this timeline's future, and one of us is going to get shot. If I change that outcome, I don't really stop it. Depending on the intensity of the paradox I create, I could enter an entirely alternate timeline where we both survive—a timeline B. But then I've duplicated the streams, and I have no idea what will happen to the other me in timeline A who didn't get shot. Will anyone save him?

The only way I know for sure how to avoid a duplicate timestream and not double my problems is to *not* change the events. But then one of us gets shot. How do I manage that?

All things considered, a change to the timestream will still be preferable to dying, but if there's a way to save us that doesn't involve condemning alternate selves to a worse fate, then I at least have to try.

I'm still puzzling over a solution when we reach our destination.

It's a typical New England farmhouse. Another reason I don't love colonial times is that the houses are pretty boring. Nine windows symmetrically spaced around a door in the center of a rectangle. Sloped roof. Chimney in the middle. I guess they hadn't thought up front porches yet. I'm helped from my horse under the watchful eye of the big dude I've decided to call Smiley. He seems the type of guy who ought to have a name that's the opposite of his actual appearance. Tiny would work too.

Tiny Smiley shoves me toward the house.

"You're going to stay inside and shut up," the guy in the wig says. I've decided his name will be Wiggy McWigerson. "You give us any trouble, you get a beating. Got it?"

"Wouldn't dream of giving you any trouble," I say. "Not with such charming hospitality."

Wiggy scowls at me but points toward the door.

The sun has disappeared below the horizon, and twilight is taking a grip on the landscape around the farm.

As I'm approaching the corner of the house, I notice two hitching posts jutting from the ground at the side. The spot from the video.

Shit. That doesn't bode well.

A door opens ahead of us. They have a friend. He's wearing a coat with shiny buttons and epaulettes on the shoulders. I recognize the outfit from the video too. George Washington Mask. The shooter.

"'Bout time you made it back. Expected you half an hour ago. Who's this?"

"Apparently they sent us a second hostage," Wiggy says.

"What for?"

"Do I look like I know?" Wiggy throws up a hand. "You know Franco never tells me shit. It's like he thinks we're mind readers or something."

The man in the doorway appraises me. "A younger one. Maybe they just wanted a spare, in case the Quickly girl won't give up the clock on the first try." He looks at Smiley. "Go unsaddle the horses. We won't need them anymore tonight."

Smiley crosses his arms. "You better not get to thinking that because I'm dressed up like a slave, and we're in olden times, that I'll be taking orders from you."

Epaulettes considers the big man and frowns. He turns to Wiggy. "Fine. *You* go unsaddle the horses then. Somebody has to do it."

Wiggy looks exasperated but doesn't argue.

I'm led into the house by Smiley and shoved into an open room. A stone fireplace dominates the far wall with various cooking implements hanging from the mantel. Cast iron skillets and heavy fire pokers catch my eye, but I don't have time to consider possible alternative uses for them because I am marched toward a wooden rocking chair in one corner of the otherwise open room.

Smiley shoves me into the chair and glares at me, as if securing me there with just his mind. It's working. My hands are only loosely tied in front of me, but I have zero desire to get up and piss him off. He strides over to a door in the corner. When he swings the door open, it reveals a pantry lined with wooden shelves. The shelves are loaded with preserved fruits, sacks of flour, beans, and barrels of what might be beer or mead. The pantry isn't only storing food, however. Seated among the canvas flour sacks and casks of beer is a man in a floppy shirt like mine. He lifts his head.

It's me.

Smiley gestures for the other me to get up, and as he exits the pantry, our eyes meet. His eyebrows raise but he doesn't speak. My other self isn't bound, but he notes the guns in our captors' hands and maintains a passive silence. I likewise keep my mouth shut as Epaulettes drags another chair over next to mine and deposits the other me in it.

"May as well get the video done." Epaulettes pulls a phone from his pocket and fiddles with the camera settings.

"Mym isn't going to comply with this, you know," the other me says calmly. "I don't know why you think taking me hostage is a good idea."

He's wrong, but I just keep my mouth shut and stare at the floor.

"Shut up and look at the camera," Smiley says from beside me. His fingers grasp my scalp and yank my head up, forcing me to look at Epaulettes.

"It's too dark out," I say. "I've seen this video. It happens during the daytime."

Epaulettes stops the camera and glares at me. "What are you on about now?"

"I've seen the video. My guess is that you'll get a message from Franco, sometime tonight. He's going to give you new instructions on what to do with us. You'll send the video to him after. If you do it now, you're just wasting time."

"Bloody know-it-all time travelers. You're the reason we're out here, you know? So nobody tells us what to do every damn second. Get up." He walks over and grabs me by the shirt, pulling me to my feet. He looks like he's going to punch me.

At that moment the front door opens and Wiggy McWigerson walks back in.

"Hey. Got a ping on the TPT. Supposed to tune in for a message from Franco sometime tonight. Says he's got new instructions for us."

Epaulettes releases his grip on my shirt, then turns to berate his companion. "Hey. I didn't say nothing about scheduling more calls. You were just supposed to take care of the horses."

"What, and I don't get free will around here?" Wiggy scoffs at him. "You're gettin' to be as bad as Franco. Who died and made you the boss?"

Smiley turns and engages in the bickering too. While they're distracted, I pivot and pilfer a flat, cast iron plate from the mantel and shove it up under my shirt. It's not the easiest feat with my hands bound, and its weight threatens to pull my pants down as I tuck it away. But by the time Epaulettes turns back around, I'm standing quietly with what I hope is an innocent-looking expression on my face.

"Fine. Screw it. Get these two back in their cell. I'm tired of all this nonsense. We've got a government to change here. Our mission is more important. I'll deal with this warp clock shit in the morning."

Smiley grabs me by the arm and shoves me toward the pantry. My other self is plucked from his chair in the same manner and forced inside as well. The heavy wooden door slams shut and is secured from the other side.

My older self slowly turns to me, the concern evident on his face. "You said you've seen tomorrow on video. Tell me you came here with a plan."

I reach under my shirt and awkwardly pull the cast iron plate from my waistband. I drop it onto the lid of one of the barrels. "Honestly, I'm kind of making this up as I go. I'm hoping you might help me with the details, because come morning, one of us is getting shot."

20

"There is a common misconception that love is without cost. I would argue that we pay for love daily, and the currency it requires is time." -Journal of Dr. Harold Quickly, 2001

"It's not that I'm not happy to see you," the other me says. He brushes a hand across his brow. "But I was kind of hoping for a bigger rescue party."

After being unceremoniously locked into the pantry, it only takes a brief look around to reveal that there is little chance of escape. There are a few wooden barrels and multiple bags of grain but no windows and little that could be used to help us. The floor is dusty and only dimly lit by a single candle burning in the corner. I sidestep a loose potato on the floor. "They treating you okay?" I ask.

"Not really. But they haven't started chopping off fingers yet or anything, so I guess it could be worse." He keeps his voice low to avoid being overheard by anyone on the other side of the door.

My other self unties the knots at my wrists, letting the ropes fall to the floor.

He has a shirt similar to mine with a lace-up collar. Had we both been wearing the same clothes in the video? I can't recall.

He picks up the cast iron plate I've pilfered from the mantle. "Is this part of your master plan?"

"Worked in *Back to the Future III*."

The other me looks skeptical. "He stole it from a Clint Eastwood movie first though, right?"

"Yeah. I think so," I say. "But I've only ever seen the *Back to the Future* version."

"Either way it's a very Hollywood solution." He appraises it doubtfully. "You don't have a better plan? With two of us, it at least evens the odds in a fist fight."

"We can't attempt any escapes until after that video tomorrow, otherwise it'll create a temporal paradox," I explain. "We have to go through with it."

"The video where one of us gets shot."

I nod.

"You know which one of us it is?" He rocks the cast iron plate back and forth in his hands.

"Actually no. Both of us had bags over our heads in the video. I just know it was the guy on the right that gets shot."

"When do they do it?" my other self asks.

"Not sure. It's outside. The hitching posts."

"And you saw that exactly? One of us gets shot for sure?"

"Kind of hard to forget."

He sets the plate down and moves over to the bags of grain. He's made himself a sort of couch out of them. "And there's no changing it without creating a paradox."

"I suppose we could try, but it would be breaking a lot of rules. It would almost certainly make a new timestream."

"We'd duplicate ourselves again," he says. "But shit. We've had enough of that already for one lifetime. If we create another timeline and we all survive, we'd have to share the rest of our lives with more versions of us. You'd have to share Mym. I'd have to share my daughter."

I consider the mess my life has been since becoming a time traveler. I've definitely had my fill of other selves. But then again, I'm not sure I can even claim to be the original version of myself anymore after all the timestreams I've survived. And I'd rather be alive than dead. My eyes fall on the cast iron plate. If he doesn't plan on using it . . .

"How is Mym?" he asks.

"Terrified, I imagine. She's probably worried sick about us."

"Us? Does she know I'm here?" He looks hopeful. "Mym from your time?"

"How much do you know about what's going on?" I ask.

He crosses his arms and leans back against the wall. "Not much. I've been in here since this morning when they grabbed me, but they haven't been especially chatty. I only know they're after something Mym has, and they want to use me as leverage."

"Not just you." I slump to the floor beneath a set of shelves, then explain what I know about the warp clock.

The other me listens carefully until I mention the part about how it shuts down all the chronometers.

"Whoa, hold up! So no one else will be able to get to us once they have it?"

"Not unless we find this clock and get the chronometers turned back on," I whisper, encouraging him to keep his voice down.

"Wow. That's bad. I didn't even know that was possible," he mutters.

His statement and this situation confirm one thing I was fairly certain of before but had to be sure about. He's not me. Well, I suppose I should say, I'm not going to be him in the future. Whatever life I lead from here won't wind back around in a causal loop and leave me in his place again, because I would most certainly remember the day I've just had.

"I also met your daughter."

The other me sits up straighter and looks me directly in the eyes. "Where? Is she okay?"

"For the moment. But we need to get back to her."

It takes rather longer to give him the story of my day with Piper, even the abbreviated version. He looks at times shocked and other times relieved to hear that we even survived. When I get to the part about Franco, he gets angry.

"An arena full of the worst people in history? And they put a little girl in there? I thought these guys were a bunch of numb nuts, but I didn't think they were downright evil. Who does that?" Frustrated, he rubs a hand through his hair, then stands. "Her mom is going to be horrified."

The mention of the older Mym stirs another issue to mind. Since it seems like we aren't going anywhere, I figure I may as well ask.

"What happened with you two? In the future? Piper let on that you weren't living at home anymore. Did you get . . ." The word seems stuck in my throat. ". . . divorced?"

The other me shakes his head. "Not officially. I guess you can say we're separated. Whatever that means as a time traveler." He pulls a jar of fruit preserves from the shelf, pauses, then offers it to me along with a wooden spoon. I reach forward and take it eagerly. It's been so long since I've eaten that I've passed beyond hungry. My stomach seems to sense that relief is near, however. It does a little flip in my abdomen as I spoon the first of the peaches into my mouth.

"I wonder if my Mym even knows I'm here," he comments, grabbing his own jar of fruit from the shelf.

"Was it that bad?" I ask, garbling through a mouthful of peaches.

"It's just been a while since I've seen her."

I consider the man before me. He's perhaps ten years older than me, but he has a definite air of resignation as he settles back to his seat.

"I don't really want to pry, but I feel like it might be important that I do. You mind letting me in on what happened? I don't mean to be insensitive, but Mym and I are doing pretty great these days. Life is good. I'm surprised it could ever get so bad."

"I remember those days," Ben says. "The easy times."

"I wouldn't call it easy," I object. "We have our share of arguments. Nothing catastrophic though."

"Why would it be?" Ben shifts his position on the bags of grain. "You have it made right now. No real responsibilities. Nearly inexhaustible funds. You can get up any given morning and travel anywhere in the world. You can relive the same day if you want. You're young, in love, and you're totally free."

His statement feels like I'm headed toward a cliff. "Yeah? And?"

"I'm just saying that you're still living the honeymoon. It can't last forever."

"It's been a couple of years," I argue. "At least I think it has . . . Things are still great."

"You have the conversation about kids yet?" He cocks an eyebrow at me.

I narrow my eyes. "Sure. We've talked about it. We're going to wait awhile."

"And you think that's what she wants? To wait?"

"It's what *we* want," I clarify. "We're not ready to settle down yet."

My other self sits up straighter, then leans toward me conspiratorially. "I'm going to fill you in on a little secret, since I actually have the voice of experience to back me up. *You* are the one who doesn't want to settle down. Mym has been ready for a long time. Since before you were married. She's been a time traveler her whole life. She's not the one craving adventure and freedom anymore. You're the only one left in that boat."

I set my empty jar of peaches on the floor and study the ring on my finger. "We've had the discussion."

"And you'll have it again. But let me give you another tidbit. Getting dragged into parenthood backward won't work. If you don't look it in the eye, you're going to get run over."

"Time travelers have kids," I say, finding myself echoing Mym's own argument. "It can't be that much more complicated than for any other couple."

"You don't think so?" My other self studies me. "Has anything about being a time traveler made your life *less* complicated?"

I have to admit he has me on that one. Whatever my life has become, 'simple' clearly doesn't apply any longer. If it did, I wouldn't be sitting in a pantry in 1777 talking to a parallel self from the future.

"So what happened then? You were a bad dad?"

My older self looks away. "I wish it were that simple. I wasn't a bad anything. It just took me too long to figure things out." He crosses his arms and looks back to me. "It's not like we didn't do things as a family. We planned trips, had adventures. I took Piper to meet Pierre Lallement and his Velocipede before I taught her how to ride a bike. She once had a guitar lesson from Jimmy Hendrix. We definitely made our share of memories. I was always good at the grand gestures. It was the little stuff that I sucked at."

"How do you mean?" I ask.

"I think I just wanted to live life to the fullest. It's so much potential, you know? A multiverse? All of time? How are you supposed to live a normal life and do basic stuff in the face of all that? Any night of the week, I could be meeting pop stars, presidents, kings even. Every damn day could be extraordinary.

"It's an addiction though. Nobody tells you that. Turns out I should have just paid attention. That's what it is in the end. Paying attention to the little things. The people closest to you. For all the grand plans I had, I missed out on the things I never realized were special. Or I always ducked out right after. I felt like I owed it to myself. Piper would get the flu, and I'd feel like seeing her through it meant I needed a reward. Held her hair back while she threw up, and I thought that meant I deserved a week to myself in the Old West. Went to a PTA meeting and listened to her principal complain? I'd better go hang out with Bon Jovi for a weekend. I thought I was being heroic, sacrificing my precious time for little menial shit when I could have been out there living it up. Like I deserved a medal every time I emptied the damn dishwasher."

"I can relate to that more than I'd like," I say.

"Of course you can," Ben replies. "You're me." He tosses away the jar lid he's been fiddling with. "I know Mym had her share of side trips too. She took off sometimes to get space. But not as often as I did. She might have a night with the girls here or there—have her chance to unwind—but I'd come back with a beard and a contact list full of entirely new friends that I'd want to keep up with. There was always another trip or party planned. I was ready to commit to anyone else's time but mine."

"Kind of ironic," I say.

"It just built resentment in the end. For both of us," Ben says. "Mym waited around for me to be happy with just us. Our family. Our life. I never got it until it was too late.

"Kids are smart. Especially Piper. You might think you're fooling her, popping in and out of her life and pretending like you've been there the whole time. But she knows. She always knows."

"So what's the solution then?" I ask. "Assuming we get back? I don't think the world is going to let us quit time traveling. "

"Time travel doesn't matter," he replies. "Linear or time traveler, you just have to stay together. Stay for all of it. Because none of the other stuff really matters in the end. The universe is going to go right on existing without you. History ... the future ... all of it. It's all out there, and it's going to be perfectly fine whether you show up or not. Your kids, though ... nobody but you can do that job."

"Kids? As in plural?"

Ben smirks. "That part's up to you. You get your own story now, I imagine." He stands up, stares at the door, then reaches a hand out to help me to my feet. "If we do get out of here, do yourself a favor and try to get things figured out a little quicker. Don't be me, okay? I think you can do better."

"What about you?"

"Yeah. I can do better too." He brushes off his hands and picks up the cast iron plate I stole. "Okay. So what's this plan of yours? How is this going to work?"

My plan is embarrassingly vague at the moment, but I do my best to explain. "I'm just thinking whoever gets shot should wear that ... and not die."

"Is that what happened in the video?"

I recall the scene of the man in the hood taking the bullet to the chest—the blood wicking into his shirt.

"No. It's not exactly how it happened." I begin searching the shelves and cupboards in the pantry. I rummage through jars until I find one filled with preserved cherries. "We'd still need blood."

The other me stares at me skeptically. "Cherry blood?"

"Look man, I'm just doing the best I can here. I'm trying to make this work."

He sighs and nods. "Okay. I guess I see where you are going with this. You're trying to recreate what you saw on the video."

"I'm trying to *cause* what I saw in the video," I reply. "Maybe I didn't see someone die." I find a leather water costrel on the shelf, stoppered with a cork. "I hope I just thought I did. Maybe what I really saw was something like this." I hold up the jar of cherries alongside the leather water bag. "Fake death. Followed by wildly successful escape later."

"Is the rest of your escape plan this bad?" my other self asks.

"I don't know because we haven't come up with it yet, so I'll have to get back to you on that."

We spend the next half hour exploring the pantry for any tools to aid in our plot. I salvage some twine from the neck of a grain bag and a leather thong that previously held together a bundle of candlesticks. We successfully fabricate our version of body armor. When I'm done trying it on, I'm almost feeling confident. But we still have one big problem. We don't know which one of us will take the hit.

"You said it was the guy on the right?" he asks. "Any distinguishing characteristics?"

"Not really," I reply. "Oh. Except the one who got shot had a rip in his pants."

My other self looks down at his knees, then at mine. When his eyes find mine, I understand the question.

"Yeah, I don't know how it happens. Could be in the fall after. I just know the guy who gets dragged away has a rip."

"Doesn't really help us much."

"I agree."

We debate the logistics of how to determine our fate for a while longer. Eventually we end up drawing straws, or in our case bits of string, for who has to wear the homemade armor. I end up with the short piece. It'll fall to me to make sure I'm the guy who ends up with the gun pointed at him.

"I guess it's only fair, since I came up with the idea." I keep my voice calm, but I imagine my nerves still show. He is me after all. He can probably tell.

There isn't time to discuss the subject much more because someone lets out a whoop as he slams the front door.

"We did it! She gave it up!" I recognize the voice belonging to Wiggy.

The other men stir somewhere on the other side of the door. "What, already?"

"Yeah. Apparently we're the ones who make it happen. The hostage video does the trick."

"We haven't even sent one yet," Smiley replies. "They sure?"

"Sure as shootin'. We just have to send the video tomorrow, then we're in the clear. After that, it's game on for the rest of our plans."

I turn to the other me. "You know what they're up to in colonial times? What's their game here?"

He keeps his voice low, even though I doubt our captors could possibly hear over the sound of their jubilation. "I heard them talking about it. They came for the Constitution. It gets ratified next year. They plan to make some changes."

"Rewrite the U.S. Constitution? Which parts?"

"A bunch of it. The slavery part for sure. Heard them talking about that. I think they have some other changes in mind too."

"Well, I can't really fault them for trying to fix that. Saving the United States a hundred years of slavery sounds like a great idea. But they have to know it will make major changes to any future timestreams. What's the end goal there?"

"Your guess is as good as mine," my other self replies.

Eliminating Hitler, writing slavery out of U.S. history—I have to admit that these guys seem to have noble intentions. But the execution leaves a lot to be desired, especially if it means murdering me as part of the plan. Hard to empathize with that.

We listen to the men outside the door for a little longer, but it becomes more difficult to hear once their enthusiasm dies down. We're soon left with only indecipherable murmurs.

I pace the narrow confines of the pantry, then open myself another jar of fruit. I snag a bag of walnuts as well. If I'm going to get shot tomorrow, it's not going to be on an empty stomach. I find a place to settle down in the corner. My other self repositions himself on the bags of grain. He picks up something that has fallen to the floor, and I recognize it as one of the bags used to cover our heads during the abduction.

"You get to see much coming in?" I ask.

He shakes his head, then holds up the fabric sack. "Mostly blindfolded. Just enough to know it was a dirt road."

I describe the ride in from the barn where the time gate was. Whatever happens, it's a good idea for both of us to know the way out. My other self seems to have no trouble picking up on what I'm saying, even when I'm fumbling with how to phrase things. One benefit of being the same person is that he gets how my mind works and what the important details are to pick up on. He in turn fills me in on where the horses are kept and other information I missed coming in.

Once we experience the shooting, assuming we're both still alive, our options will be a lot more open. We can run, fight our way out, do just about anything it takes to escape. No paradoxes will ensue. At least none we know of. We'll be freed from my knowledge of the future. It's just a matter of surviving till then...

I fiddle with my homemade body armor some more, filling the leather costrel with a mixture of water and cherry juice. I get the whole set-up affixed to my chest underneath my shirt. It's terribly uncomfortable, but I have no idea what hour of the morning these guys are going to come for us. I'll need to be ready. The frilly-looking shirt does a fair job of disguising the contraption on my chest but it still looks a little bulky. Am I crazy to think this could ever work? I wrack my brain for a solution I'm missing, but it's hard to argue with a future I've already seen happen. For now, it's the best option I have.

Before long, my mind settles back to Piper waiting for me to return with her dad. What will happen to her if I don't make it back? The candle in the corner gutters and then goes out, leaving only a single glowing ember at the tip of the wick. I lose sight of the other me and can only hear his breathing. He might be falling asleep.

Despite the stress of the situation, my body is crashing too. Physical exhaustion is catching up to me. Before I succumb to the pull of sleep, I ask one last question of the darkness.

"You think when we get out of here, maybe we should give up time travel?"

My other self answers from the dark. "I'd like to have a future where I see my daughter grow up. Time travel or no time travel, I'll take any version where that happens."

I let the words linger in the dark and ponder them. All things considered, I would too.

21

"Time travel offers flamboyant excitement and the intoxicating high of bold adventure, but a linear life often hides its joys in moments easily overlooked by those rushing from peak to peak." -Journal of Dr. Harold Quickly, 2018.

Something is very wrong.

When I open my eyes in the morning, I'm aware of two disturbing facts. One is that the big man I've nicknamed Smiley is standing in the doorway pointing a gun at me. The other detail takes a moment to register but bothers me far more.

My other self is sitting up on the grain sacks he's turned into a bed, and he already has a bag over his head. That in itself would be bad enough, but there is a far more disturbing sight at knee level.

His trousers are ripped.

"Wait, you're getting this wrong," I blurt out.

Smiley doesn't blink. He merely waves the gun at me. "Get up. We're going outside."

"You're making a mistake," I stammer. Though in reality it's me who has made the mistake. I should have been smarter than to assume I could rig this reality to work in my favor. Wiggy steps into the doorway, only he's not wearing his wig today. His short spiky hair jabs out at all angles, untamed at this hour of the morning. He grabs my arm and pulls me to my feet. "Come on, Travers."

The cast iron plate attached to my chest slides a little as I get up, and I use one hand to maneuver it back in place. "Listen. This is very important. When we get outside, I need to be on the right."

Wiggy isn't paying any attention. He's simply binding my hands in front of me. My mind is racing to catch up with the situation. My other self is just standing there. His hands are already bound and he's not struggling at all. Has he given up? How on earth did he tear his pants since last night?

The bag goes over my head before I've had time to think anything else.

"The right! You understand?" I beg my question of the interior of the canvas bag. Wiggy ties something around my neck to secure it.

Shit. How do I fix this?

I'm shoved forward and guided across the room toward the front door. The steps slow us down, but after a brief delay, we're outside. I bump against someone and hear my own voice from next to me.

"Don't worry, it's going to be okay."

I'm glad *he* feels confident.

Dirt crunches beneath my shoes, and I'm pushed to the left, guided around the corner of the house. I don't know why they are using the side of the house as a backstop for this. It seems like a stupid idea to shoot toward a house, but I've got far more pressing things to worry about.

"I need to be on the right, okay?" I repeat my plea to anyone listening. "Please!"

"Will you shut up?" Smiley says from somewhere ahead of me.

"It's important. Please make sure I'm on the right."

"You're on the right already. You happy now?" Wiggy is tying my hands to one of the hitching posts. I try to verify that he's telling the truth, but I can't hear where they put my other self. I've lost track of him.

"Ben? You okay?" I ask to my general surroundings.

I don't get a response. Why won't he answer me?

"Will you please shut him up?" The third voice is facing me. Epaulettes. His voice is vaguely muffled. I recall that he's wearing a rubber mask. "We need to get this done. You have the camera started yet?"

"Keep your damn mouth shut, you got it?" Wiggy hisses the words at my ear then walks away to join Epaulettes.

This is where things get real. If they've successfully positioned me where I asked, I'm about to get shot. The cast iron plate is still pressed against my chest. The leather water bottle too. I positioned it where I thought it should be last night before I fell asleep, but I've been jostled quite a bit since then. Plus, I think I've changed things now by switching places with my other self. Will the bullet still hit the same spot it did in the video? From what I remember of history, colonial muskets were hardly what you'd call accurate. What if I get shot in the head?

"They didn't say which one. I guess we get to pick." It's Epaulettes speaking again.

Shit. It's about to happen.

My mind is racing, and my heart is going a thousand miles an hour. Please God, let them hit me in the same spot as on the video. This plate has to stop it. Has to. I really don't want to die.

The blast from the gun is deafening. I duck and flinch involuntarily. Shit.

I do a mental inventory of my body. Did it work? I didn't feel anything. My ears are ringing a little but that's all. Am I in shock or something?

The thump comes from my left. A body hitting the dirt.

No.

No no no.

They lied.

"Okay, you got that recorded, right?" Epaulettes says. "Send that back."

I'm frozen, shocked into silence until someone finally pulls my bound hands away from the hitching post.

"You bunch of bastards!" I blurt out. "You said I was on the right!"

"You were on the right," Wiggy replies. He pulls the bag from my head.

"No I wasn't!" I exclaim. "He was!" My other self is lying prone in the dirt.

"Oh, you meant right like from what the camera sees?" he replies. "Yeah, that's true then. But I guess that makes it your lucky day."

I turn to look at the man being dragged away by Smiley. He's bleeding. Real blood. There's no way that's cherry juice.

I'm going to be sick. The bile comes up and I try to choke it back down.

Wiggy takes a step back. "Don't you dare throw up on me."

My mind is reeling. I've failed. Completely and utterly failed. How could I have messed this up so badly?

"Get that body buried," Epaulettes says. He pulls the rubber George Washington mask from his face. "Man it's hot in this thing."

"What do we do with this one?" Wiggy asks.

Epaulettes turns to face us. "The hell if I care. Apparently the video already worked. It's not like we need him anymore. Get rid of him. Actually, no. Put him to work. He can dig his own grave." He grins at me. "You dig a good enough hole, we won't have to bury you with your clone."

Wiggy has a pistol. He gestures for me to follow the trail of blood left by Smiley and his grim burden. I've lost control of my own senses. The smell of dirt and the color of blood is all that's registering in my brain. The sight of the body now lying near a brilliantly red maple tree at the edge of the woods brings on a strange sort of cold clarity. Smiley had the forethought to leave a shovel by the tree.

It was always going to be this way.

Nothing I did mattered in the slightest.

I arrive at the blood-red maple without much conscious thought. Smiley steps over to me with a knife and severs the ropes around my wrists. He reaches for the shovel and stabs it into the ground next to me, letting it protrude from the grassy earth. The moment my wrists are free, my hands are under my shirt, my fingertips finding the edge of the cast iron plate. I yank hard on it, doubling over as I break the twine that was binding it around my neck and chest.

"What the hell are you..."

I come back up with as much velocity as I can manage, the iron plate in my hands connecting with the big man's jaw, silencing his question and knocking his mouth shut with a bone-crunching click. The leather water bottle explodes with a gory-looking jet of cherry juice that splatters across his face and up into the leaves of the already red tree. Smiley's eyes roll back in his head as consciousness leaves him. The effect is breathtaking. At least it is for Wiggy, because as I spin around to face him, his mouth is hanging open, and his gun hand is sagging limply toward the ground.

Smiley thuds to the earth behind me. Caught up in the spectacle of what has just happened, Wiggy realizes the danger too late and can't get the pistol raised fast enough. I hurl the cast iron plate directly at him. He ducks instinctively and attempts to block the blow with his forearms. The maneuver buys me the time I need to pluck the shovel from the ground and step into my swing. His gun hand comes up, but decades of baseball playing haven't failed me. Eye on the ball. The blade of the shovel connects with his hand at full force.

The clang of metal on metal is loud enough to obscure whatever noises occur from his breaking fingers. The gun sails into the grass. It takes a few seconds for the pain to register in Wiggy's face, but he drops to his knees clutching his wrist. A wail comes out of his mouth as he attempts to move his fingers.

I stride through the grass and pick up the pistol.

"We... we were going to let you go..." Wiggy stammers, cradling his broken hand. "You would have been fine."

"And I suppose you think he's fine too." I incline my head toward my other self.

"It was just... just business, man." A tone of pleading creeps into his voice as I check that there is a bullet in the chamber of the gun. "It was for a higher cause."

"What higher cause?"

He wavers. "I mean, we were just doing what the boss man told us. He's changing things. Making the world better."

I don't care about better. I just want out of this nightmare.

"What did you do with the warp clock? Where is it?"

"I never saw it. I swear."

"Someone has to have it. Who picked it up from Mym?"

"I don't know."

I take a step closer and level the gun at him. "You sure you don't want to rethink that answer?"

"Okay, okay!" He leans away. "Vanessa. She had it. She's the one who picked it up."

I lower the gun.

"Look, man. I swear it wasn't personal against you or nothing."

"Then I trust you'll feel the same way about this." I raise the gun again. He cringes and closes his eyes.

I pull the trigger.

Wiggy flinches with the gunshot. When he slowly opens his eyes, his gaze notes the position of the gun, aimed several inches to the left of his head.

"Next time, I'll *make* it personal." I pivot the gun back toward his face.

Both of his hands go up. His right hand has already begun to swell. "We were going to let you go. I swear."

"You were going to bury me," I say. I glance at my other self's body lying near the trunk of the tree. "And you still are." I gesture to the shovel on the ground. "When I leave, you bury me. And you mark the grave. And you don't ever forget this, you got it?"

"I got it. A hundred percent." He lifts his arms a little higher.

"What the hell is going on out there!" Epaulettes comes storming out of the farmhouse. He's shrugging back into his jacket and still carrying the long colonial musket.

I turn and fire a few rounds into the side of the house. He ducks and swears, then beats a retreat for the safety of the house.

"Remember. You bury me. And you mark the grave."

Wiggy nods vigorously. I take one last look at my other self lying prone in the dirt, then break into a run, fleeing into the woods.

I run for several hundred yards without any plan or thought for direction. Then the situation slowly works its way through my otherwise addled senses. I need to hurry. They'll know where I'm headed. They may try to cut me off. They'll have horses.

I spin around to get my bearings. Morning sun is in the east. I head south till I hit the road we arrived by. At first I cut through the woods parallel to it, staying out of sight, but the woods become too dense. I'm forced back onto the road. The road is little more than a rutted path with twists and turns that obscure vision for any measurable distance. I can only hope that if they come after me, I'll at least hear them coming. I probably would if I had a chance. Unfortunately, opposition appears not on the road behind me but on the road ahead.

I round a curve and find myself facing a column of several dozen infantrymen. Two officers on horseback are leading them. No one gives an order, but several of the infantrymen take it upon themselves to raise their weapons at my sudden appearance.

"Halt! State your business, sir," one of the mounted officers says. He raises a hand to stop the infantry march and takes a look at the state of my clothes. I still have the pistol in my hand, but I doubt it even looks like a weapon to him. I keep it at my side.

The uniforms aren't red. I take a guess and assume that I'm dealing with Patriots and not British loyalists.

"Hey," I manage. "I'm . . . I'm searching for Benedict Arnold."

Which side was he even on at this point? At least either way there is a chance I'm right.

The officer focuses his gaze on my face. His brow furrows with concern. "We are likewise in search of Major General Arnold. Do you possess information regarding his whereabouts?"

I do, in fact, know his location, but these guys would never believe me. Not that I should let that stop me.

"If you lend me a horse, I can take you to him," I suggest. "There are men looking to harm him. They kidnapped General Arnold and are holding him prisoner. I was a prisoner myself until I escaped. But I can show you where they are keeping him."

The officer appraises me skeptically. "Your manner of speech is strange, sir. From which company have you been detained?"

"Uh, First Company," I say. If I'm going to make up a number, I may as well start with a number that has to exist. "But we have to hurry."

I can tell I'm walking a thin line with this guy, but I keep my mouth shut, and he eventually consents to bring me a horse from the back of the column.

"You know the location where the Loyalists are holding him?"

"I do, and I can show you. It's not far."

"What is your name, sir?" the officer asks.

"Benjamin Travers."

"I am Colonel Daniel Morgan. My men and I will see to these traitors."

And so, in a matter of minutes, I am riding hard with a group of early American patriots, headed for a time gate to the future. The oddity of the situation is not lost on me, but I don't have long to ponder the experience. After several miles of riding, I manage to locate the barn where I first arrived. Another horse is already tied up outside. Its sides are damp with sweat.

Has Epaulettes or one of the other men beaten me here?

I dismount from my horse cautiously, and am followed to the door by Colonel Morgan and several of his men. They fan out around the barn, readying their muskets. Before entering, I pull the pistol from the waistband of my pants. I crack open the door to the barn and peek my head in. There's no sign of anyone inside, but someone has activated the time gate. The multi-colored swirl is still oscillating between the emitters. My way out.

I close the door and address the colonel. "I think it's best if I go in alone at first. If I don't come out in five minutes, then come in after me."

Colonel Morgan pulls a watch from the pocket of his waistcoat. "Five minutes, you say."

"Give me that much. If I'm not back out, then come find me."

If I'm not back in five minutes, they'll have no idea where in time I am. I'm not telling them that though.

I make it indoors and close the barn door.

There's no one else here. That's fairly clear. Whoever has come in and activated the time gate left in a hurry.

I study the control pad and check the last coordinates. They are far into the future. Twenty-second Century. I recognize the location coordinates. Yesteryear Adventure Park. That's my destination too, but I dial the time back to the coordinates where I left Piper in the 1950s.

My hand hesitates briefly over the actuation key, but then I punch it. She needs me now, even if I did fail her. I don't know what I'm going to tell her.

I clear the chamber of the pistol and tuck it into the waistband of my pants. I search the area around the gate for the shirt and leather jacket that were taken off of me when I got here, but someone must have taken them.

The time gate is pulsing with light as I take my position in front of it.

I don't know if the colonel's pocket watch was running fast or if he just got impatient, but the barn doors swing open to reveal the cluster of patriots and their muskets pointed in my direction. Colonel Morgan has a sword drawn. Mouths drop open at the sight of the time gate's brilliance.

"What the devil is that?" Colonel Morgan says. He takes a step closer, lowering his saber.

"I'm afraid your general isn't here, colonel," I say. "But if I see him on the other side, I'll be sure to send him home."

I don't wait for his response. There are too many muskets still aimed my direction. I step into the swirling temporal ether and make the crossing.

It's only been a minute since I left. Piper is still waiting, face expectant. She leans around me, waiting for the next person to come through the gate. I take a step closer.

"Piper."

She's still watching the gate. After a moment she must realize that no one else is coming through. The gate powers down.

Her eyes find mine.

"Where's my dad?" Piper is staring at me hopefully. I don't know how to say what I need to tell her. I take a knee in front of her and force the words to come out.

"I'm so sorry, Piper, but... your dad isn't coming home."

She searches my face, looking for answers to the questions I know she has. After a moment, I can tell she knows. The noise that comes out of her mouth next isn't a word. It's not a scream or a cry either. The sound pierces me nonetheless, and I understand its meaning perfectly.

It's the sound of her heart breaking.

22

"Remember that there is a camaraderie to aging alongside your friends and family. Time is a war, and the ones we fight beside are waging the same battles."- Journal of Dr. Harold Quickly, 1916

There is something absurdly cruel about our location. Surrounded by amusements and rides, concessions and carnival games, every part of our environment is designed for smiles, joy, and laughter. I'm not the first parent to carry a crying child through a theme park, but the sobbing girl in my arms won't be consoled with cotton candy or skipping the line to a water slide.

Piper's tears have soaked my neck. Her crying is snotty and ugly and raw. I'd be surprised if she weighs sixty-five pounds, but the weight of her in my arms is compounded by the guilt of my failure. Whether I chalk it up to improper planning, poor decision-making, or just sheer cowardice, I've failed to bring her dad home. I'm responsible.

People are staring. Some are trying to hide it. Other observers wear their judgment and scorn openly. I know that I'm currently filthy. I'm dressed in a strange amalgamation of 1700s shirt and post-millennial trousers. I've got an inconsolable child in my arms and have no idea where to even go next. I'm lost.

I'm clearly a terrible father, even as a substitute. Is this all Piper has to look forward to now?

Yesteryear Adventure Park is having a banner day. Despite our current pain, business is booming, and the rides are packed with patrons. As I navigate the crowd on my way out of Liberty Village, I do my best to keep my head down. We reach a turnoff near a covered bridge that looks slightly less busy, and I take the opportunity to set Piper down on a bench. She's still crying, but her sobs have lessened. Bystanders go on with their day of amusements, losing interest in us. That's perhaps the most cruel fact of loss. No matter how much we suffer, life still goes on—mostly oblivious to our pain.

Piper sniffs and attempts to control some of the snot coming from her nose. I don't have a handkerchief, or even a tissue. Getting up, I cross the pathway to a malt shop and snag a napkin from a serving stand outside.

"Hey, mister. Those are for customers," the teenage hostess says.

"Got a crying kid over here with a runny nose. You can have it back after if you really want it."

The hostess scrunches up her face in disgust and goes back to inviting people into the malt shop.

Just before I reach Piper, a figure down the pathway catches my eye. Perhaps because of her contrast with the mostly white clientele here, the tall black woman stands out. She's striding confidently through the crowd, a wrapped bundle under one arm. It looks heavy. She's making for the entrance to the Old West town.

Vanessa.

I get to Piper and extend the napkin for her. "Hey. I just spotted Vanessa, and she's carrying something that I think could be our warp clock. We need to see where she's going."

Piper wipes at her face, but her eyes are still red when she looks up at me. "I want to go home."

"I know you do, kiddo. But we have to find the way out first. She might be willing to help us."

"I want Mom." Another tear runs down her cheek. "I wish she was here instead of you."

The comment stings but I can't blame her. "You and me both. Come on. We've got to get moving or we might miss our only chance."

Piper looks physically and emotionally spent, but she gets to her feet anyway. "That-a-girl."

I attempt to take Piper's hand as we walk, but she yanks it free from my grip. I try to ignore the scowl on her face. I lead us forward, picking up the pace as we search for Vanessa in the crowded Old West zone. We pass saloons full of lively music and recorded voices. Farther along the street, a couple of actors in cowboy hats are staging a gunfight. Spectators have gathered around to witness the show, blocking access to the rest of the road. The actor in the black hat has a bushy mustache and is taunting the hero in the white hat. Kids are looking on in awe, a few with tin sheriff badges pinned to their shirts.

"That's her," Piper says, her voice flat. She points toward one side of the crowd. "Over there."

Vanessa has been brought to a stop by the crowd around the entertainment. She's attempting to circumvent the throng, edging her way up onto the porch of the general store. When she reaches the door, she elbows one of the onlookers away and disappears inside.

"She's getting away," I mutter.

I break into a jog and Piper reluctantly follows a few paces behind.

When I reach the door, I open it and peek inside. Unlike the tavern in Liberty Village, the general store is more than just a façade. The building is a catch-all merchandise store. Some items are offered in period style, but there are plenty of modern toys and games for kids. A few exasperated-looking parents are browsing the shelves with their children. Piper follows me inside and sticks close.

We push past the curtain in the back amid protestations from a cashier.

"It's okay. We're with her." I nod toward the back.

The young woman at the cash register frowns and reaches for a telephone.

"Good luck calling your manager. I'll bet this is way over his head."

The back of the general store is broken into two sections. One side is a storage area with a door to an employee bathroom. The other side has a solid wood door that's hanging slightly ajar. Pushing through it, we find ourselves in a completely empty room. The bare wood floors meet paneled walls at every side. The door itself is unremarkable but has a decidedly modern-looking lock on it. Upon closer inspection, a portion of the lock swings aside to reveal a touchscreen control pad. I shut the door.

There's another time gate here somewhere. I gesture to the panel and invite Piper to have a look. "Can you see where she went?"

Piper frowns, but reluctantly steps to the control panel and begins playing with the controls.

"She went to the future. Back to the bad place."

I study the coordinates. The decrepit theme park. My finger hovers over the activate button. My heart is still thrumming in my chest. Is this what a panic attack feels like?

The moment stretches into two. Then more. I work to control my breathing.

"What are you doing?" Piper looks from the control panel to me. "Are we going there or not?"

"Not yet."

I spin on my heel and grab Piper by the hand. I tow her out of the store.

"I thought you said we needed to talk to Vanessa." She attempts to pull her hand away again, but this time I keep a firm grip.

"We do. But there's something I need to do first."

The showdown outside has ended. The white-hatted cowboy has shot the gun out of the villain's hand and restored order to the town.

I lead Piper away from the crowd and back to the medieval section of the park. It takes a bit of searching, but I finally find the snack stand with the grouchy cashier I attempted to barter with earlier. I leave Piper at a picnic table before heading toward the food stand. The cashier spots me walking up and reaches under the counter. When he straightens up, he lays Vanessa's multi-tool on the counter. "Figured you'd be back. Thought that deal might be too good to be true."

"I don't want that. We still have a deal. I want the food."

The cashier takes another look at the multi-tool. "Really? How much food?"

"Let's start with one of everything you've got."

Pipers eyes widen when I bring two trays of food to the nearest table. It's mostly junk: pretzels, hot dogs, paper bags of popcorn, and half a dozen other options. We'll probably feel terrible after eating it, but we already feel terrible as it is.

"Mom never lets me eat like this in the future," Piper says. "She says it's a good way to . . . die young."

"That's because your mom is smart and clearly knows best. This is just all I can manage at the moment."

Piper looks unsure. For a moment I'm worried my gesture will go completely to waste, but I know she has to be starving. I chew on a piece of pretzel and watch her. She's slow to start, but eventually she begins to eye the food. She carefully picks the hot dog out of the bun. Once she gets a few bites down, she looks less wary. After she's finished the hotdog and moved on to a candied apple, she starts to look more herself. "Why are we doing this? Are you scared of going back to the bad place?"

"I'm scared of going just about anywhere right now. Seems like every decision I've made lately has been the wrong one. But I figured if I could . . . if there was an opportunity to do one thing right by you . . . then now might be the time. I know I haven't been much good as a dad so far, but . . . I don't know. I hoped I could at least make this one good thing happen before leading us into the next inevitable disaster."

I don't get a response.

I lean in a little closer. "Look. I know I'm not your real dad. I know you wish your mom were here instead of me. I wish it was different too, but I want you to know that whatever happens from here, I'm not bailing on you. I'm going to do my best to . . . step up."

I wait for some kind of response.

Piper considers her hunk of pretzel. "This food isn't gravitized. If we make another jump right away, most of it won't even come."

"Yeah, that's true." I take a sip of water, then select a French fry from the tray. "But it'll be okay by the time we get back to the gate. I'm sure your dad taught you the rules, right? I know I would. Traveling right after eating is gross. Especially bad for carpets." I stare at the fry in my hand, then toss it back to the tray.

"I know all that already." Piper toys with with the stick of her apple then slides her tray away. "You're still not my real dad. You'll never be him."

I sigh, then dig my corndog into some ketchup. "He's probably a lot smarter than me when it comes to raising kids."

Studying Piper, I can't help but notice how much she resembles her mom, especially the way she's looking at me now. I set the corndog down. "I'm really, really sorry. I'm sorry I couldn't get him back for you."

Piper looks down at her hands and fiddles with her napkin. "Are you going to tell mom? About what happened?"

I fold my hands in front of me on the table. "Yeah. Yeah I will."

"What happens when we get back? What happens after?"

"I have no idea."

"Will you still be my . . ." She looks up at me with questioning eyes but trails off. "You'll still get me back, right? Back to mom?"

"I'm sure trying to get us there. That's the goal."

"But you don't know for sure that you can?"

"If I said I did, I'd be lying. And I don't want to lie to you. Not again."

Piper doesn't look up at me for a few moments, but when she does, she looks a little less lost. I recognize the strength in her eyes, even if it's still shrouded in sadness. It's another look I've seen from her mom.

"Are you done being scared now?" she asks.

"Probably not. You ready?"

Piper looks me in the eye for a long moment, then nods.

"Okay, then. Let's go."

When we get back to Frontier Town, the cashier at the general store is busy helping a customer. She never notices us slip into the storage area. We find ourselves back in the empty room and twist aside the cover for the time gate controls.

"You think the gate is in the doorway?" I ask. "Or maybe one of the walls?" I still can't figure out where the emitters are.

Piper shrugs.

"Okay. Only one way to find out, I guess. Go ahead and activate it."

Piper selects the next available time slot after Vanessa went through, then punches the activation button. A brilliant light washes over my feet. Then the floor disappears.

Gravity is a bitch.

I hate falling at the best of times, but suddenly plummeting through the floor into a whirl of temporal soup has to be the least enjoyable method of time travel I've experienced so far. I'm grateful that the drop is short.

Piper and I crash into a makeshift landing pad made of a dozen dirty couch cushions. I roll off the pile and onto the dusty floor. Looking up, I find that someone has installed the exit of the time gate in the ceiling of the room we left. We've landed back on the same floor we just fell through, but a long time into the future. Unless gravity somehow reverses itself, we're not getting back out the way we came in.

A temporal trapdoor.

Piper gets to her feet and brushes herself off. I get up a little slower. "Okay then. Let's see where our elusive friend got to." Piper follows me out of the dusty back rooms to the front door of the general store. The termite-eaten door almost falls from its hinges as I drag it open. We step onto the dilapidated porch.

The Old West town looks even more brittle and dry. Years of sun and wind have eroded the paint from the storefronts and left a haze of abrasion on all the windows. It's a ghost town now. If it weren't for the sun-faded restroom signs on the building across from us, it might even pass for a real western town and not a theme park.

The bang makes me jolt.

Splinters shower my face, torn from the roof support pole next to me.

It takes me a moment to register the noise as a gunshot. I move just before the second bullet thuds into the wall behind me.

"Get down!" I tackle Piper to the floor, then scramble to get her behind a few barrels sitting on the porch.

The street has gone quiet again. Whoever shot at us could be anywhere.

The sliding doors are open on the feed store across the street. There's a hotel and saloon and some sort of music hall. Plenty of cover for a shooter.

"Who's shooting at us?" Piper whispers.

"Can't see 'em."

I pull the pistol from the waistband of my pants and check the magazine. The gun has eight bullets left. I won't be getting any more around here.

Peering around the barrels, I look for any sign of our attacker. As high up the pole as the bullet hit, they must have been down the street somewhere.

After a solid minute of waiting, I gesture for Piper to get ready. "We're going to head the other direction. Behind the building. We'll sneak around."

Piper still looks frightened, but she nods. On my signal, she takes off and I follow immediately on her heels.

I'm expecting a bullet in the back every step of the way, but we make the corner of the store without being shot at.

The back of the general store opens onto a circular fairway. A decrepit wooden roller coaster arches overhead, and the line for waiting riders twists beneath it. Unlike the authentic main street western atmosphere out front, this avenue hosts a variety of Old West themed carnival booths. There are rusted tin targets in the shape of pigeons dangling in a shooting gallery. Another game is modeled after a bank robbery. A robotic cowboy is seated in a barker's chair, frozen in place with one arm extended, beckoning guests closer.

I keep the pistol ready as we search for an exit, trying to evade whoever might be out to get us.

"Howdy, partner," the metallic voice crackles through a speaker behind us. It's accompanied by a background of old-time piano music.

I spin to find that the robotic cowboy has come to life, straightening up and tipping his hat to Piper. "Care to test your skills at the Lone Star Shootin' Range? Five chances only costs you a nickel. Hit a target and choose from one of these fabulous prizes." His rickety arm extends toward the bare shelves beside him. "Have you got what it takes, partner?"

Piper squeezes closer to me and we move on, trying to get away from the clattering of the robot's rusty joints. The only route that gets us away from the shooter leads beneath the deteriorating coaster. Neither seems like a safe choice, but I opt for the route without the bullets. A quartet of animatronic miners is positioned alongside mining cars at the entrance to the ride. One is inside a mining car with his hands in the air. A bunch of dirty signs illustrate the safety procedures of the roller coaster. One reads "Caution: Fun Ahead."

"Drop it."

The voice startles me, but I try not to make any sudden moves. As I turn to find the speaker, I discover Vanessa aiming a handgun at me.

"Hey. I've got a little kid here," I say moving to block Piper. "Be careful with that."

"Put your weapon on the ground."

I lay the pistol gently on the walking path.

"Now back away."

Piper has her hands up. We both back away from the gun.

"What did you do with the warp clock?" I ask.

Vanessa keeps her pistol aimed at me while stooping to pick up the one I left on the ground. When she straightens up, she looks me up and down. "Aren't you one of Franco's hostages? How'd you get away?"

The question throws me off. She doesn't recognize us?

She keeps the guns aimed at my chest. "Give me one reason I shouldn't shoot you right now."

My brain is rushing to catch up to the situation. "Because you don't. You'll have a chance to shoot us later, and you won't then either."

"You trying to predict my future?"

"We just came from there," I reply.

Vanessa is about to say something when a clatter comes from behind her.

"Howdy there, folks!" One of the mechanical miners shuffles his way around his mining car. He takes a step toward us. Vanessa swings a gun around and shoots, blasting the top of the miner's head off. Piper and I both flinch.

"Shit! This place gives me the creeps," Vanessa mutters.

But despite the damage she's caused, the mine cars and miners are still moving. They rock back and forth in their designated area, and the one without a head still invites us to line up. He waves a rusty arm. "Riding alone? Today's your lucky day. Fastest way to enjoy the Old West is in our single rider line."

Something above us shudders, and a small cloud of dust and dirt rains down around us.

I look up to find that one of the ride's cars has started ratcheting its way up a track. It's already near the apex of the first hill, but part of the track is rusted away. The missing section is directly over our heads.

"Oh shit. Look out!" I push Piper away as the car tips over the missing section of track. Piper pivots toward the open air of the fairway as the car crashes down through the structure's support beams. Debris cascades around us. I'm struck by something heavy and sprawl into the dirt.

"Dad!"

I shake my head to clear the haze from my mind. Piper is back at my side, pulling on my arm to help me up. A fractured chunk of wood slides off my back and onto the ground. A sickening groan is coming from behind us. When I turn to look back, I find Vanessa on the ground, her leg pinned beneath a section of fallen track. She's frantically trying to free herself because, directly overhead, another ride car is working its way up the damaged rails, headed for the same point of failure.

I debate for just a moment, then push Piper onward. "Go. Get out of here!"

"She's stuck!" Piper replies, pointing back toward Vanessa.

"I know. Get out into the open. I'll be right there!" Once Piper is moving, I spin around and race back for the fallen car. Vanessa's eyes are wide. A pistol is still at her side, but I don't even bother to kick it away. There's no time. I lift the rail pinning Vanessa's leg as she pries up on it from below. She gets her foot out not a moment too soon. The car above us teeters and falls, crashing its way down through the already damaged supports. This time even more support beams splinter. Vanessa screams.

Timber and steel rain down around us. It's disorienting and I've suddenly lost sight of the way out. I cover my head with one arm as I search. Spotting a momentarily unobstructed path, I pull Vanessa to safety, diving to the dirt in the open fairway. Once we're clear of the collapsing ride, I immediately search for Piper.

She's nowhere to be seen.

"Piper!" I spin around. How could I lose her? "Piper!" My stomach clenches in my gut. She has to be here. She made it out.

Vanessa is wide-eyed. "I saw her running."

"Which way?"

"Back toward you."

No. No no no. I sprint for the wreckage, hurling aside scraps of wood and scouring the rubble for any signs of Piper. She was out, wasn't she? Why would she run back in?

The roller coaster is in ruins. Twisted metal track curls through the wreckage of fallen cars and lumber. Wood beams have splintered into fragments from the force of their destruction. How will I even see her? Could anyone survive this?

This can't be happening. Not her. Not this little girl.

"Dad?" The voice sounds far away and tentative, but it's there. I flinch and spin around, looking for the source. "Piper? Where are you?"

"Dad! Help!"

She's under here. Under the wreckage.

"Keep shouting, Piper. I'm coming!"

"I'm over here!"

There. A small hand is protruding from the wreckage. She wiggles her fingers.

I scream at Vanessa. "Help me! Help me get her out!"

I rush to the spot Piper is buried and squat to grasp her hand. "Are you okay? Are you hurt?"

"I think... I think I'm okay." Her grip is strong.

Vanessa reaches my position and helps me lift away an aluminum panel that is obstructing my view of Piper. When we set it aside and look for her, I'm shocked at what I find.

Piper is curled up on the ground in a ball, seemingly imprisoned by mechanical arms and legs. She's under the clustered group of animatronic miners who greeted us as we walked in. Their now smashed bodies are positioned over her, forming a barrier. If they hadn't been there...

I push aside a pair of the mechanical arms and pull Piper from the wreckage by her armpits. I scoop her into my arms and hold onto her. "Thank God."

Piper wraps her arms around my neck. "I tried to come back for you."

"You're crazy, you know that?" I say. "You could have been killed."

"I got saved," Piper says. "They saved me." She turns to look back at the mechanical miners. They are still frozen in their protective positions, leaned out and over the spot where Piper had fallen, their backs still bearing the weight of much of the wreckage that had rained down on them. The mechanical men are silent now, no signs of life or movement, but there is no denying the oddity of their positioning. Did they really move to save her or was it just a lucky coincidence?

I hoist Piper higher in my arms and carefully carry her across the wreckage.

Vanessa reaches the open path ahead of us. She stays standing as I collapse to the ground with Piper. I look up to find her staring at me.

"What?" I'm panting and out of breath.

"Why'd you come back for me?" Vanessa asks. "I tried to kill you."

"I don't know. I figure this makes us even. You helped us. On the train and in the arena. I wasn't going to let you die."

Her brow furrows. "The arena? What arena?"

It hasn't happened to her yet. This Vanessa is just starting her day. She hasn't gone to kidnap Hitler yet. No gold rush. No arena.

"You'll know," I explain. "Next time you see us, we'll be in your helicopter's gun sights. I'm trusting that you'll remember us."

"I have no idea what you're talking about. I ought to haul your ass back to Franco right now."

"What did you do with the warp clock?" I ask. "Was it you? You're the courier?"

Vanessa appraises me skeptically. "It's done. The warp clock is delivered. He's got it now."

"Who does? Your boss? Is he here somewhere?"

Vanessa slowly backs away. "I'm out. You consider yourselves lucky that I'm not ratting you to Franco. You saved me, and I owe you for that, but now you're on your own."

"There's got to be a way out," I reply. "How do we get out of this damned park?"

"Just pick a gate, man. We all have our ways out now. We're rewriting history."

"We need to go back. Back to the time we came from."

"There's no going back now." Vanessa turns and starts walking away. "You'd better pick a past you can live with. History is all changing."

In a matter of moments she's disappeared up the path.

I turn back to Piper. She's dirty and disheveled but alive and unhurt. I'm taking it as a win.

She gets to her feet first, then helps me up. I groan a little as I stand. There's a stinging pain in my leg. It doesn't feel like more than a scratch, but as I look down at my legs, I freeze.

My pants are torn. A single jagged cut in the fabric runs from one side of my knee to the other.

"Are you okay?" Piper is watching me. "Are you hurt?"

My mind is racing to catch up with the situation. The video. The shooting. Torn pants.

Piper is looking up at me, her face still bearing the tearstains from our conversation before the collapse.

It takes time, but my mind finally organizes my thoughts into coherent words.

"I think your dad might still be alive. And I think I know how to save him."

23

"There are few teachers as instructive as your past or as inspirational as your future." -Journal of Dr. Harold Quickly 2275

The real problem with time travel is keeping yourself ignorant of the future. When you know what's coming, you have time to think about it. And when the future isn't good, that's an even worse problem. As Dr. Quickly always says, you can't change the past. What happened, happened. I would add an addendum. What you *know* is going to happen, is going to happen, because you're an idiot and did things wrong the first time.

I've seen the past. It's now my future. And I'm not going to like it.

Piper doesn't know. She can't know.

Standing near the wreckage of the collapsed roller coaster in her now disheveled clothing, she's starting to look like a street urchin. Our frequent gate jumping has at least removed some of the dirt from our day, but we're both tired and we're still just as lost as we've ever been. The warp clock is here somewhere—the way home. I thought I would be the one to find it, but I was wrong about that. It seems I have another destiny.

I lead Piper out of Frontier Town and back into the heart of the park.

"Where are we going?" she asks.

"We need to find a gate that'll get me back to 1777 again. Back to your dad."

"I want to come this time."

I shake my head. "I know you want to help, but that's not going to work."

"How do you know?"

"Because I was there. I've seen what happens. If we change it, then we split the timeline. We could end up with two of us. Or more copies of your dad. Who knows what kind of paradox that might create. We can't risk it."

Piper frowns. "I could help. Maybe this time I could be there and not change anything. I could hide . . ."

"Hiding is good but you're going to do it here. I'm going to get your dad and I want you to wait."

"I don't want to stay here. It's scary," Piper argues.

"I know, but if you want your dad back, it has to be this way. And I know you want him back."

Piper looks like she wants to argue more, but she stays quiet.

It takes a few minutes to reach a time gate. I locate the gate in the Green Dragon Tavern as it's the one I went through the last time. I study the controls when we reach it. The gates we've been using are apparently on a shared network of some kind. The problem with Franco's system of stolen time gates is that they are low on options for exit times. Many of the time slots I would like to use have been used up by other travels. The exit unit paired to this gate has been a lot of places in its day. Unfortunately I have only one destination left in me.

I turn to Piper and take a knee.

"We're going to try this again. I need you to do me a favor though. When your dad comes back through this gate, don't wait for me. Show him where we last saw Vanessa, and see if he can find where she took the warp clock. I know he'll get you home, but he'll need your help."

"What about you?" Piper's brow furrows.

"Don't worry about me. I'm gonna be okay." I gently brush a strand of hair away from her face. "If you guys get the warp clock back on, your mom will bring the cavalry so fast it'll make your head spin. You're going to be fine."

The little girl in front of me is putting on a brave face, but she's still just a kid. She's been through so much today already. It pains me to be leaving her again, but I'm not the version of me she needs. If I don't go, I doom her to a lifetime without him.

I extend a hand to Piper. She cautiously raises hers to mine.

"It's been a pretty exciting day. I'm glad you were the one I got to spend it with." I shake her hand. When I let go, Piper opens her mouth to speak but then closes it again. I get back to my feet and activate the time gate controls. The temporal emitters flicker to life, casting their eerie colors across the gate.

I take a breath and try to steady my nerves for the crossing.

"Wait." Piper takes my hand and turns me around. Then she wraps her arms around my waist, hugging me hard.

"What's that for?" I ask, laying my arm across her back.

"Because even if you're not my real dad, you're still a good one."

I pat her gently. It takes all of my resolve, but I slowly unwrap her from me. I hold her shoulders as I look her in the eyes. "If it was up to me, and I did get to have a daughter, I'd want her to be just like you."

A tear runs down Piper's cheek, and her lower lip has developed a quiver, but at least this time it's for the right reasons. She looks like she wants to say something else, but I have to go. I'm not going to let her down again.

"I have to go now, okay? Be patient. Your dad is going to be right back."

Piper wipes her eyes and nods.

Brave girl.

I wish I could see the woman she grows up to be.

I turn and face the gate. If I don't go now, I'll never hold together. I take a step and plunge into the ether.

L imited options. That's what I've had to work with. And a long history of bad luck. I half expect to meet another group of men with guns when I step through the gate, but for once I'm given a break. The barn is empty.

It's mid-afternoon. According to the time gate settings, I've arrived prior to my earlier trip. I'm once again unarmed. I have no advantages in my favor except one—a little bit of time.

I exit the barn and look around. The scene is quiet except for a continual splashing sound to my right. Cautious of being seen, I creep around the side of the barn to ascertain its source. The sight of the water wheel and the generator answers one of my previous questions. I wondered why these temporal fugitives positioned their time gate so far from Arnold's property, but having a steady source of power makes sense. This water wheel will attract far less attention with the locals than running noisy gas generators or displaying mysterious solar arrays.

It takes a moment to get my bearings, but I don't have a lot of time to waste. I break into a run along the riverbank, headed for the road to Benedict Arnold's property. My captors are going to be arriving before long, so I'm forced to use the woods again. I really can't risk running into Wiggy and Smiley on their way to send Arnold through the time gate. But if I can get to the house while they are gone, I'll have fewer eyes on me and might be able to work out a plan.

A plan.

There is something fundamentally wrong with plotting my own demise. My brain doesn't want to admit that's what I'm doing, but I am. There are ways out. I could run. I could abandon all the rules of time travel and commit to my own survival. But at what cost? I've seen this future. They shoot me. They send the video to Jermaine Clevis. He sends it to us. That starts us down this entire journey to rescue my other self. We lose the warp clock. I end up here.

If I choose something else now—create a paradox—it'll fracture into a new branch of this timestream. Then what? They don't send the video? They do but it's different? Some other version of Mym and I go off on this adventure? Another version of the warp clock goes missing. We are still stuck. No one saves us. I'll have duplicated all of our problems. Another me gets to make this choice. Will he succeed in saving Piper's dad or would he chicken out too? Another Piper loses her dad. The girl I know gets left to die in an abandoned theme park in the future.

I'd escape but end up living or dying somewhere in the 1700s in this timeline, far from everyone I know and love. They'd never even know what happened or what choice I'd made to cause it. But I'd know.

No.

That can't be my legacy.

We all have to go sometime. There's a good chance that when I die here, no one else would know either. Except me. Literally. If I save my alternate self, he has a chance. He can get back to Piper. He can find the warp clock. He can live the life I never will. And I won't have failed everyone. I won't have inflicted the results of my own cowardice on the rest of the universe and the people I love. Piper will have a chance to grow up.

I think that's a legacy I could die for.

If I can get there on time.

My run through the woods is noisy and exhausting. I force my way though brambles and leap over fallen logs. I let the exertion wipe the doubts from my mind. It feels good to be breathing. My beating heart feels good in my chest. I pass into a glade filled with sunshine and have to pause. Maybe it's just my emotional state, but the world looks like a beautiful place. The trees are putting on a brilliant display of autumn leaves, and the breeze is just the right temperature. The earth is vibrant and sensual and alive. I walk gratefully to the widened riverbank, my heels sinking into the sandy pebbles. At the water's edge, I kneel and scoop a handful of the refreshing current to my face. I splash myself twice, then cup my hands and scoop some for a drink.

In my time I'd think twice about drinking river water. Here, under the current circumstances, I have little to lose.

I'm still drinking when I notice I'm being watched. With the sound of the river and my own noisy breathing, I never would have heard them if it wasn't for the little child's burbling cry. Two adults are frozen like statues near the riverbank opposite me. A family. The native man is bare-chested and knee deep in the water holding a forked spear. His partner is on her knees on the riverbank, a string of fish in her lap. The little wild-haired boy is perhaps two. His tiny fingers are clutching a stick. He's been scribbling in the sand or perhaps just digging. He has his mother's jet black hair and his father's strong nose.

The man with the spear considers me. He doesn't seem tense or overly concerned, but he keeps his eyes on me nonetheless. The woman gets up from the sand, abandoning the string of fish in order to scoop up her son. She balances him on her hip and holds him with both arms.

I rise slowly, my chest still heaving, but my body is calming down. The little family is expectant, waiting for some indication of my intentions. I raise my hand, palm open to them. It's not really a wave, but it seems to convey the message. The man lifts his head just slightly. The woman turns and says something to her partner. She's hugging her child close. He responds in their language, then steps out of the water and scoops up the string of fish. The trio moves away from the river, climbing a grassy embankment and stepping into the cover of the woods. The woman and child disappear beyond the trees. The man reaches the tree line and pauses. He turns back to consider me one more time. He transfers the string of fish to the hand holding the spear, then lifts his free hand palm out toward me. He smiles.

The next moment he walks into the woods and vanishes.

I don't know why the scene I've witnessed matters to me, but it does. There have been times I've wondered what it would be like to witness life before modern explorers changed the continent. Even before I was a time traveler, the idea fascinated me. But this little happy family is more than that. They are living in their own sort of twilight—the remnants of a changing world. Whether they know it or not, time is moving on.

The beginning of the end.

I could be wrong. With Smiley and Epaulettes here to change the Constitution, maybe that will change the future of the American

Indians. Perhaps their destiny is more hopeful than mine. Maybe I'm just jealous that they are experiencing a family life that I never will. Either way, it's making me sad. I squat and splash myself one more time with a handful of water.

It's time to go.

I reach the farmhouse without encountering Smiley or Wiggy. They most likely passed on the road without me hearing them. They aren't home yet in any case. When I sneak up to the barn where they are keeping the horses, the one I rode in on isn't present. I don't recall the exact coloring of the other horses I came in with, but I'm fairly certain they aren't here either.

That just leaves Epaulettes and the other me.

And this is where things get tricky. I have no idea what to do next.

I exit the barn and keep my eyes on the farmhouse. I have to assume Epaulettes is in there guarding my older self. It's now a waiting game. Somehow, some way, I've got to replace my other self, but only after he's had a conversation with me later in the evening.

I creep slowly from the barn toward the farmhouse, my eyes flitting between the pair of windows on this side of the house. Is anyone watching?

I'm about halfway there when my luck runs out. The back door swings open.

Shit.

I drop to my belly in the tall grass. Have they seen me?

Lying prone on my stomach, I fight the urge to flee, at least till I know whether they've seen me.

I recognize the pair that exits easily enough. Epaulettes is prodding my other self along in front of him using a musket. My other self is bound at the wrists, but his hands are in front of him. A useful fact, as the two are making for an outhouse situated at the back of the clearing.

As soon as they are far enough away that I think they won't hear me, I jump up and sprint for the door they just exited. I make it to the steps and take one last glance in their direction before slipping inside the house.

Okay. I'm inside. Now what?

Looking around the room, I search for places to hide where I won't be discovered. There isn't a lot to work with. I have no idea where my captors will be throughout the night. The spartan furniture doesn't leave a lot of options. I need to be close enough to the pantry to sneak in and get to my other self. It's hard to know where to hide out here when all I saw the whole night was the inside of the pantry.

The door to the pantry is hanging open. My other self hasn't constructed his bed of grain sacks yet. The sacks are still piled up at the back wall past the wooden barrels. I take a closer look at the barrels, noting that while two of them have sealed barrelheads held tight with metal bands, the third barrel near the back is a different style. It has a lid with a handle. I didn't pay much attention to it when I was in there before...

I cast a quick glance out the window. Epaulettes is still waiting outside the outhouse. Apparently my other self is taking his time in there.

I slip into the pantry and lean over the front barrels to lift the lid on the one in the back.

Potatoes.

The barrel isn't full. Potatoes fill about a foot of the space at the bottom, but if I were to move some around...

I find a grain sack that's mostly empty and start tossing potatoes into it. I work frantically to buy myself some space. I've removed most of them when I hear the voices. They're close. I drop the sack of potatoes. One escapes the confines of the bag and bounces across the floor, wobbling to a stop near the doorway.

Hinges creak at the rear of the house as the back door opens.

Out of time.

I throw my legs over the edge of the barrel and slip inside. I wrestle with the lid for just a moment before deciding to just flip it over and face the handle down inside with me. If anyone tries to lift it, I'll be able to keep it secure.

I gently close the lid to the barrel just as my other self and Epaulettes come into view. I cling tightly to the lid handle and do my best not to make a sound.

"Get back in there. I don't want to hear any more complaining out of you."

"It wasn't really a complaint," the other Ben says. "If you're going to kidnap people after they've had that much coffee, I feel like you should have bathroom breaks in your game plan."

"Okay, wise guy. Just shut up."

Epaulettes slams the door and slides the latch closed. My other self goes quiet for a few seconds, then I hear some scraping as he rummages around the shelves. His footsteps stop near the barrel I'm in and I hold my breath, but then he begins dragging sacks away to the other side of the pantry. He's making his spot to lie down.

The position I'm in is growing uncomfortable, but I don't dare move.

I keep pressure on the handle of my barrel lid until I hear him settle down on the sacks. Even then I'm cautious, doing my best to not breathe, partly to stay quiet, also because my hiding place isn't a well-ventilated choice. Smells like dirty potatoes and sweat in here.

As the minutes go by, I finally get the courage to move. Slowly. I get my legs under me in a more comfortable position and, just before I settle back onto my haunches, I lift the lid of the barrel a fraction of an inch, peeking out to determine the situation.

My other self is lying on his back, hands resting across his chest. He appears to be asleep, or at least drowsing.

He's Piper's dad, and he's still alive.

The reality of what I'm trying to do is creeping back in on me. While I've had something to do, I've been able to keep my mind off it. Off dying.

I've been shot before. If you want to get technical about it, you could argue I've died before. I've been through some weird experiences as a time traveler, but this one is different. I'm not dealing with a flesh wound. Not a timeless Neverwhere of memories either. We're talking death. The real deal.

Looking at the man reclined on the grain sacks, I'm almost resentful. He's me, so I shouldn't be upset. I'm going to live. A version of me anyway. He'll carry on with my future life. I won't be completely gone from existence, just this particular version of me. In a multiverse full of possibilities, I've always known there had to be an ending. We all have to die. I just didn't think I'd be going so soon.

I settle the lid back on the top of the barrel and slump into a sitting position. The darkness in here just makes it worse. No distractions.

My mind goes to Mym.

Of all the people in the multiverse, she'll be the one most affected. She chose me to go through this life with. It was our combined story. No matter what happens to Piper's dad, he still won't be *her* Ben.

I know she's strong. I know she'll survive without me. Doesn't make me any less sad about it though. We thought we'd have the next fifty years or more together.

I lean my head back against the side of the barrel.

But there's that little girl.

She came back. She braved a trip into the past to come find me. To ask for my help. And I made her a promise.

She needs her dad back, and that's what she's going to get.

The sound of hooves outside inspires activity in the house. Voices.

In a matter of minutes, I'm reliving the slightly more muffled sounds of my day.

Smiley and Wiggy are back. They bring me inside.

I clutch the handle of my barrel lid and strain my ears to listen. Piper's dad is rousted from his place and forced out into the main room for the video. My earlier self is there. He argues. As I lift the lid of the barrel again, I catch sight of him through the doorway. He spins around to pilfer the cast iron plate off the mantel.

This never gets less surreal.

I hide again as my other selves are escorted into the pantry. The door slams shut and I'm officially trapped. There's no getting out of this now. If my earlier self discovers me here it would be paradox city. This pantry is probably already straining the space-time continuum as it is, hosting three versions of the same person. I have no idea what the temporal fabric of the fractal universe is doing with this fact, but I'm not about to test it further.

I close my eyes.

The sound of my other selves speaking to each other is oddly soothing. I've experienced the conversation before, so it's like listening to a replay of a favorite audiobook or a familiar song. Piper's dad begins explaining his breakup with Mym, his issues as a husband and father. I ignore the words but listen to the earnestness in his voice. His emotion is raw and honest, especially when he's talking about Piper.

He'll do the right thing by her.

He'd better.

My legs are cramped before long, but I'm not in a mood to complain. It's a good feeling to be experiencing anything at all. I've even grown used to the dirty potato smell. Maybe that's just my brain trying to talk me out of my plan.

But it's too late. I'm in this to the end now.

Nightfall comes before I know it. The two other versions of me in the pantry have settled down. I let them sleep for a while before lifting the lid on the barrel. I slip it aside and gingerly adjust my feet in the darkness.

One last danger to face.

My legs have gone numb in the barrel, so I wait for circulation to return before attempting to stand.

My other selves are breathing quietly. One of me is on the grain sacks, the other slumped against the wall on the floor. Past and future, fast asleep.

I let minutes creep past. Then an hour. I wait till the version of me on the floor sounds like he's in a deep sleep before throwing a leg over the side of the barrel. I slip to the floor, gently laying the lid aside.

Here's where things get tricky.

I edge over to Piper's dad and get down to his level. Putting one hand over his mouth, I give him a gentle shake with the other.

"Shhh. Don't make any noise," I whisper the moment he stirs.

It's hard to see in the darkness, but he doesn't sound alarmed. It makes sense. He's probably assuming I'm the version of me he was just talking to.

"I need you to do what I say, and just trust me, no questions asked." He doesn't respond immediately. "It's for Piper," I add.

"What do I need to do?"

I help the older me up. That's when he senses the other person in the room. The breathing of my earlier self on the floor is loud enough to give away that I'm not him.

"Where did you come from?" Piper's dad whispers.

"The future." I guide him the few feet toward the mostly empty potato barrel and instruct him to get inside.

"You sure you know what you're doing?" he asks.

"You said you wanted to know the escape plan. This is it."

It only takes a few seconds to get him into the barrel. "They'll be in at first light. They're going to take us outside. That's when you run. Get to the barn and take one of the horses. Then get to the time gate as fast as you can and get out of here. Your daughter is going to be waiting for you on the other side."

I give him the coordinates to the time gate that will get him back to Piper and make him repeat them several times, and I confirm the route to the barn until he's confident he knows it.

"What's going to happen to you?" he asks.

"That's already been handled."

"You're sure?"

I hand him the lid to the barrel. "What happened, happened. I'm just living it over now. I'm counting on you for the rest. Piper needs your help. Go to her."

He doesn't argue any further.

Once he's settled in the barrel, there's nothing else to be done but to wait. I take his place on the grain sacks, running through the plan in my head. I'm suddenly very tired. I'm about to lean back and fall asleep when I remember the bag for my head. Come morning, my other self can't know it's me. I scrounge around on the floor until I find the sack and a bit of twine, then slip it over my head. I secure the bag loosely around my neck, making sure I can still breathe okay. Won't do to suffocate myself before morning. I lay back on the grain sacks and work to slow my breathing. Surprisingly, sleep calls me right away.

I have strange dreams.

The leaves of the blood-red maple tree wave in the breeze.

Piper is wandering through the abandoned theme park trailed by an army of animatronic robots. Thick electrical cables twist and wind past her feet like so many snakes. The sky is full of falling stars. Meteorites.

The door creaks open.

Morning.

It came so fast.

"You that excited to be on TV that you couldn't wait?" Wiggy's voice is mocking as he grasps my wrists and binds them. When he's done, he steps back. Thankfully, he doesn't mess with the bag on my head. "I didn't bring enough rope. I'll grab some more. Wake the other one." His footsteps disappear but I'm not alone. Smiley steps across the room and wakes my other self, then backs away.

I can hear him stirring. Then he freezes.

"Wait, you're getting this all wrong!" he exclaims.

"Get up. We're going outside," Smiley orders.

"You're making a mistake here."

Wiggy's footsteps return. "Come on, Travers." He mutters curses to himself as he ties my other self's wrists.

"Listen. This is very important. When we get outside, I need to be on the right." My earlier self is desperate. "The right! You understand?"

At least I was earnest. Can't fault myself for trying.

I can't help but wonder what Piper's dad is thinking, listening from inside the barrel.

I'm helped to my feet and shoved toward the front of the house. Near the doorway, I collide with my earlier self. I can feel his anxiety. It's almost tangible.

"Don't worry, it's going to be okay." I try to sound reassuring. Technically I'm lying.

We're shoved onward and around the side of the house. I listen intently for Epaulettes. If we are all accounted for, then Piper's dad will be in the clear.

"I need to be on the right, okay?" My other self repeats his plea. "Please!"

"Will you shut up?" Smiley is getting annoyed.

"It's important. Please make sure I'm on the right."

"You're on the right already. You happy now?" Wiggy replies.

Someone finishes tying me to the post. I try to keep my heart from beating out of my chest. This seems to be happening even faster than I remembered it.

"Ben? You okay?" I jolt at the question. I forgot I asked myself that. For a moment I'm about to speak, but stop myself. If he knows where I'm standing he'll know we're in the wrong places. He needs to stay there. And he needs to live.

"Will you please shut him up?"

Epaulettes. Good. Everyone is still in their places. Despite the severity of my circumstances, I let myself smile. Piper's dad is going to make it. Even now he's probably sneaking into the barn, stealing a horse, preparing for his ride. We only have to go through the motions here now. My job is done. Piper will be safe.

"They didn't say which one. I guess we get to pick." Epaulettes is prepping his musket.

Shit. This is it.

I take a deep breath.

God. If you're up there ... I could use—

The blast still takes me by surprise. I stagger back from the impact, my wrists catching on the hitching post. It's like being punched by a ... bullet.

My knees go weak. Damn. My head is already getting fuzzy. Warmth is wicking from my chest. Going where? I teeter and fall. A swirl of color opens up in my vision. I'm plummeting into an endless abyss. The earth catches me momentarily. My senses flare. Dirt. Grass. The smells. Ringing in my ears. I gasp. A breath. I'm still here. It's not so bad. I'm cold, but my vision is clearing. No more dingy burlap sack. I'm looking across forever. The universe is expanding around me. I try to swallow. Something is choking back my breath now. It's okay. I don't need it. Not anymore.

I'm standing now. Floating maybe? Looking down on my own prostrate body. Epaulettes is there. Smiley. Wiggy. My other self is yelling, cursing their brutality. I wish I could tell him it's okay. If he could see what I see, he wouldn't be upset. How could he be? All of this is just a tiny sliver of time. His life stretches out into the forever. My life.

It's hard to be upset about my situation in the face of this much beauty. I let my anger go. It vanishes like a weight dropped into a bottomless pool. The rest of my stresses follow. There are a million colors here—a billion musical sounds. I can feel them humming through every bit of me.

It's calling. The eternity. It's been here the whole time, in every last molecule I possessed and more. It's the pulsing, vibrating fabric of space and time and a dozen dimensions I couldn't have described if I tried. But there's one I recognize. It's been a tingle in my spine in the best moments of my life. Love. Love of life. Love of this amazing, flawed, incredible universe. If I still had a spine, it would be tingling.

I take one last look around me, trying to focus on the here and the now. It's so hard. Time is an ocean with no horizon, and this little moment is just the smallest speck. I hold onto it for a final glittering second—a last instant of me, frozen in time.

Then I let go.

24

"Keep close to the people you care about. Stay in touch. Time is an ocean with many currents, and one day it may sweep away someone you love. Hands clasped in friendship are not easily parted." -Journal of Dr. Harold Quickly 1928

Strange dreams.

A blood-red maple tree. A collapsing roller coaster. A universe of color. Potatoes?

I'm being shaken awake. Someone's hand is over my mouth.

"Hey, don't make any noise."

I stir slowly. I'm propped against the wall of the pantry. I don't know when I fell asleep.

He's looming over me in the semi-darkness. Piper's dad.

"I need you to listen to me and do what I tell you to do without question. Can you do that?" He slowly removes his hand from my mouth.

"Um. Yeah, I think so. Are you working on a new plan to—" I stop talking when I realize there is someone else breathing in this room. Against the wall, asleep on the grain sacks. "Who else is . . ."

"Don't worry about him. He'll be fine." Piper's dad helps me to my feet and guides me a few steps to my right. "Put your hands out here. Feel the edge of this barrel. I need you to get inside."

"In the barrel?"

"No arguing. I didn't argue with you."

"What? When?"

"Never mind. I know this is confusing. Just get in."

I climb slowly into the barrel. It smells like potatoes. The cast iron plate I have under my shirt bumps against my chest and I hold it with one hand. "What about our body armor plan?"

"Oh, right. You won't be needing that."

I detach the plate from the strand of twine holding it on and pass it to him. He accepts it and sets it aside.

"Stay quiet in there. Come morning, they are going to come get us. That'll be your chance to slip out. Get to the barn, steal a horse, and get to the time gate. I have some coordinates for you." He lists me off some coordinates and asks me to repeat them.

I do, but then I stop to argue. "Wait. This is a date in the 2100s. I left Piper in 1958. I need to get back to her."

"A lot has happened since then. You won't remember it, but Piper is waiting for you in the future now."

"What about you?"

"I'm going to need some help here too. What did you do to escape them last time?"

"What? Escape who?"

He mutters to himself. "That's right, you won't have any memory of that either since it hasn't happened to you yet..."

"Look man, I'm really confused right now." I gesture toward the sacks of grain where someone is sleeping. "Which one of us is that?"

"We still need to get him back too. Look, when you go to the barn, get two horses. One of me is getting shot in the morning. Whichever one of me makes it, I'd appreciate it if you could help get us to the time gate with you."

"One of *you* is getting shot?" I ask. "What about the video? I thought it was a version of us with a torn pant leg. Are yours ripped?" I have a hard time seeing his knees in the dark.

My other self pushes me farther down in the barrel and picks up the lid. "Don't worry about that. Piper will be able to explain it to you once you get back. Get out of here in the morning. Save whichever one of me is alive, and get back to Piper. The rest will be up to you guys to solve."

I have about a hundred questions, but I don't get a chance to ask them. He closes the lid and silences me.

I puzzle over the situation I've found myself in, but I'm not seeing all the pieces. Like why are there two of him now?

It doesn't take long for his predictions to start coming true. The dawn brings trouble in the form of Smiley and Wiggy opening the door and trussing people up. When the commotion has died down and the two other versions of me have been led away, I lift the lid on my wooden prison and sneak out of the pantry.

He said to get to the barn.

It sounded like the others went out the front door, so I opt for the back, slipping out the door and down three steps to the dirt and weeds. A billy goat is tied to a post by a long tether and has been munching the grass down to little nubs in a wide circle. It bleats at me as I rush past it.

I don't look back. I just run. The barn is seventy yards to the west. I'm fortunate that it's a direction not visible from the hitching posts. Inside, I find three horses in their stalls. There are saddle blankets on a rack and several saddles. They're not the western saddles I've used before, but a more minimalist-looking version. I trust the general concept is the same. That leaves the matter of the horses.

It would be wise to try to pick the fastest horses, but since I have no idea how to assess that, I go for the ones that look least likely to kick me.

I'm unlatching a gate to one of the stalls when the gunshot echoes across the barnyard. I jolt. To the horses' credit, none of them are spooked in the slightest.

Someone just got shot.

The reality of the danger makes me work faster. I bridle the first horse and throw a blanket and saddle over its back.

Up at the house, someone is shouting.

I tighten the strap on the saddle, then sneak over to the barn wall and peer through a chink in a pair of the boards. I can't see anything. They must still be up at the house. How am I supposed to rescue my other self? Piper's dad was pretty vague on that detail.

The second horse backs away from me when I enter the stall, so I do my best to calm myself down before approaching it. I won't be rescuing anybody if I get a hoof to the face.

Fortunately the horse lets me bridle and saddle it without further complaint. I lead the two horses to the door of the barn and pause to look out. Three men are walking across the field, headed south. One is dragging a body. Wiggy has a gun pointed at Piper's dad and is forcing him along. All three are headed toward a blood-red maple tree.

The sight of the tree gives me pause. I get a strange feeling of déjà vu. My dream. But I saw it closer in my dream, didn't I?

I'm too far away to get the jump on them from here. There's no way they wouldn't see me coming and just shoot me off my horse. I need a better plan.

The edge of the woods is only a dozen yards away behind the barn. The trees wrap all the way around the clearing, ultimately joining the red maple tree. I can get there, I'll just need to move quickly.

I lead the two horses around the barn and into the woods without being seen. I mount the calmer of the two and lead the other by the reins. I encourage my horse into a trot, and it deftly dodges thickets and ditches, even nimbly leaping over several fallen logs. This is clearly not its first time navigating the woods. Dexterous as my mount is, I fear the amount of noise I'm making. When I get closer to where my other self is being held prisoner, I slow the horses to a gentle walk, then stop when I hear voices.

Through the trees I can just make out the figures of Wiggy and Smiley. Wiggy has a pistol that isn't very colonial, and he's using it to guard Piper's dad, who has been given a shovel and is in the process of digging a hole.

Okay. He's still alive. So far so good.

Smiley is standing near the body of the other man. He's staring down at it with a curious expression on his face. Does he sense something is off?

Smiley squats next to the body. What is he doing?

I shift a little closer to get a better view. It looks like he's untying the twine around the victim's neck. That's not good. If he removes the bag he'll see the switch. Will he recognize that it's not me? My stomach sinks as he reaches for the bag.

I need a distraction. What would get someone's attention in colonial times?

I cup my hands to my mouth and shout. "The Redcoats are coming! The Redcoats are coming!"

Smiley and Wiggy both look up. Wiggy immediately aims the gun at the woods.

Oh this was a bad idea.

It's too late now. I dig my heels into my horse's sides to spur it forward. The animal responds immediately, leaping forward into a run. The second horse neighs loudly as I pull it along, eight hooves now pounding through the underbrush.

The commotion is enough to make Wiggy take a few steps back. Piper's dad must have recognized my yell. He got the message. He takes a two-handed baseball bat grip on the shovel and turns on Wiggy. The kidnapper doesn't have time to react. The shovel blade collides with his skull with a resounding crack, and the previously conscious man goes thudding to the ground, raising a puff of dust, a few startled insects, and sending several of the fallen maple leaves fluttering about.

That just leaves the big man.

Smiley is tall. He's muscular and strong and an intimidating specimen of a human being. There are zero circumstances I'd like to tangle with him one-on-one. But I'm not one-on-one. I've got a horse. As I come galloping out of the woods, headed straight for him, Smiley turns and falls to his face in the weeds. Smart decision. My horse leaps cleanly over him and skids to a stop at my command.

I'm starting to love this animal.

I pull on the reins of the second horse and encourage it forward till Piper's dad can grab ahold of its bridle. The older me is looking up at me with wonder. "You know how to make an entrance."

"You said you wanted an escape plan. Welcome to the only plan we've got."

"I'll take it."

I study the face of the other me. "So you're you? Or are you the other one?"

Piper's dad looks to the body lying near the base of the maple tree. "I thought it would be me to get shot, but it was 50-50. I didn't know."

Smiley is getting back to his feet. He looks angry.

"Come on. Time to go!" I shout.

Piper's dad grasps the saddle of the horse I brought him and pulls himself up. He's more efficient at it than I am. He must have had some practice sometime in the next decade of my life.

Smiley roars and charges at us. My horse sees him coming and sends a sharp kick in his direction that instantly stops Smiley in his tracks. My horse then breaks into a run for the road.

It's official. I love this horse.

Piper's dad is on my tail in a flash, racing along next to me.

Smiley shouts his displeasure into the cloud of dust we leave him in.

I cast one last look at the body on the ground as we flee. I don't understand what has happened here exactly, but I hope my other self knows what he's doing. He promised I'd have answers. We just have to get out of here.

Our horses thunder down the road, navigating the ruts and bends with practiced ease. As we pass a particular grove of trees, I get a strange feeling of déjà vu again and slow my horse to a walk and then a stop. Piper's dad reins his horse in as well.

"What's wrong?"

"I just have a weird feeling we should get off the road. Someone is coming."

The road ahead looks quiet for now, but my gut is telling me otherwise.

My other self peers down the road. "That's right. There were soldiers on the road last time."

"Last time?" I ask.

He shakes his head and guides his horse into the woods. I turn my horse and we follow. My premonition comes true almost immediately.

A column of soldiers comes around the bend up ahead. They are led by a bold-looking Patriot officer on a white horse. As the column passes, we keep out of sight. In a matter of minutes they've moved on.

"You certainly called that one." Piper's dad says. "I would have run right into them again, and I even knew better."

"You've got a lot of explaining to do," I say.

"It'll make more sense to you when we make it back." He leads the way through the trees and onto the road again. We reach the barn with the time gate without further incident, and Piper's dad enters the coordinates to get us back. I unsaddle and unbridle the horses, turning them loose to run free. I give my horse a grateful scratch between the ears, and it whinnies at me before breaking for the road home.

As the colors swirl from the emitters, I put a hand to my older self's shoulder. "Thanks for saving me, man. Here I thought I was coming to save you."

He turns to me with a somber look in his eyes. "You already did save me. Trust me, I should be the one thanking you." He extends an arm and invites me to step through the gate ahead of him. I still don't know what he's talking about, but I don't need further invitation. I want out of this place. I step through the gate.

Yesteryear Adventure Park.

I had hoped I could be done with the bleak and desolate version of this place from the future, but that's where I find myself again. I don't have time to look around because I'm instantly tackled by Piper.

"Yes! He did it!" She's grinning as she wraps her arms around me. "I knew you would make it. You had to!"

"Whoa, hey there! Good to see you too."

She's somehow dirtier than the last time I saw her but seems otherwise unhurt. I wrap an arm around her and step away from the gate. "How'd you get here? Are you okay?"

"I'm fine," she says. "I came here with you. We followed Vanessa and you saved me from the roller coaster."

Roller coaster? What's she talking about?

Piper's dad emerges from the time gate, and she rushes over to him. He grins and opens his arms. "Hey, there's my girl."

She flings herself into his arms and hugs him even harder than she hugged me.

I'm still unsuccessfully trying to solve the riddle of what has happened when they finally separate. It's a heartwarming sight seeing them back together in any case. Whatever happened, I like the results. Piper's dad walks to the controls for the time gate and pulls the plug on it.

"Let's keep the revolution in the past for a while. We've had enough of that." When he's done, he turns back to me. He picks up a bundle from next to the time gate and hands it to me. I recognize it as my shirt and leather jacket. "Here. Found these next to the gate on my first trip. Thought you might want them back."

"Thanks. I wondered who ran off with those. Glad it was someone trustworthy." I take the shirt and jacket and immediately change into them.

Piper's dad gestures to the deactivated gate controls. "We think these gates operate on some kind of shared network. Piper said you guys have already found most of them. I think it's best if we shut them all down. No telling who might come looking for us."

"We'll be trapped," I say. "Without the gates, we're stuck here."

"But I don't think we need to leave," he says. "Piper says the warp clock is here."

I turn to look at Piper. She is still holding her dad's hand.

She addresses me. "We tracked Vanessa. We saw her with a package. You said you thought it was the warp clock, so it's here now."

I run my fingers though my hair. "Okay. Slow this down for me, okay? You guys keep talking about things I said and did that I don't remember at all. What happened back there?" I gesture to the powered-down time gate. "I went in to save you and things got completely confusing."

"Let's walk and talk," my other self says. "You two can lead us to the other time gates you've found, and Piper and I can try to explain."

We step outside the façade of The Green Dragon Tavern and move past the dried up recreation of Boston harbor.

"You were a hero," Piper says. She's looking up at me with something akin to wonder. "You saved my dad, just like you said you would."

"When?" I ask.

"You remember me waking you up in the middle of the night and stuffing you in that barrel?" Piper's dad asks.

"Yeah. Pretty hard to forget."

"That was your idea. You did it to me first. You came back for me and replaced me in that pantry. Then you took a bullet so I could get away."

"*You* were the man with the ripped pants from the video," Piper adds. "You tore them when you saved me from the roller coaster."

I look down at the legs of my trousers. Neither pant leg is torn. "That sounds awfully noble of me, but I never experienced that. Does that mean you guys changed the past to get me out? What about the paradox that would create? If you duplicated the escape, it would mean there are two separate timestreams now."

"We're getting to that," my other self says. "From what I can gather, you decided to come back and save me because you believed Piper needed her dad more than she needed you. You sacrificed yourself and died back there in 1777. I escaped and came back here. But Piper had more pieces of the puzzle."

Piper holds up my digi-lens sunglasses. "It was in the video. It was there from the beginning."

I take the sunglasses from her. I put them on and toggle the power switch. The red battery light is flashing angrily at me and threatening to shut the lenses down, but I'm able to start the video where Piper has paused it. It's the scene with the Gladiator.

"Mym Travers. This message is for you alone. You will hand over the warp clock at the location we tell you, at the time we tell you, or people you love will die." He gestures to the man with the camera. "Feed in the video. Show her the price she'll pay if she refuses."

The man with the camera fumbles with something, then aims the camera at the floor while he attempts to play the video. The Gladiator grumbles, then the man with the camera straightens it again. "There were two files with the same name for some reason," he complains. "Not sure why they sent it twice. Okay, here we go."

The video switches to the scene of Piper's dad and me tied to chairs while being threatened.

"Did you hear it?" Piper asks.

I lift the lenses from my face to see her better.

"There were *two* videos," she says. "Two video files with the same name."

I'm slow to pick up on what she's saying. "Two different videos of the shooting?"

Piper's dad chimes in. "Like what would happen if the goons in 1777 sent multiple files."

"Or they sent one video file but from two different timestreams..." I say.

"The video you were sent showed the timestream where you came back and were shot," he explains. "But there was always a second scenario. A video you were never shown. If we were to watch that video, I'm betting it would show the events of the second timestream we just experienced together. I knew that I could go back, pull the same stunt you did, and the end result would be both of us still alive. It had always happened twice because there were always two different versions of the 1777 timestream."

"You duplicated the timestreams, duplicating us there, but each of us died to save the other?"

"That was the plan anyway," Piper's dad says. "I went back in trying to duplicate your sacrifice, but it was 50-50 odds. In my case it was my other self that got shot. I failed on that front. But the thing that gives me some comfort is knowing that he would have chosen the same thing.

Any one of us would have gone through with it for the other. You proved it."

"So I went back in time, hid you, and died in your place, but you escaped, created an alternate timestream and saved me the same way? Two of us died back there, and we're the two that survived?"

"Exactly." He puts his hands in his pockets.

"How did you make the extra timestream?"

"When I went back in, I picked a time before you arrived and unplugged the gate during the period you should have shown up. You couldn't arrive there when you would have. It was a paradox. Enough to change things and set me down a different path. It was Piper's idea."

I turn to Piper and rub my head. "It's enough to give me a brain cramp . . . you figured this out all on your own?"

"I told you I know how time stuff works," she says.

"Sounds like I owe you my life."

"I needed you," she says.

Dropping to a knee, I smile at her. "I'm glad you feel that way, even though you've got your real dad back now."

Piper shakes her head. "No. You don't understand. I meant the other me."

I squint in confusion. "Wait, what? What other you? There's another one of you now too?"

Piper's dad takes her hand again. "Piper told me about how she came back to Harry's funeral to find you. It makes sense that she would choose that weekend. It's the weekend Mym and I found out."

"Found out . . ." I look from his face to Piper's. "Found out what?"

My other self grins at me. Piper is smiling too.

"Oh whoa. Seriously? Mym is . . ."

"Pregnant?" he asks. "Yeah. We found out the morning after the funeral when she started not feeling well. I thought it was just something to do with the service, but . . ."

I look at the little girl in front of me.

She really is my daughter—a version of my daughter anyway.

"You knew the whole time," I said. "Here I was thinking I wouldn't be having kids for years and acting like you were someone else's future. You knew."

Piper searches my face. "Are you mad?"

"Mad?" I open my arms to her. "Oh gosh, how could I possibly be mad about this?"

Piper steps forward and wraps her arms around my neck. I squeeze her tightly.

When she steps back, she's smiling. "Maybe when I'm born, I can come visit? It'll be kind of like having a little sister."

"Let him at least tell your mom first," my other self says.

Mym.

She's going to be a mom. She's going to be so thrilled.

I get to my feet again. "Well, in order to tell her, I need to find her first." I look around the desolate theme park. "Or give her a way to find us."

Piper's dad rests an arm across his daughter's shoulders and turns to me. "You have a plan?"

"Yeah," I reply. "Let's find this damned warp clock. It's time to go home."

Author's note. For the temporally curious, a detailed unraveling of the time travel twist in chapters 23 and 24 is available at the back of this book.

25

"Hurrying through life is like dumping out your ice cream to get to the cone. If that was the point, they'd offer it as a flavor called 'empty regret.'" -Journal of Dr. Harold Quickly, 2582

It's time to end this.

One would think that with a slew of time gates at our disposal, we'd have plenty of exits from this broken-down park. The trouble with time gates is that they come in pairs. They only provide limited locations to jump to. When the entire network has been set up by a con man, the exits are nowhere you really want to go. Plus, the Gladiator's gates are a bunch of nearly used-up single points in time. Being black-market stolen goods, he doesn't have them hooked up to any of the Central Streams where activity could be tracked. Even if we were to find a decent decade to escape to, it wouldn't get us any closer to home. There's only one way out of this mess.

But before we can find the warp clock, we need to make sure none of the other convicts can come back to stop us first.

As I pull the plug on the time gate in the Gold Rush ride, we check the map again.

"Is that all of them?" Piper's dad asks.

"There's one more time gate symbol on this map," I reply. "Over in Industrial America. We haven't been to that part of the park yet. And there's the one in the general store in Frontier Town that comes out of the ceiling. No idea how we can reach that one."

"High ceiling?"

"Yeah. You fall through the floor of the store in 1958 and come out of the ceiling here. It's terrible. You'd hate it."

The other Ben nods. "Okay. Let's leave that for last. Let's knock out the one in the Industrial Revolution section."

We wander out to the main thoroughfare of the park. A sort of central plaza hosts shops from a dozen different eras. Most have broken windows and some have even suffered fires, but it seems like a central hub to the park.

"According to the map, Industrial America is to our right, near the entrance gates." I point to a sign that indicates an exit. It's a cluster of arrows pointing different directions. Some have broken off and are lying in the dirt. I study the remaining signs with curiosity. "You know what's weird about this place?"

"You narrowed it down to one thing?" My other self is surveying the plaza skeptically.

"Bird shit," I say, pointing to the sign. "Why isn't there any bird shit anywhere?"

"There's no birds," Piper says.

I squint at the sky. "Whatever happened to the world here, I don't think much made it through."

I scan the clouds for any sign of life but find none. The only things moving are a few ragged curtains fluttering in broken windows.

We march on toward Industrial America.

I can tell what the original appeal may have been. The smokestacks and machines on display in this zone of the park are almost cartoonish in shape. The paint that hasn't been eroded features bright colors like purples and greens. This industrial revolution bears little resemblance to the sooty reality of history.

Old cars line the avenues. I spot several Ford Model As along with the ever-popular Model T. But there are plenty of other vehicles on display as well. A sign names a 1900 Olds to our right, and overhead there are aircraft fixed to poles, cheerily dive bombing the streets with pilots frozen in mid-wave. The skeletal contraptions hardly resemble modern planes at all. It was a simpler time with an enthusiastic population on the brink of a promised bright future.

"This place is surreal." Piper's dad has been making similar comments throughout the park as we've given him the tour of time gates we've visited. I consult my map once again and point ahead to a building adorned with many oversized cogs and gears.

"The Hall of Industry. That looks like our target."

Piper takes my hand in hers, her other hand still holding onto her dad. "We'll all stay together this time, right?"

I squeeze her hand. "You betcha."

We walk toward the building hand-in-hand. We've nearly reached the doors when a great groaning and squealing erupts from the front of the building. One of the oversized gears begins to turn, shedding rusty flakes of steel as it does so. The other cogs and gears on the façade of the building begin to move as well, lurching and grinding in a deafening chorus of screeches. Piper releases my hand in order to cover her ears.

"What on earth is that all about?" Piper's dad shouts over the din.

"Can you make it stop?" Piper shouts.

Then, just as suddenly as it began, the display jolts and quivers, arresting its motion and freezing in place again.

"Oh thank God," the other Ben says. "I thought it was going to liquefy my brain with that racket."

I study the now-motionless façade of the building. Whatever caused the commotion has passed. I look down at Piper. It's almost like it listened to her... A few flakes of rust drift down in a dusty sort of drizzle, but otherwise the mechanism looks to have given up. The door to the building stands slightly ajar.

"You want to go in there?" Piper's dad asks.

I double-check my map. "What I want isn't really a big factor anymore," I reply. "But if we really want to shut these guys down..."

The front door is propped open to accommodate a heavy-duty power conduit that runs from the interior and up the outside wall. The thick wires snake their way up the face of the building and disappear onto the roof. I don't know who installed them, but they definitely aren't original. Calling it a trip hazard would be putting it lightly.

The situation inside is even worse. More conduit writhes across the floor making it resemble the snake pit in *Raiders of the Lost Ark*. I get a vague memory of my dream. None of the cables are actually moving that I can tell, but nothing would really surprise me at this point.

The Hall of Industry is apparently some sort of museum. Glass display cases dot the entrance, and several costumed robots are on hand to greet patrons.

At least I assume they are robots. Protected from the sun and wind, these animatronic creations have fared much better inside, and some of them are eerily lifelike. As we approach, a young newsboy in overalls and a cheese cutter hat twitches to life, waving a newspaper at us. "Extra! Extra! Read all about it! Marconi's radio transmits across the Atlantic!"

Piper screams.

The newsboy lowers his paper, and his head pivots on his neck in a jolting fashion. He fixes his eyes on Piper. His voice comes out at a lower volume this time. "Why are you scared of me? Aren't you having fun?"

Piper's dad steps in front of her protectively. "What the hell?"

The newsboy jolts again and looks up at him. "Welcome to the Hall of Industry. Would you like to witness the birth of mankind's greatest achievements?" The robot waits expectantly for an answer.

"What are these things?" My other self looks to me.

"Hey!" I address the newsboy. "Can you understand us?"

The newsboy rotates his entire torso to look at me. "Want a paper, mister?"

"How did you know she was scared?" I ask, pointing to Piper. "You understand what a scream is?"

"Would you like to try the guided tour of the museum?" the

newsboy asks. "One of our mobile guides would be happy to assist you."

"I want to know why you just said that," Piper's dad insists. "You some kind of synth? How do you know what we're saying?"

The newsboy straightens up and smiles at us. "One of our guides has been requested. Please wait here to be assisted."

A loud bang emanates from beyond a partition. All three of us jump. The bang repeats itself, like something heavy colliding with a metal object. The noise continues but doesn't seem to be getting any closer. I edge around the partition, cautiously searching for the source of the racket. Piper and her dad linger near the entrance, ready to flee at the first sign of trouble.

The banging is coming from a doorway. A metal door is jammed partway open, and every few seconds a figure propels itself forward and slams into it. The door is blocked by a fallen concrete pedestal. To my surprise, I recognize the figure attempting to exit as Nikola Tesla.

"What the hell is it?" My other self shouts from the lobby.

"An inventor in a closet."

Tesla spots me and pauses. "Would you be so kind as to assist me, sir? I seem to be impeded."

I approach the door cautiously but stand clear of the pedestal. "Hey. What's the deal with this place? Who's running it?"

Tesla cocks his head attentively. "This museum is the property of Yesteryear Adventure Parks, Inc. A subsidiary of United Machine."

"United Machine?" It's a name I've heard before. "Aren't they the ones that develop the first synthetic humans?"

"Yesteryear Adventure Park employs the most advanced technologies available to ensure maximum enjoyment of our parks."

I look around the area of the museum we are in. A few of the bulbs are flickering in the display cases. "Looks like you haven't had much business lately."

"We are working hard to improve park attendance. But if we can make just one child excited about history, we call it success. That is our philosophy at the Yesteryear family of parks." His eyes wander past me to where Piper and her dad have drawn slowly closer. "Because children are the future."

"You think that thing is safe?" The other Ben has his hands on Piper's shoulders.

I consider the size of the pedestal blocking the doorway, then address Tesla. "We've decided to forgo the guided tour. We'll just show ourselves around."

Tesla studies me for a moment, then bows and backs away into the darkness beyond the doorway.

Piper's dad watches the doorway warily. "This place creeps me out."

"Yeah. Let's find this time gate and get out of here." I pick my way over more fallen debris as we wend our way through the museum. Several dioramas illuminate as we pass, showing early life in an assembly line or working in various factories. Once again, the reality has been highly stylized, with happy workers smiling away as they assemble car parts or textiles. A few of the dioramas seem to be missing pieces. Robotic workers wave empty hands instead of tools and simulate loading parts into non-existent machines. Their equipment has been either moved or stolen.

One diorama makes me pause. It shows the evolution of automated robots, tracking their use in factories and production, all the way to the point where they have taken humanoid form. Several members of the theme park cast are featured. I recognize the white-hatted cowboy from Frontier Town. The final, most recent entry in the timeline, shows the United Machine logo and a plaque that forecasts the future of robotic intelligence. The plaque reads: 'United Machine will continue to employ the most modern technology in this park and the world, ensuring a bright future for both humans and robots alike. One day we will stand hand-in-hand to welcome that future."

There are no more entries. Whatever future United Machine experienced next on the timeline, it obviously didn't warrant a mention in the museum. Or no one was around to make it.

I follow the winding path, and it leads to the rear of the museum that opens up to an open warehouse where a variety of mobile steam engines have been parked. We locate the space on the map where the time gate should be located, but the contraption we find there is far bigger than any time gate. It's a sort of tunnel, ribbed with steel columns and walls patched together from various other pieces of the museum displays. The basic frame of the structure reminds me of a small aircraft hangar, though the tire tracks on the floor appear to have been made by road vehicles. The far end of the tunnel concludes with a rolling industrial door. There are canisters spaced along the columns, and the glass sight gauges of the canisters show a familiar-looking blue fluid.

"Is this what I think it is?" I ask.

"Looks like an industrial-sized gravitizer," my other self replies. He taps on one of the cylinders. "They must have used this to gravitize all their equipment before taking it through the time gates."

"I wondered how they managed to gravitize a helicopter," I mutter.

There is a control panel on one end of the tunnel. It closely resembles Dr. Quickly's design but has a placard on it labeling it as the property of ASCOTT. More of the Gladiator's stolen goods.

According to the symbol on the map, we should be on top of the time gate. "It ought to be right here," I say.

The time gate is indeed there, but it takes us a few minutes to recognize it. The reason we missed it walking in was because of its sheer size. Two posts that resemble flag poles are mounted to hinges near the entrance to the gravitizer tunnel. A third, thinner post connects the two at the top. In total, the device must involve at least a hundred temporal emitters. The hinges make sense, considering it would be a nightmare to try to reach the top by ladder to make adjustments or repairs. Instead, the entire gate can be brought to floor level. A solution I can appreciate.

"This one doesn't have a plug." Piper is standing near the control panel for the tunnel. The time gate has been hardwired into the tunnel controls via a thick conduit that runs along the outside of the tunnel and continues to the rolling door.

"There has to be a way to kill the power," the other Ben says. "At least a circuit breaker panel. Maybe we can trace the power back to its source."

"Looks like it goes out that way." Piper points to the rolling industrial door where the conduit runs under the rubber weatherstripping. "Let's follow it." She releases her dad's hand and runs through the gravitizer tunnel to the door's controls.

I follow her at a more cautious pace, eyeing the gravitite dispersal arrays along the walls. If this had enough juice to gravitize a helicopter, it has to be a powerful machine. When we reach the door, Piper punches the green open button, and the motor of the rolling door begins ratcheting its chain up the pulley system.

When the door is fully raised, I step onto the back loading ramp of the museum and look past a row of wildly misshapen topiaries to what appears to be the exterior entrance to the park. Electronic turnstiles punctuate a steel fence, and a long-abandoned trolley has been overturned and stripped of various parts. The scene could pass for a normal parking lot if it weren't for the odd amalgamation of vehicles collected around what appears to be a ticket office.

Everything from WWII era trucks to wooden wagons have accumulated there. They've been used to transport a windmill, multiple steam engines, and what appears to be a massive mechanical crank of the type powered by livestock. Several cables run from the roofs of nearby buildings, and another bundle is wired into a massive solar array out in the parking lot. Something is taking a lot of power.

To my surprise, there are a half-dozen weatherworn humanoid figures plodding around the mechanical crank, like so many oxen. Despite the deterioration of their faces, I recognize Marilyn Monroe, Benjamin Franklin, and a bedraggled Charlie Chaplin. Mohammed Ali looks especially disappointed to be there. Unlike the historical figures I met in the arena, I'm confident these are all robots.

I descend the back steps of the museum and make my way toward the ticket office.

Strange lights flicker inside. Blues and reds. There are noises as well —a clattering and clunking as though someone is working. Somebody has certainly gone through a lot of effort to outfit this hub with sufficient power. A figure passes by a window and vanishes quickly. But then the face comes back and studies us through the glass. Wild white hair and a bristly mustache give away the countenance of one of the most famous faces of all time. A moment later, the door to the ticket office bursts open and Albert Einstein comes striding out. His clothing is torn in places, and a patch of synthetic skin on his forehead has been scraped away, revealing a fraction of the metallic skull beneath.

He marches forward a few paces, then stands calmly in front of the ticket office, appraising us. A sign flashes above him, the illuminated words sliding off-screen and reappearing again in an eye-catching banner. Ticketing, Reservations, and Information Kiosk.

I read it twice before it sinks in.

I take a step back.

We've discovered the orchestrator behind the Temporal Fugitives escape. The boss man they've all been talking about. It's been this theme park the whole time.

I've found TRIK.

26

"If time travel doesn't confuse you from time to time, you're probably doing it wrong." -Journal of Dr. Harold Quickly 2109

"This was you?" I shout toward the robotic Einstein. "You're the one who broke the Gladiator and his gang out of prison? The one who has been orchestrating the changes to the past? A ticket office?"

The robotic Einstein hobbles forward on stiff-jointed legs. "Have you enjoyed your stay today at Yesteryear Adventure Park? Can I interest you in an annual pass?"

"We almost died!" I shout. "What the hell are you trying to do?"

Einstein cocks his head and addresses Piper. "You've been our first guest in many years. I hope you will come back again with friends. Children are our future."

I consider the robot standing in front of me. Does he really not get it? Does he not understand what we've been through?

"Your park is a death trap. It's a falling-down heap of rusting garbage. Why are you still operational?"

Einstein pivots to face me. "Customer satisfaction is our primary focus at Yesteryear Adventure Parks. If you have been unhappy with your visit today, we would be happy to extend you a credit to be used toward a future visit."

"There's no reasoning with this robot," the other Ben says. "If he has the warp clock in that shack of his, we just need to take it."

"Yeah," I mutter. "This place is cuckoo. Let's see if he's got it in there."

I walk past the robot and make for the ticket office. Several bundles of conduit clog the doorway, but as I step over them, I get a view of the mess inside.

It's a control center. Video monitors, gate controls, communication displays. It's all here. But it's more than that. One entire wall of the office has been dedicated to a glowing, flashing network of computers. They are connected to a single point. The warp clock.

I wasn't sure what I expected. Abraham's handiwork has never failed to impress me, but this is a level of complexity that I've never seen. At its heart is a glowing, swirling ball, the colors and consistency of the ether that emanates from the time gates. But this ether looks more condensed somehow. It keeps flashing and changing, its brilliance increasing and decreasing in irregular waves. It looks as though someone has sought to contain a raging, magical beast behind the glass. Every few seconds the light vanishes, darkening the glass, but then the colors return, flaring back to life and splashing against its container.

It's fascinating.

Around the ball of light and color there are rings that look like they physically restrict the shape of the central orb. Controls.

"Heads up, Ben. You've got company!" Piper's dad shouts from behind me.

I turn to find the robotic Einstein entering the office.

"You are an unauthorized person. This area is restricted to authorized park employees only. Please return to the public use area for your safety."

"I need to know how to use this thing," I say. "How did you shut down the chronometers?"

"The Ticketing, Reservations, and Information Kiosk welcomes your questions. In this case, your query would be better assisted by park management."

"There is no more park management, Tin Man. You're all that's left of this place."

The robot goes silent, and for a moment, I think that he might have gotten the message. But when he looks back up, his gaze is indecipherable.

"In the event of an inadequate resolution from management, I must ask you to exit the park."

"Happily," I mutter as I work to disconnect the warp clock from the wall.

A strong hand settles on my shoulder. "That is the property of Yesteryear Adventure Park. Your immediate departure is required." His grip tightens on my shoulder, and I'm suddenly flung to the floor, crashing to the tile.

"Oh, hell no," I say when I recover from the surprise. I climb back to my feet and point to the warp clock. "That device is the property of Dr. Harry Quickly. My family. I don't care what you think you are doing here, but it's coming with me."

Einstein widens his stance. "This device is currently in use as part of our Improved Attendance Directive. It now aids in our primary objective—the continued influx of new customers."

"Your park is a wasteland!" I shout. "Whatever happened to this timestream, there are no more guests. I don't know what apocalypse went on out there, but I'm sorry to tell you, they won't be coming back."

"That is why the Improved Attendance Directive is using all equipment at our disposal to reach a more innovative solution. We have determined that attendance at the park has dropped due to negative events in human history. That is why, logically, we must change history."

I blink and try to understand what he's saying. "Hold up. That's what's happening here? You're using the time gate technology to try to change the attendance at your theme park? That's not how time works!"

"We have had assurances from technical contractor Maxwell Franco that if he was granted access to the equipment he left stationed in this park, he would be able to change history per our directive. History is the cause of our drop in ticket sales and is therefore in error."

"You're definitely changing history all right, but you have no idea what you are doing!"

Einstein cocks his head and takes a step closer. "To the contrary, this park is an excellent collection of historical data. Based on the information in our museum collections, the most harmful events in human history were inspired by very few individuals. We intend to eliminate those events from time. If the human beings that inspire destruction are removed from history, history will be improved. When history is improved, guests will once again return to the park."

I run my hands through my hair. "Oh, you poor stupid robot. You don't even know you got conned. This park isn't an accurate compilation of human history, and Franco wasn't even a real employee. He was running an illegal time travel tourism racket out of your park. He didn't *leave* his equipment here. He got caught by ASCOTT and went to prison!" I look at the computer systems in the office. "I don't know how you contacted him, but if he told you he could fix your problems . . . You got conned, okay? He just wanted an escape route to anywhere the authorities wouldn't find him. He may have done your bidding, but you were a means to an end."

"Mr. Franco assured this office that his objectives were in line with our own. We also recruited a number of his other associates eager to assist in our project."

"I hate to tell you this, Einstein, but people lie."

The robot stares at me intently.

"How are things going in here?" Piper's dad appears in the doorway with Piper close behind.

"Me and Ticketbot here were just having a little discussion about how he needs to adjust his priorities. He's the reason Franco and his gang are out of prison. This whole damn park is—" I fling my hand out to indicate the scope of the park and inadvertently strike Piper in the head. The blow knocks her back a step.

"Ow."

She's snuck up behind me, presumably to get a better look at the warp clock.

"Oh hey. Sorry about that," I say as Piper rubs her forehead.

"It's okay," she mutters.

"Inflicting harm on a child is a serious offense," Einstein says, his voice deepening. "Your presence in the park is no longer permitted."

"It was just an accident, Einy," I say. "Calm down."

Einstein immediately replays a video image on one of the display screens of my hand hitting Piper in the face. "The safety of children is paramount at Yesteryear Adventure Park. It is the only directive that overrides all others. You will be escorted from the park by security."

"We're not going anywhere," I say.

"Uh, Ben, you might want to be more polite," my other self says. He jerks his thumb toward the parking lot. "Because we have company."

I follow his movement and spot the arrivals he's talking about.

He and Piper walk out the door to view the scene unfolding outside.

The ticket office is being slowly surrounded by an army of figures. Cowboys, knights, Revolutionary War soldiers. Robotic actors from all over the park are accumulating around us. Some are in rough shape, missing hands or faces, but others have come prepared for trouble, armed with period weapons. I trust that none of the muskets or crossbows are functional, but the swords and pickaxes look dangerous enough.

"Security will escort you out of the park," Einstein says.

"You're using robots for security?" I ask.

"The park is experiencing shortages of human personnel. I have had to make changes to the staff."

"Stand down, robot," I say. "I know you're programmed with safety protocols, but you need to let us have that device."

"The Improved Attendance Directive cannot be deactivated. It is our primary objective."

"You know what, Einstein? You're an idiot." I try to get around him to reach the warp clock again, but he intercepts me and grabs for my shirt.

I catch his wrist and yank hard, wrenching his arm around behind his back until something pops. His shoulder lets out a puff of smoke and then his arm goes limp. I shove him into a desk and he topples over. His arm comes away in my hand.

"Domo arigato, Mr. Roboto."

Piper screams.

I spin around to check the doorway, but Piper and her dad are gone. I rush to look outside and find them in the fairway surrounded by robots. The other me is being dragged away by a pair of bulky metallic figures. He's trying unsuccessfully to escape their grip by repeatedly kicking at their legs.

"Hey! I need a little help here!" He calls to me. Piper is pulling the arm of one of the robots carrying her dad, but it doesn't pay her any attention.

I rush toward them, still carrying Einstein's robotic arm. I swing it at the first robot that gets in my way, knocking her aside.

Pretty sure that was Betsy Ross.

Other androids move to block the way.

I fight my way through several more of them, but they are encircling us from everywhere now. Several have decided to raise weapons in our direction. I bowl through the last of the opposition and shove one of Ben's captor's away. With an arm free, he's able to escape the grip of the other robot. We turn back-to-back amid the throng of angry androids.

"What the hell did you say in there?" my other self says.

"Things didn't go exactly as planned." I brandish Einstein's arm at a robot version of Frederick Douglass.

"I'm thinking you should have been more polite."

I take a swing at the nearest robot, a mustached cowboy. Einstein's arm catches him under the jaw and dislodges his head. It tips back and then tumbles from the robot's shoulders, dangling by thick bundles of wiring. The robots around us watch their compatriot teeter and fall to the concrete, but the results aren't good. Instead of being deterred, they seem to ratchet up their intensity. Frederick Douglass swings a fist at me and catches me in the jaw. I stagger back from the blow.

Piper does her best to stay close to us. "Stop it! Stop it!" But the robots continue to ignore her, concentrating their efforts on her dad and me. I put an arm around her and try to stay clear of the horde.

Looking toward the ticket office, I note that Einstein is back on his feet, and the route back is blocked with row upon row of robots. He's creating a perimeter and forcing us toward the exit gates.

"Wait. I have an idea!" Piper shouts. "I know what to do!" She ducks under my arm and sprints through a gap in the robots, headed back toward the museum.

"Wait! Piper!" her dad shouts after her. He rushes to follow. Babe Ruth is lumbering toward me with a baseball bat, so I have no choice but to retreat.

It's tough going. The other Ben and I are forced to work together to fight our way through the increasingly violent throng of androids. It seems as though the rougher we get with them, the more aggressive they become. We are assaulted by a cadre of historical characters from Mark Twain to Henry VIII. Mary Todd Lincoln seems to really have it out for me. She keeps trying to crush me with a broken flag pole that's welded to her hands. It's becoming increasingly harder to avoid the blows.

Piper has an easier time. The park security protocol seems to be granting her immunity. She's able to slip through the crowd of robots and run up the ramp to the loading door of the museum. She turns and shouts to me. "Bring them this way!"

"Bring them?" her dad says. As he's speaking, one of the robots lunges forward, swinging a broadsword. It sweeps his legs out from under him, and he hits the ground hard.

"Ben!" I dash back into the crowd to get to him, barreling into the robotic knight just before it uses the broadsword to impale my alternate self. I knock the robot to the ground, and we skid along the concrete.

I scramble back to my feet and rush to the other Ben, hastily shoving away more of the androids. He's hurt pretty badly. The broadsword was dull, so luckily it didn't cut him, but the blunt force of the blow was enough to lame him. Dropping Einstein's arm, I help Ben up, throwing one of his arms over my shoulder so I can drag him away from danger.

We reach the loading ramp and are gifted with a slight breather as the robots are slower to execute the incline.

"There must be a way to shut these things down," I gasp.

The other Ben winces in pain but then raises his eyes to the museum. "Looks like my daughter is on it." He points inside the museum's warehouse. The lights on the gravitizer are on.

"Come help me!" At the far end of the tunnel, Piper is struggling to push one of the poles holding up the time gate. I carry my older self through the industrial-sized gravitizer to join her.

"What are you doing?" her dad asks. "You're trying to get it down?"

Piper is indeed lowering the time gate, working to get the thing horizontal. "It's going to work. We just need to use it on the robots."

I'm confused about what she means till she points to the open area beyond the time gate. "It's like the gate in the store. The trap door. We can do it here!"

"That's brilliant!" I see what she's trying to do now and move to the pole on the other side. I pull the locking pin out and start lowering the gate to the floor. By the time we have the gate horizontal, the first of the robots is already coming through the tunnel.

"You think this thing has enough juice?" I ask, eying the gravitite canisters along the wall. Piper merely moves to the system controls and starts punching buttons. I drag her dad across the open space inside the time gate, then lay him on the ground on the far side of the temporal emitters. He looks worried.

"You realize you're about to create a bunch of time traveling robots, don't you? Pretty sure that's how *The Terminator* started."

"If they go anywhere but here, I'll be happy," I reply. I rush back to the tunnel opening just as Piper activates the gravitizer. Blue electrical energy flickers and arcs along the walls, then bolts of electricity connect with the robots lumbering their way through. The energy crackles and pops, and the faces of the oncoming horde take on an eerie glow. The industrial gravitizer is far more powerful than any device I've seen employed for this. The gravitized energy is blinding. I'm forced to put up a hand to block my eyes.

I turn to Piper. "Get out of here before this thing shocks you!"

"We still need to turn on the time gate!"

That's a problem. With the gate on, we're not going to get across it. Whoever designed these controls clearly didn't plan to run both machines simultaneously and definitely not with the gate lying horizontally on the floor.

The first of the robots is almost on me—my nemesis, Mary Todd Lincoln.

"Go. I'll operate the controls," I shout. "Run!"

Lincoln's wife raises her flag pole club.

"Now!"

Piper sprints away across the concrete floor and leaps over the edge of the time gate on the far side. I catch the First Lady's swing and groan from the blow, going to one knee as I absorb it. She's still getting shocked by the gravitizer, and I can feel the energy from the machine coursing through me. My skin tingles with it. When I come back up, I use all of my strength to swing the robot around and send her sprawling onto the concrete in the center of our now-horizontal gate. She skids across the floor with her bloomers showing. For the next couple of seconds, she kicks and waves her arms wildly like a beetle on its back.

I hope Honest Abe will forgive me for what I'm about to do.

The rest of the robots are almost on me. They are still getting zapped and gravitized by the machine. I locate the schematic for the network of time gates linked to this one. There is only one left available, the gate in the ceiling at the general store that we were unable to unplug. It'll work. How about tomorrow . . .

"Watch out!" Piper yells. Mary Todd Lincoln is back on her feet, and Babe Ruth is closing in from behind me. I punch the activation button for the time gate, and the floor lights up with the brilliance of the temporal emitters. Waves of energy merge with one another across the gate and finish the connection. Mary Todd Lincoln plummets into the ether.

I dodge a swing from Babe Ruth, then another. His second swing brings him right to the edge of the time gate. When he swings at me again, I roll under the blow, spinning around to kick him in the leg.

He teeters and falls, tumbling backward and vanishing through the floor.

"It's three strikes and you're out, Babe."

The only ears close enough to hear my joke are the ones on the throng of androids pressing toward me. They don't look amused.

Getting to my feet, I angle for space to maneuver, but there's not much left. The swarm of robots has reached me. I grab the closest one and hurl it into the colorful abyss behind me. The next one won't budge as easily. One of the other robots is holding onto its back. They're getting smarter.

"Dad!" I turn to find Piper at the nearest side of the time gate. She's holding a couch cushion from one of the museum displays. She tosses it over the edge of the time gate, and it lands amid the swirling ether but doesn't sink. No gravitites.

"The floor is lava!" Piper shouts.

"What?"

"The floor is lava!" she shouts again. "Just play the game!"

God, she's brilliant.

I wrestle one more robot over the edge and into the ether, then judge the distance to the couch cushion Piper has thrown. I make the leap.

I land on my hands and knees atop the cushion, and true to its temporal limitations, it doesn't budge. My toes dip into the colorful swirl of the time gate, but when I pull them back up they're still with me. I center myself on the non-gravitized cushion and turn to watch more of the robots tumble into the time gate. The ones at the back haven't realized the danger. They press forward, shoving their counterparts over the edge. Row upon row of historical figures reach for me on my cushion, lose their balance, and fall into the ether. I can only imagine that they are landing in a heap, sometime tomorrow.

I turn to Piper and her dad on the far side of the gate. "It's working!"

Piper is grinning, and her dad has made it to his feet, though he is standing on one leg and leaning heavily on Piper for support.

As I watch Nelson Mandela and John F. Kennedy go tumbling into the near future, I can't help but smile. Here's a sight I never would have imagined. It's oddly satisfying to watch.

I'm turning to point out Mahatma Gandhi to Piper when cold fingers close around my ankle. My leg is yanked from under me, and I'm pulled violently off the cushion.

My fingers grasp at the foam and fabric just before I'm hauled under the current of timeless color.

"Dad!" Piper's shout is suddenly cut off.

I find myself dangling from the ceiling of the back room in the general store. My hands still grasp the cushion on one side of the time gate, but my body has been pulled into tomorrow. My legs are being clawed at and tugged on by a roiling mountain of androids beneath me. They have piled up on the floor and are now climbing over one another to get to me. It's like a seething robotic mosh pit.

I'm forced to kick Mother Theresa in the face to free myself from her metallic grasp. I use all my strength to haul myself upward, reaching to gain the top of my cushion again. I get an elbow up, then my head. I find myself back at floor level in the museum warehouse, straining to remain in the present, while my legs and lower body are still dangling into tomorrow.

"Dad! I'm coming!"

I turn toward the shout and find that Piper and her dad have thrown more objects on top of the time gate, and she's using them to work her way toward me. They've found a number of wooden folding chairs and lobbed them over the perimeter of temporal emitters. Piper is clambering from chair to chair to try to reach me, but more robotic hands are now protruding from the ether. Nearly all of the androids have exited the tunnel and fallen into the temporal ether, but their sheer numbers are bringing them back.

Piper leaps from the chair she's on to a closer one, extending a hand toward me. I clasp her wrist and am able to edge my couch cushion closer to her chair. Using its stability, I'm able to climb up out of the ether.

It's several yards in any direction to get to safety, and the number of robots protruding from the floor is increasing. I recognize the broken flagpole of Mary Todd Lincoln protruding from the floor close to the tunnel.

"We have to turn it off!" I shout. "I'm not sure we can make it!"

"I can make it!" Piper is eyeing the distance to the tunnel mouth. She drags one of the chairs she's not using around in front of her and steps onto it. I help her move the now vacated chair in front of that, allowing her to progress. Something thuds into the bottom of my cushion, nearly dislodging me, and I'm forced to leap up onto the free chair instead.

"I'll look for more chairs!" Piper's dad is watching anxiously from beyond the perimeter. "Hang on!"

"No. I can make it!" Piper is watching the space between her and the tunnel where the broken flagpole is surfacing like the fin of a shark amid the waves.

"Watch out for that—"

My words come out too late. Mary Todd Lincoln surges from the ether, riding some unseen swell of the android pile beneath her. Her expression is pure robotic rage. She swings her flagpole hard toward Piper's chair.

But Piper is too fast. She leaps over the swinging weapon, soaring through the air, before planting a red sneaker cleanly atop the first lady's head. And then it's another flying leap, over the remaining temporal soup to land safely in the confines of the gravitizer tunnel. She jams her hand into the time gate controls. The gravitizer tunnel and temporal emitters instantly go dark.

Mary Todd Lincoln loses her head.

Scanning the concrete around our now unassuming folding chairs, I find a multitude of robotic digits and appendages have been left in the present. None of them are moving anymore. I get down from my chair and rush across the now solid floor to Piper. She runs into my arms.

"We did it!"

"I don't know how you thought of that, but you saved our butts," I say.

"You say to think your way out, talk your way out, or fight your way out. I went with plan A."

I muss her hair. "And it was brilliant."

We find her dad on the other side of the emitter array with a smile of relief on his face.

He hugs his daughter, then turns to look at the now vacant tunnel to the outdoors. "What do you think happened to Einstein? I didn't see him go over the edge."

"I don't know. I hope he's out of security guards now. It's time to get that warp clock back."

Piper takes both of our hands again. "Come on. I've got an idea for that too."

27

"If the purpose of life isn't learning to love one another better, then I've completely misread all of the encounters I've had in time. And if I'm wrong, I'll stay wrong. I'd rather be remembered as a kind-hearted fool than an uncaring genius." -Journal of Dr. Harold Quickly, 1942

The robotic Albert Einstein is in poor shape.

We find him standing outside his kiosk looking mildly unbalanced. I suspect a lot of that issue is because I broke his arm off, but at least some of it looks mental. Despite the turmoil of our day and the hell he's put us through, I can't help but feel a little bit sorry for him.

"Mr. Einstein!" Piper calls to him as we get close. "Mr. Einstein!"

The robot looks up and pivots to face her. His face contorts into a smile.

"We have a deal for you." Piper lets go of our hands and forges ahead to face the android. "If you let me have the warp clock, I can make more people come to your park."

Einstein's back straightens and his eyes widen. He takes a few steps closer. "The Improved Attendance Directive is our chief priority."

"I know," Piper says. "If you let us use the warp clock and call our friends, we can bring more people to visit. We'll even buy lots of tickets."

"Could I interest you in an annual pass?" Einstein asks.

Piper turns to look at us. "Well, you'd have to ask my dad. He has the credit card."

Einstein turns to us expectantly.

I put a hand to the side of my mouth and whisper to my other self. "I feel like there's a lesson here somewhere about how credit cards work."

"I'll leave that conversation for the teenage years," he replies. "You have to pick your battles." He turns to Einstein. "I think an annual pass would be excellent. I'll take two."

"Same from me," I reply. "In fact, if you let us operate the warp clock, I'll buy a lifetime membership."

Einstein grins a wide smile. "You are in luck, because we offer a universal lifetime pass good at all of our affiliated parks. That would make today a very good sales day."

I can't help but smirk. He's a crackpot old robot and a few circuits short of true intelligence, but at least he's dedicated to his job.

Turning around, the android hobbles back to the ticket office on rickety joints. I follow him inside, cautious of any more surprises. Once in the door, the robot stands aside.

I size up Abraham's device. The core of the clock continues to vacillate between flashes of brilliant color and moments of darkness.

"I just need to undo what you've done to our chronometers."

"I've darkened all frequencies that indicated they were temporally linked to external devices," Einstein says. "If you tune the clock to reconnect with those frequencies, the corresponding devices in those timestreams will once again be usable."

"I don't exactly know what you're talking about, but if you mean getting rid of the dark spots in the middle of this thing, then I think I can manage that."

Extending my hands to the rings around the edge of the clock, I move one of them clockwise. A purple glow brightens within the clock. The next ring increases the blue hue. Studying the colors represented in the sphere, I notice most of the red to yellow spectrum is missing, and the vibrational hum of the device is sporadic. I find the dials that increase those colors, and the frequency of the dark spots reduces. After a few minutes of adjustments, the dark moments stop altogether, and the light in the center of the clock glows pure white. It hums evenly. I step back from the device. Did it work?

"I have fulfilled my end of our bargain," Einstein says. "As for yours?"

He's watching me expectantly.

"Um. My wife has my wallet. You take PayPal? Bitcoin? What are you running these days?"

"I've created you a user account. An eBill will be sent to your universal public profile."

"What if I don't have one in this time—"

"Mom!" Piper's shout echoes across the parking lot.

Looking out the window of the office, I spot vehicles arriving in the parking lot. More are racing into view, some with men and women in riot gear hanging from the sides. The motorcade of vehicles is a welcome sight, but not as much as the two figures climbing out of the lead vehicle. Both of them are Mym.

I turn to Einstein. "You're about to get the influx of visitors you wanted."

Piper ducks under a turnstile and races toward her mom. One of the Myms goes to one knee and opens her arms wide. Piper rushes into them.

The other Mym is scanning the fence. Searching.

My Mym. I step past Einstein and off the step of the ticket office. As I come around the corner, Mym spots me. She doesn't wait, but breaks into a run to get to me.

"Ben! You're okay!"

I grin as she rushes through the turnstile and into my arms. I didn't realize just how much I missed her till this moment. I wrap my arms around her as tightly as I can.

After the initial embrace, she pulls away and searches my face. "You're not hurt? That video..."

"That part takes some explaining," I say. "But I had help."

Piper's dad limps up to us and smiles at Mym. "He said you'd come. Not a single doubt."

Mym reaches for his hand and holds it. "We got here as fast as we could. This timestream is really obscure. Once the chronometers were reactivated, it still took us a week to find our way here. We didn't want to make you wait that long though."

"Grateful you didn't," he replies. "I'd guess the resort's accommodations are a bit less than five star anymore."

A squad of armed ASCOTT agents rushes by, scouring the park for threats. Someone shouts when they discover Einstein and several of them take up defensive positions, training their weapons on the ticket office robot.

I detach myself from Mym and move toward the kiosk.

"Hey! We have an arrangement with the robot," I shout. "Don't shoot him!"

The one-armed android meanders toward the agents. "Welcome to Yesteryear Adventure Park. If you would like to purchase speed passes to our most popular attractions, I would appreciate if you form an orderly line. I regret that our online purchasing system is temporarily unavailable."

"Stand down, synth!" one of the agents shouts.

Einstein continues toward the agents. "You are speaking with the Ticketing, Reservations, and Information Kiosk. If you would like to speak to a representative—"

Gunfire erupts from one of the agent's weapons, then another. Einstein staggers back, showering sparks on the concrete. There are now gaping holes in his outer case. He pivots slowly toward me and raises his hand before being hit with several more bullets. The robot tips and then falls, crashing to the ground in a heap.

Piper shrieks.

I turn to find my older self hugging her tightly to him. Piper's eyes are glued to the robot.

Looking past them, I spot a new cluster of men near the gates.

ASCOTT director Jermaine Clevis has arrived. He strides forward flanked by several bodyguards. When he reaches my position, he sizes up the smoking wreck of Einstein, then looks around the broken-down theme park. "Mr. Travers. Of all the timestreams to find you in, we never would have thought to look here." He turns to shout to his agents. "Any sign of our Tempus Fugitives?"

I answer his question myself. "Your team is going to have their hands full rounding them up. I can show you where they are, but the first priority needs to be a rescue operation."

I explain where Abraham is, and what Franco, the Gladiator, has going on in his timestream.

"An arena? Full of history's villains? What an outrageous idea," Jermaine replies. "I'll have my men on it immediately."

He's true to his word. After I show him one of the maps and the locations of the time gates, his agents swarm through the park to apprehend the escapees.

I locate Mym again and take her hand. The other Mym and Piper's dad are now speaking quietly near the turnstiles.

"I talked to my future self on the way here," Mym says. "It sounds like they had a challenging go of it. Life hasn't exactly gone according to plan."

"Yeah, I need to talk to you about that." I hold both of her hands as I face her. "There's a reason Piper chose your dad's funeral as the day she returned to. It wasn't coincidence she picked that day."

"I know," Mym replies. "I—I was sick the day after you were taken. I thought it was just nerves at first, being worried about you. But then I took a test." She looks up at me, searching my face. "You know what it said already, don't you?"

"I know, and I couldn't be happier about it."

Mym smiles. It lights up her face. "You aren't upset? It's going to change... everything."

I nod and take a deep breath. "Well, if the last few days have taught me anything, it's that learning to be a parent is no joke. But I think I'm ready. I don't know if our daughter will turn out exactly the same as this Piper, but if she does, I'd be thrilled."

I look for our alternate daughter and find that Piper is standing over the disabled robot. We walk over to her and I rest a hand on her shoulder. "How are you doing, kiddo?"

Piper keeps her eyes on the robot. "Is he dead?"

I glance from the broken android to the still-blinking lights of the ticket office. "I don't know that it was ever really alive, so it's hard to say."

"It wasn't really his fault though, was it?" Piper asks. "Trying to fix the past. Lots of people wish they could do that."

"And for lots worse reasons," I say. "But I don't think he picked the right friends."

"You think if someone else had offered to help him, maybe it would have been different?"

"I don't know. Hard to say what anyone else's future will turn out to be." I look to where my alternate self was last talking to his wife. He and the other Mym are hugging. Piper notices too and beams.

I wrap my arm around my Mym and kiss her. The future just got a lot more fun.

By midday, ASCOTT teams have reactivated and entered each of the time gates. Finding Abraham was top priority, and thanks to the nature of time travel, when they rescue him from the Gladiator's arena prison, it's only a couple of hours after I left him. They capture the Gladiator the moment he reappears from the involuntary trip I sent him on.

Piper and Mym are equally thrilled to see Abraham exit the time gate.

He meets us with a weary but undaunted smile on his face.

"I had confidence that you would find a way to stage a rescue," he says to me. "Your talent for survival and thinking on your feet continues to serve you well."

"I couldn't have done it without your help," I say. "And Piper was the real hero. If it hadn't been for her, I never would have had a chance to save anyone." I turn to my alternate daughter. "I assume you two know each other?"

Piper smiles at Abe. "I've learned a *few* things from him."

"Our paths do tend to cross from time to time," Abe says, returning her smile. "You have a bit of competition in the chronometer repair department. Piper is even building her own custom device at my shop."

I consider the old watchmaker. "You've known I had a daughter before all this? And you never told me?"

"I figured that's what you might call *family* business. I assumed you'd want to find out on your own."

"Oh, speaking of chronometers . . ." Mym reaches into a bag she has slung over one shoulder. "I brought some spares." She hands one to each of us. "Pretty sure you'd like the option again."

I gratefully slip the chronometer onto my wrist and latch the band. It feels good.

"Who's taking home the warp clock?" I ask. "I'd like to keep a close eye on that thing, especially now that we know its existence is public knowledge."

"I've been meaning to develop a fail-safe for the system," Abe says. "I think now may be that time. If you don't mind, I would appreciate being able to ensure this sort of event never happens again."

"You won't get any argument from me," I say.

Mym smiles at him. "Well, as long as it's staying in the family. Sorry to tell you, Abe, but you're stuck with us. We count you in that category too."

Abraham grins. "There are worse fates, to be sure." He heads for the ticket office to see about disconnecting the warp clock.

The Tempus Fugitives are rounded up. It takes the ASCOTT teams multiple trips to 1777, but all of the escaped convicts are brought in. Director Clevis approaches me as the agents load the prisoners into vehicles.

"It seems you've managed to increase the number of escapees for us, Mr. Travers." He gestures to where Smiley, Epaulettes, and Wiggy are being held. Their doppelgängers from the alternate timestream are being loaded into a parallel vehicle. The criminals are giving their own selves dirty looks.

"Sorry if they take up a few more jail cells at Rookwood this way," I say. "But it beat the alternative. You have any idea what will happen to all these new timestreams they created?"

Jermaine sighs and crosses his arms. "We're going to survey the damage. If their activities yielded results we can live with, we may end up adding them to the list of approved timestreams and allow visitors. It seems this park robot they were following did have some noble intentions. But we all know that doesn't always make much difference when it comes to results. In the end, some of these timestreams may bear very little resemblance to the originals they came from. They made some drastic changes."

I spot Vanessa being lined up behind Sal and a very dejected-looking Jorge. They are being loaded into one of the vehicles. "That woman saved my life. When it comes time for her hearing, I'd like to be there."

Jermaine runs a finger across the palm of his hand and scribbles something, no doubt seeing more than I do from his perspective. "I've made a request. I suspected you may want to be present for *all* of the hearings, considering what happened here. I trust you know that we discovered two bodies in the duplicate timestreams. Are you aware of their identities?"

"I am."

"And what would you like us to do with the deceased?"

"I'd like to have custody of them," I reply. "I know of a place they should go."

"Very well," Jermaine says. "I'll have my people arrange things per your request."

I'm glad he doesn't ask me to explain the situation in more detail. I imagine there will be time for that later.

Another group of technicians has arrived in the park, but these don't look like ASCOTT agents. Dressed in gray with matching company logos on their jackets, the team is analyzing the ticket office.

"Who are those people?" I ask.

Jermaine makes more invisible notes on his hand. "Representatives from United Machine. The system running this park was one of their early designs. They mean to study the anomaly that occurred here and determine what it means in terms of their synthetic intelligence programs. And of course to keep it from happening again."

"Do they have any idea what happened?" I ask.

"Their speculation is that the AI running the park may have developed its own survival instinct over the years it was left abandoned, and used that to make new decisions and strategies. While it wasn't able to untether itself from its core programming, it's clear that this system was far more advanced than was ever intended. It may be that you have inadvertently discovered one of the evolutionary steps of the technological singularity—a leap ahead for robot kind, as it were."

"I'd rather I hadn't," I reply. I begin walking us over to where Mym is talking with Piper.

"I'm sure that when the investigation is concluded, you'll be given credit for your role in the discovery," Jermaine says. He rests a hand on my shoulder as we walk. "Who knows, Mr. Travers? Perhaps one day you'll even be famous."

When I reach Mym and Piper, I turn and shake Jermaine's hand. "Thanks for the rescue, director. Tell United Machine they can keep the credit. We'll just head home."

"It could be an astounding discovery. If you wanted to consider becoming a member of ASCOTT, I'm sure I could speak a few words in your favor and make sure that you get the recognition you deserve from the scientific community."

"I have all the recognition I need. As long as the people I care about still like me, I'm plenty famous enough." I move to Mym's side and take her hand. I drape my other arm around Piper's shoulders.

"Famous among a rather small group of time travelers," Jermaine argues.

"Not a group, director. We're a family."

28

"It's easy to imagine that time travel can fix any issue, but truth be told, there are some problems that can only be solved by living one day at a time." - Journal of Dr. Harold Quickly 2021.

"I don't know how he felt at the end," I say. "I don't know what it was like to die. I don't think I'm ready to know."

Standing in this grassy prairie, I feel a long way removed from the events of the last few days, but the reality is still with us, etched in granite. Mym slips her hand into mine and looks down at the gravestone.

"Some part of you must have been more ready than you think. At least he was."

It's a strange feeling to think that only a few pivotal hours separate the life I'm living now from the life that ended in 1777. It was a single twist in the timeline, but one that gave me a second chance.

Reading the names on the nearby headstones, one fact is fairly clear. There may be a multiverse of realities, but my time in any of them will eventually have to end. The grave for Piper's dad is near mine. A row beyond it, there are several monuments for Dr. Quickly overgrown with wildflowers. I recognize engravings for Abraham and Cowboy Bob among the scattered other graves. There are even a couple of headstones with Mym's name on them.

"Does it bother you?" I ask. "Knowing that there are times out there when you didn't make it? Alternate endings to your story?"

Mym holds onto my arm and looks up to the clear blue Montana sky. There are no meteorites to watch today, but this spot isn't far from the hillside where we first lay talking under the stars. It makes me wonder if she's recalling that night too.

"I think part of me is okay with knowing that there are versions of me that have died," she says. "I remember how terrible it was the first time I lost my dad. And when I've lost friends. But I think that knowing they've been through it already—been to where we're all headed—it makes the thought a little less lonely. I feel like the biggest part of our adventure is yet to come, but we'll have friends when we get there.

"When I look out the window of the farmhouse and see the graves out here, I used to be sad or scared, but not anymore. It's just a reminder that the universe has more to show me, and some piece of me is already there experiencing it."

"You don't think that makes us somehow lessened? Like pale copies of the originals?"

Mym stretches up and pulls my face toward hers, standing on tiptoes and pressing her lips to mine. She kisses me softly and slowly, then drops back to her heels. "Did that feel like I love you any less?"

I can't contain the warm feeling rushing through my body—the electricity of her touch. "No. It most certainly did not."

Mym wraps herself around my arm again and leans her head onto my shoulder. "Good. Because we have a lot of life left to live."

Mym and I are still hand-in-hand when we walk back into Cowboy Bob's farmhouse. His resident housekeeper, Connie, is baking something delicious-smelling in the oven. The long wooden table is set for a meal, but Piper and a younger version of Dr. Quickly have commandeered one end and are busy wrapping a package.

"It won't do to keep it now. Otherwise it won't ever end up in our collection later," Harry is explaining. "What is it I always say?"

Piper mumbles in a monotone. "I know. What happened, happened. You can't change the past."

"Exactly," the scientist replies. "But sometimes we must be the ones to ensure that the past happens."

I squeeze Mym's hand, then leave her in the kitchen to go see what Piper and Dr. Quickly are working on. I rest a hand on Piper's shoulder and look over her head to discover that the package they are wrapping contains the framed photograph of Piper in the welders goggles—the same art piece that we spotted in the museum in Rome.

"Tying up some loose ends?" I ask.

Piper still sounds exasperated but she nods. "Grandpa says I have to send it to the museum or my whole life won't make any sense."

"I didn't phrase it like that," Harry replies. "But it's true. Creating temporal paradoxes is—"

"Universally irresponsible," Piper and I complete his sentence in unison.

"Well, yes. Exactly." Dr. Quickly surveys both of us. "I see my work here is done. I'll see if Connie needs my help taste-testing dinner." He checks his pocket watch and heads for the kitchen.

Piper and I look at each other and laugh. We finish wrapping her package, and I help her position it near the front door. When we get back to the kitchen, her parents arrive through the back door. They are holding hands. Piper runs to them. "Are you *both* staying for dinner this time?"

The other Ben looks at his wife and smiles. "Yeah. I think we will. Don't want Grandpa to think we're only using him for his babysitting services."

"I'm not a baby," Piper argues. "I'll be ten any day now. If you would let me have my party already."

"Well, you know what terrible tyrants your mom and I are about birthdays. Only letting you have one a year and all." He looks at me and winks.

"That reminds me," my Mym says from the kitchen. "What day did you choose for her birthday? Did you pick it or just let it happen when it happened?" She's absentmindedly resting her hand on her belly.

"My birthday is February 29th," Piper says. "Because I'm a leap child."

"Ha. Makes sense," I say. "Doesn't that mean you should technically only get a birthday every four years?"

Piper scowls at me as though I have completely betrayed her. "No! It means that my birthday can be whatever day I want. Or it should be."

Mym smiles from the kitchen. "Would you recommend that day as a birthday? Do you think we should pick the same day for our Piper, or something else?"

"Yes!" Piper exclaims. "Then we can have the same birthday! We can have parties together and share presents. It will be like having a twin sister. Only she'll be little, and I'll have to teach her all about time travel."

"I'm glad you don't mind sharing," Piper's mom replies. "But it might be a while till you're teaching anyone to time travel. Let's concentrate on sticking together." She looks across the room to my Mym, who smiles gratefully.

"Okay, dinner is served!" Connie announces from the kitchen. She waves a wooden serving spoon at us. "Buffet style, because Lord knows I can never tell how many place settings to put out around here. More of ya'll could be popping in the door at any moment."

"You know you wouldn't have it any other way, Mrs. A." Our host, Cowboy Bob, descends the staircase into the hallway, followed by Abraham. "Don't pretend you don't love every bit of this life."

Connie blushes as he enters the room. "Oh, you know I'm not complaining, Bobby. A full house is a happy house in my book. Don't care how many of you there are. At least this way, I don't have to learn as many new names!"

I grin as I move into the kitchen and take a plate.

Before long, all of us are seated around the farmhouse table. We pass salt and pepper shakers and pats of butter around as we get situated. Dr. Quickly pauses before we dig in and lifts his glass. "I'd like to propose a toast."

I elevate my wine glass.

"There are many times and places worthy of note in this wild and wonderful universe, but few could bring the joy of the evening we are sharing right now. So here's to the present moment. If we never have another, we can still count ourselves blessed."

"Hear, hear!" I raise my glass. The others cheer their agreement as well. Mym sips her sparkling water and smiles. Her blue eyes crinkle at the corners. She looks happy.

As I look around the table full of faces from my past and future, Dr. Quickly's words make sense. I couldn't have put it as eloquently or as succinctly, but he's accurately summed up my feelings about the life and family I've stumbled into.

I've come a long way since my first accidental trip on a rainy Wednesday night in 2009. It's been an exciting ride. I have no idea where the future will take me from here, but I'm not in a hurry.

I'll find out in time.

Thanks for reading! Want more of the story? Enjoy the bonus epilogue and deleted scenes, plus sneak peeks at future books by Nathan Van Coops. Get your free bonus eBook here!

https://dl.bookfunnel.com/ufwrynwfg9

You'll also get two free time travel stories when you subscribe to the monthly newsletter at www.nathanvancoops.com. See you there!

ACKNOWLEDGMENTS

This book is better than I could have made it alone because of the help of a large number of dedicated readers. I'd like to thank the members of **Beta Team Bravo** for helping me through numerous revisions and providing me with not only your support and critique, but also your friendship.

Especially:

Alan Rothberg, Alissa Nesson, Amanda Bildeaux, Amy Spicka, Art jury, Barb Brown, Ben, Benjamin Wiechel, Bernie, Bethany Cousins, Bill Hamshire, Bill McCarthy, Blanche Padgett, Bob Garel, Bob Stocks, Brad Friedlander, Brad Hammond, Brett Parker, Bruce, Bruce Kunkle, Caroline Ruth Molloy, Chantal-Lise Mirman, Chris Collins, Chuck, Chuck Scro, Cindy Williams, Claire Manger, Claire Palmer, Cle Montgomery, Colleen Chamberlain, Connie Nealy, Corey Scott, Cosmin, Crystal Ley, Dan McCrory, Dane Bishop, Darleen Rodriguez, Dave, Dave Bennett, Dean Thibault, Diane Bates, Dorothy Hill, Dwight Brooks, Elaine, Elaine Davis, Elenora Sabin, Eric Slade, Erica Howe, Fiona Holden, G4rrid00, Gabrielle, Gary C Smart, Geoff Elliott, Gerry Cohen, Ginelle Blanch, Gloria Chadwick, Gordon K Brown Jr, Harry Sweigart, Helen, Ian Macfarlane, James, James L Morse, Jan Butterick, Janet Cervantes, Jason Wolverton, Jeff Marcum, Jeffrey Braisted, Jerry

Simmons, Jim Brown, Joan porter, John Jennings, June Høstan van Riel, Karen Lefkowitz, Karen Stansbury, Karl M Killebrew, Kay Clark, Keith A. Marshall, Ken Robbins, Kristine Taylor, Lacy Harvey, Larry Dietz, Lauren-Grace Kirtley, Laurie Flynn, Linda Kerekes, Lisa Mages-Haskins, Logan DeVane, Maarja Kruusmets, Malcolm, Marcus Baker, Marijelle Bartholomew, Marilyn Bourdeau, Marilyn Gast, Mark Hale, Matthew, Matthew Rapp, Maurice Druck, Melanie S Tippett, Melissa Pritchard, Michael Clarren, Mike Brown, Mike Reed, Milian Glafira, Missy Burrows, Mitchell Berdinka, Neill Gerstbauer, Nispar, Paul Ness, Philip Boynton, Randi, Randy Chrust, Randy Webster, Ray Clements, Revella, Rich Cross, Rob Stephen, Roger Rubinstein, Rogerio Faco Franklin, Ron flood, Sally Kendall, Sean, Sean Hull, Sean Moynihan, Seb Fosdal, Stephen Bishop, Steve Hawkins, Steve Shaw, Susan Davies, Tammie, Ted Casey, Thomas Dunleavy, Tim Wright, Timothy Mason, Tod, Todd Margarita, Tom, Tonny Worstell, Tracy Haynie, Uli Dericks, Veronica, Von Whitlock, Walt Taylor, Walter Jones, Wendy Burrell, and Yvonne Mitchell.

A special thanks to to my friend and editor, Emily Young, who makes every book I write shine that much brighter.

And to my lovely wife, Stephanie, and our darling daughter, Piper, for being my constant inspiration. I love you.

-NVC

THE TIMESTREAM TWIST

Time travel can be tricky. Need help unraveling the temporal knot of a twist in Chapters 23 and 24? You aren't alone. As the author, I laid awake till 2 am one night puzzling through it and making sure the action didn't violate any of the rules of the multiverse. Here is a detailed explanation of the events that Ben experienced:

Caution: Spoilers.
If you have not read through chapter 24 of the book yet, don't read this.

Okay. Here we go.

Our hero, Ben Travers, watches a video in which two versions of himself are held hostage. In that video, one captive has a torn pant leg and is shot.

Ben knows that Piper's dad has been kidnapped and is being held hostage in 1777.

Ben enters a time gate arriving in the late afternoon on an autumn day in 1777, but is immediately captured.

We will call the events of this timeline, Timestream A.

Timestream A

Ben is taken to the Benedict Arnold house and put in the pantry with Piper's dad. At this point neither of them have a tear in their pants, and it is impossible to determine which of them will be shot.

The two men cannot escape prior to the shooting because Ben has seen the shooting occur on the video. Changing the events would not change the past but would instead create an alternate timeline, Timestream B, duplicating all of the residents of Timestream A. The reason they don't want to attempt this is because, while the future of the 1777 timestream would be duplicated, the rest of the multiverse would not. There would be two versions of each Ben for a total of four Bens, with only one version of Piper and the original two Myms because they are not present in that timestream. The Bens would be obligated to share their lives between four of themselves, and they want to find a better solution. As an alternative solution, Ben attempts to create body armor like *Back to the Future III*.

In the morning, Ben wakes to find that his companion is already hooded and awaiting the shooting. He also discovers that the other hostage now has a tear in his pants. He doesn't know that this is the future him and not Piper' dad. Piper's dad is now hidden in the potato barrel.

Ben and the other hostage are led outside and the hostage with the torn pant leg is shot. Ben escapes, rushing to the time gate, only to discover that someone has already gotten there on horseback and gone through to a different destination. (This is Piper's dad but Ben doesn't know that yet.)

Ben jumps to 1958, picks up Piper and then travels to the future, arriving in the desolate theme park. While saving Piper from the collapsed roller coaster, Ben tears his pants. He realizes that the man in the video who was shot was not Piper's dad. He now knows it was him.

Ben travels back through the time gate and arrives in 1777 a couple of hours prior to his original trip. He escapes to the woods before his captors show up, sneaking to the house and hiding in the pantry in the potato barrel. His earlier self arrives and has a conversation with Piper's dad. When they are asleep, Ben exits the potato barrel and wakes Piper's dad, hiding him in the barrel instead. He tells Piper's dad how to get to the time gate on a horse, then takes Piper's dad's place, putting the hood over his head to conceal his identity from his earlier self.

In the morning, Ben takes the place he knows will be that of the victim in the video, sacrificing himself and dying, but knowing that at least Piper's dad will live. His earlier self escapes, continuing the time loop he has just completed.

This is the end of the actions in Timestream A.

Timestream B

Piper's dad, having escaped the events of Timestream A, arrives back at the theme park and finds Piper. He explains what has happened to the other Ben who chose to take his place. Piper is unhappy with this solution and points out that there were two videos of the shooting on the cameraman's camera. She interprets this to mean that there are two timestreams and one video came from each one. Piper's dad realizes that there is still a chance to save Ben if he's willing to make the same sacrifice.

Piper's dad enters the time gate, arrives in the afternoon prior to when Ben arrives and unplugs the time gate during the time period when Timestream A Ben is supposed to show up. This is paradoxical for the events of Timestream A and therefore creates a new timestream: Timestream B.

Piper's dad goes to the farmhouse, repeating the strategy Timestream A Ben used, waking a confused Timestream B Ben up in the middle of the night and hiding him in the potato barrel. This is where chapter 24 begins for our narrator Ben. The events preceding this moment are unknown from his point of view.

Confused Timestream B Ben has no knowledge of the events that occurred in Timestream A. He doesn't know his other self has died in that alternate timestream. He escapes from the house.

Piper's Timestream A dad has never seen the video of the shooting from Timestream B. Presumably no one has other than the men who sent it. He takes a guess at which position to take, but his Timestream B other self ends up getting shot.

Timestream B Ben rescues Timestream A Piper's dad and the two return to the theme park. This is the end of the events of Timestream B.

Back at the park, Piper explains to Ben that he is in fact going to have a daughter and that she didn't want her alternate self to grow up without a dad.

The final results of this timestream duplication are:
    Timestream A Ben=deceased
    Timestream A Piper's dad=living.
    Timestream B Ben=living
    Timestream B Piper's dad=deceased.

There are two versions of everyone else in timestreams A and B including Wiggy, Epaulettes, and Smiley. A total of 6 bad guys that now need to be dealt with. No one else outside the 1777 timestreams was duplicated. Piper, the Gladiator, and all of the other characters existed in separate, unconnected timestreams.

Timestream B Ben shares the history of Timestream A Ben up to the night of the potato barrel in 1777, but they lived their divergent stories simultaneously in the alternate timestreams, leaving Timestream B Ben the survivor and able to carry on their life.

I contend that occasional time travel knots are good for the brain, but I hope this explanation was helpful in unraveling this one.
   -Nathan

ALSO BY NATHAN VAN COOPS

In Times Like These

The Chronothon

The Day After Never

Clockwise and Gone

Faster Than Falling

In Times Like These Books 1-3

Copyright © 2018 by Nathan Van Coops

All rights reserved.

No part of this book may be reproduced in any form or by any electronic or mechanical means, including information storage and retrieval systems, without written permission from the author, except for the use of brief quotations in a book review.

Cover design by Damonza.com

Author photo by Jennie Thunell Photography

❀ Created with Vellum

Printed in Great Britain
by Amazon